Long Time Coming

"Heartwarming, drama-packed, and tender in just the right places."

—*Romantic Times*

Long Time Coming

Vanessa Miller

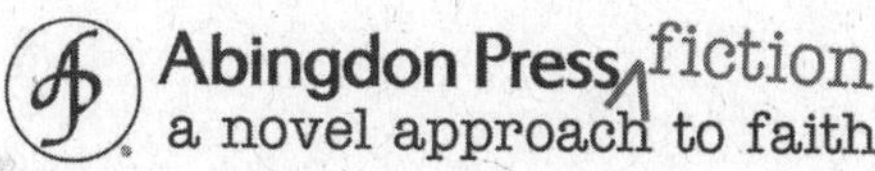

Nashville, Tennessee

Long Time Coming

ISBN-13: 978-1-4267-0768-1

Published by Abingdon Press, P.O. Box 801, Nashville, TN 37202
www.abingdonpress.com

Published in association with the Natasha Kern Literary Agency, Inc.

Scripture is from the King James or Authorized Version of the Bible.

Cover design by Anderson Design Group, Nashville, TN

Library of Congress Cataloging-in-Publication Data

Miller, Vanessa.
Long time coming / Vanessa Miller.
p. cm.
ISBN 978-1-4267-0768-1 (pbk./trade pbk., adhesive - perfect bdg. : alk. paper)
I. Title.
PS3613.I5623L66 2010
813'.6—dc22
2010035449

Printed in the United States of America

2 3 4 5 6 7 8 9 10 / 15 14 13 12 11 10

To my best friend, Rhonda Bogan—for the good times and the not-so-good times. I'm glad I had you around. Stay strong.

Acknowledgments

I am old enough now to recognize the value of lifelong friendships. Friends sometimes come and go, but the ones who stick with you through the good and the bad are precious indeed. I have had two such friends: Rhonda Bogan and Seana Reeves. I met Rhonda in the second grade and Seana in the seventh. In the time since then, we have each experienced great sadness and great joy.

One such time of sadness occurred when Rhonda was forced to watch her twenty-seven-year-old cousin lose an unexpected battle with cancer. Rhonda shared with me her sorrow in having to say good-bye to her cousin, but also her joy in knowing that her cousin had accepted the Lord and would live forever in heaven. Although *Long Time Coming* is not that particular story, it was inspired by the loving way in which my friend retold her cousin's final days. So, I would like to thank Rhonda for sharing her heartbreak and joy with me.

I would also like to thank Linda Behnken at the Hospice of Dayton, who provided me with the information I needed concerning hospice patients. Patricia Hill of Action Adoption Agency was a wonderful resource for everything I needed to know about the adoption process. Through writing this book, I learned that there are some truly giving people in this world, and I'm grateful I was able to speak with a few of them, if only for a moment.

I also need to thank my agent, Natasha Kern, for finding *Long Time Coming* a home. The Abingdon Press team has been wonderful to work with; I can't say enough about them. Barbara Scott works tirelessly to ensure that each book in this line receives the attention it deserves. Maegan Roper, the marketing/publicity manager, has already begun working on publicity angles for the book, and I absolutely love my book cover. There have been many others within the Abingdon Press organization who have worked on this book, and although I might not know the names of everyone who had a part in bringing *Long Time Coming* to life, I'd like to say thanks—your efforts were not in vain.

Finally, I must thank my readers. I'm so thankful that you all continue to read my books, and I hope that you will fall in love with this book and the characters within as much as I did.

Prologue

The double doors opened, and the guests stood as Deidre Clark came into view. She was a vision in white. Small clusters of sparkling beads accented the front and back of the bodice and traveled down the wrap of the skirt. Her veil was covered with the same sparkling beads that accented her gown. The princess-style headpiece was pinned to her hair and the veil flowed down her back. Her mother had asked that she not cover her face with the veil. Loretta Clark's pastor had taught them that the veiled bride held secrets that the husband would have to uncover. But Deidre's mother didn't believe that a husband and wife should have secrets.

The musicians began to play, and the soloist stood.

"Are you ready?" Deidre's uncle asked.

She looked at her uncle, standing in for her beloved father, who had died way before his time. She pondered her uncle's question for a moment. Was anyone ever ready for such a thing as matrimony? She looked down the aisle at her groom, Private Johnson Morris. He'd told her when they met that he was career military. His dream was to one day wear general's stripes like his hero, Colin Powell. Johnson had lots of dreams, and Deidre wanted to help him achieve them all. She nodded. "I'm ready."

Still behind the double doors and not quite in the sanctuary yet, Deidre took a step as the soloist sang, "*At last, my love has come along.*"

Although some might say that this particular song wasn't appropriate for a church wedding, Deidre requested it anyway. She had been terrified that no one would ever want to marry her. But Johnson had come into her life and swept her off her feet at last. She took another step and then her wedding coordinator stopped her.

The woman lifted the veil and put it over Deidre's face. "There . . . simply beautiful," she said as she gently pushed Deidre toward the sanctuary.

"*My lonely days are over*," the soloist continued.

Deidre kept walking once the veil had been placed over her face. But as she neared her groom, Deidre's thoughts turned to a conversation she had had with her mother earlier that day.

Loretta had walked into her dressing room, kissed her on the cheek, and then asked, "Did you tell him?"

Deidre turned toward the full-length mirror and smiled at her image.

"Did you tell him?" Loretta asked again.

"Not yet," Deidre said. She could see her mother's eyes fill with worry as she glanced at her. She turned back to the mirror, choosing to ignore her mother. This was her day—her never-supposed-to-be day—and she wasn't going to let anything spoil it, not even reality.

She was standing next to Johnson now. They recited their vows, and the preacher pronounced them husband and wife. Deidre let out a sigh of relief as Johnson lifted her veil of secrets and kissed her.

1

Twenty-three and played out. Like the words of a tired old blues song, Kenisha Smalls had been strung and rung out.

"Too young to give up," she chided as she pulled herself out of bed. But when her feet hit the floor and her knees buckled from unexplained pain, she reminded herself that she had actually lived a hundred dog years, lapping at the crumbs from underneath other folks' tables, and being kicked around by more good-for-nothings than she could count. A few years back, Kenisha thought some good would have to come into her life to even out the bad. But when James, her first baby's daddy, got arrested for armed robbery, and then Terrell, her second baby's daddy, got himself shot and killed trying to be a kingpin, she'd stopped praying for the sun to shine through her drab days and resigned herself to embrace the rain.

Guess that's how she'd hooked up with Chico. Kenisha had been dazzled by his olive skin, wavy hair, and bulky arms. Dazzled by his corporate job and technical school education. Of course, all that dazzling occurred before her responsible boyfriend started hanging around her crackhead brother, Kevin Carson. By the time she had given birth to her third child, Chico had quit his good-paying job so he could give crack his undivided attention.

Now the only time Kennedy saw her crackhead father was when he made his first-of-the-month visit. Begging for a loan that he knew his broke behind couldn't pay back. She remembered the first time she refused to give Chico her rent money. He'd punched her in the face so hard her teeth clickety-clacked. Grabbing the iron skillet that she'd been frying chicken in, she'd chased him out of her house. When she walked back in and saw Jamal, her oldest child, standing in the kitchen holding a butcher knife, his eyes blazing with fury, she swore right then that she would have nothing more to do with Chico and his crack demon.

Shaking her head to ward away bad memories, Kenisha grabbed a washcloth and towel from the hall closet. Jumping in the shower, she allowed the hot water to assault her weary bones. As the steam filled the small bathroom, she wallowed in the horror story her life had become. What next? How much can happen to a person before the Almighty decides it's time to pick on someone else?

"Ah, dawg." She knew she'd forgotten something. Bumping her head against the tiled wall of the shower, she turned the water off and stepped out. She had an appointment that might make her late picking up Jamal from school. Not wanting to leave it to chance, she decided to call her sister Aisha Davis to see if she could pick up her son.

Before she could get her clothes on and make it to the telephone, Chico knocked on her back door. She was familiar with his knock. It was the first-of-the-month, "baby, can I please get a loan" kind of banging that rolled through her head twelve times a year.

"Don't I have enough to deal with?" She picked up the pink frilly robe James had bought her on her fifteenth birthday. It had been soft and pretty, but the drudge of life had worn on it. Thought she would have replaced it long ago. But the kids kept coming, and the men kept leaving.

She picked up Jamal's leather belt, secured her tattered robe, stalked downstairs and flung open the back door. "What do you want, Chico?"

"Ah, girl, quit tripping. You know you're happy to see me. Them hazel eyes of yours sparkle every time I come over here."

She ran her hands through her short layered hair as the skeleton strolled up to her and puckered his lips. The five-day stench and sunken cheeks made Kenisha back up and give him the hand. "If it's money you want, my welfare check hasn't even arrived yet."

Crossed eyes and a deep sigh accused Kenisha of misjudging him. "How you know I didn't come over here to see my beautiful little girl?"

"Did you happen to get a job and bring your beautiful little girl some child support? 'Cause Kennedy likes to eat."

"Why you got to be like that?" He leaned against the kitchen sink. "See, that's why I don't come by more often. You always trippin'."

Kenisha opened the back door. "Boy, who do you think you're fooling? You don't come by more 'cause the first only comes once a month." A strong wind blew her robe open, exposing two bony thighs.

"Girl, you need to quit selling them food stamps. You know I like a woman with meat on her bones."

Kenisha rolled her eyes and waved him toward the coolness of the outdoor wind.

"Oh, so it's like that?" Pushing himself off the sink, he told her, "Just get Kennedy down here. Let me see my baby girl, and I'll be on my way."

"She ain't here. They spent the night over at Aisha's."

Walking toward her, he got loud. "How many times have I told you not to have my daughter over at your sorry sister's house?"

"When the telling comes with a check, that's when I'll start listening." Still holding the door open, she motioned him outdoors again.

He poked his index finger into the middle of her forehead. "Make sure my daughter is home the next time I come to see her."

He walked out. But before Kenisha slammed the door, she told him, "Yeah, right. We'll see you in thirty days, Chico."

She sat on the couch as her body shook with rage. Her rage was directed not only at Chico, but at all the men who'd promised her sweetness, then made her swallow dung. She was tired. Wished she'd never met any of them. She sure wouldn't be in the fix she was in now if she'd waited until marriage to have sex. Maybe she should have signed up for karate classes when she was six or seven. That way she could have broken her mother's boyfriend's neck that night he took all her choices away.

Clicking on the TV, she hoped to find enjoyment in somebody else's drama. Dr. Phil was putting a smile on the face of a woman whose house had been robbed and ransacked. "Ain't that 'bout nothing? My life is raggedy, but I don't see nobody offering me so much as a needle and thread to stitch it up." She turned off the TV and stood. Might as well just deal with it. She picked up the phone and dialed Aisha.

The phone rang three times before Aisha's angry voice protruded through the line. "What have I told you about calling my house so early?"

Caller ID wasn't meant for everybody. It was 10:45 in the morning. And Aisha's lazy behind was still in bed, screening calls. "You need to get up and fix breakfast. My kids have a hot meal every morning."

Aisha yawned. "Your kids ain't no better than mine. They can walk downstairs and fix a bowl of cereal just like the rest of them monsters."

Rolling her eyes, Kenisha wondered why she'd agreed to let Diamond and Kennedy spend the night over at her sister's house. But she had been too tired to get on the number 8 bus and pick them up. Blinking away unwanted tears, she allowed her fist to smash against her living room wall.

Ever since her doctor had told her about the cancer eating away at her body, her walls had gotten punched. When her doctor told her that having sex at an early age was one of the factors for cervical cancer, she'd wanted to kill the men who had paraded through her life, taken what they wanted, then left her diseased. "I need you to pick Jamal up from school today."

"Oh, no. I've already got two of your kids over here. Dawg, Kenisha, I've got four kids of my own. What makes you think I want to babysit another?"

Grabbing some tissue, and wiping the moisture from around her eyes, she said, "Look Aisha, I've got an appointment." Kenisha's third radiation treatment was scheduled for today. She'd missed her second appointment when Aisha promised to pick up her kids, but never showed. "It's important or I wouldn't ask."

Kenisha heard the rustling of the sheets as her sister sat up in bed.

"What's so special that you can't pick up your own son?"

"Nothing special. Just another rainy day."

Deidre Clark-Morris sat behind her oak desk trying to decide whether to respond to her emails. At last count, she had seventy unopened messages. She just couldn't make herself read another parent complaint about the athletic programs she was forced to cut. And she didn't have the patience to deal with teachers complaining about old textbooks. The superintendent had already given her his sorry-about-your-luck look the last time she told him that she needed to replace the textbooks.

Today, she didn't have the energy to fight. Deidre had other things on her mind. Consuming things. Things between her, Johnson, and God. *Please God, don't let it come.*

It was her monthly cycle. Due yesterday, but thankfully absent. If *it* didn't show up today, maybe she'd finally have some good news to report to Johnson.

Another email appeared in her inbox. This one was from Johnson. The header read, "How are you doing?" On an ordinary day, a simple message like that from her husband would have put a smile on her face. Would have made her think of the "When a Man Loves a Woman" song.

But today was not ordinary. This was the day she would either get her period or be pregnant. So she knew that her wonderful, loving husband's email really meant "After seven long years of wishing and waiting, are you finally pregnant?"

Leave me alone. Those were the words she wanted to shout back across the email line. But salvation in the name of Jesus, and a couple deep breaths stopped her tirade. Consigning Johnson's email to the same devil the other seventy could go to, Deidre signed off her computer. It was 3:30; the students had been gone since 2:50.

"It's time to go."

A knock at her door stopped her from packing up. "Come in."

Mrs. Wilson, the stern-faced second-grade teacher, walked in with little Jamal Moore in tow. Deidre knew Jamal. Had greeted him several times in the hallway. He was always well groomed. One of the first things she noticed about Jamal, after his signature zigzag cornrows, was that his pants fit. Either he or his mom didn't buy into that sloppy, hanging-off-your-backside fad that most kids were wearing.

"What's up?" Deidre asked.

Pointing at Jamal, Mrs. Wilson told her, "His mother didn't pick him up. I need to leave him with you."

"I was just getting ready to leave, Mrs. Wilson. I can't stay with him today."

Mrs. Wilson gave Deidre a piercing glare. "Now, I understand that you are the principal of this school, and therefore more important than the rest of us, but you are also the one who closed down the after-care program—"

Deidre held up her hand. "The superintendent closed down our after-care program, Mrs. Wilson. Not me."

With hands on healthy hips, Mrs. Wilson told her, "I don't care if it was you or the superintendent. You didn't stop him. And you promised to take turns watching these errant children. Well, it's your turn."

Deidre looked toward Jamal. With the exchange going on in front of him, he couldn't be feeling very wanted or cared about. For goodness sake, his mother had left him to fend for himself. Abandoned him. He didn't need to listen to this babysitting tug-of-war. "Go home, Mrs. Wilson. Jamal and I will be just fine."

"What's your number?" Dismissing Mrs. Wilson as she harrumphed out of the office, Deidre smiled at Jamal. "We'll get your mom on the phone. She'll be here in no time, you'll see."

She opened her desk drawer, grabbed the Reese's peanut butter cup she'd been saving for a special occasion, and tossed it to Jamal. She stood and picked up the telephone. Her smile disappeared. The oozing warmth between her legs screamed, "Failure." With as much composure as she could muster, she put down the phone. "I'll be right back."

Picking up her purse, she ran down the hall to the teacher's restroom. In the stall, sitting on the toilet, her worst nightmare was confirmed. "Oh, God. Oh, God, no." She had done everything right. She'd used that chart religiously. She and Johnson had waited until her body temperature was at the right level. How could she not be pregnant? Banging her fist against the restroom stall, she declared, "It's my turn, God." But, no matter how much she wanted it to be, it was not her turn. Would probably never be her turn.

She put her elbows on her thighs and her hands over her face, and cried as if she'd carried a baby to full term, watched him play in the backyard, watched him grow into a young man, then held him as he slowly died in her arms.

Twenty minutes later, Jamal found her still crying. He tapped on the stall door. "Mrs. Morris, what's wrong?"

"I-I g-got my period," she blurted between gasps. She clamped her hand over her mouth as her eyes widened. The superintendent had been itching to fire her. He'd certainly do it now. How could she blurt such a thing out to a seven-year-old child?

Jamal smirked. "My mama always screams, 'Thank You, Jesus' when she gets her period. The only time I heard her cry was when Mr. Friendly—that's what Mama calls it—came late one month."

Although she hated to admit it, Jamal's statement caused her to be upset with God. Women who didn't want children seemed to spit them out, while she and Johnson remained childless.

She closed her eyes, blinking away the remnants of tears as she thought of her husband. The day they met, he'd overwhelmed her with his deep, dimpled smile. Scared her when he declared that he believed in destiny and she would be his wife. But the following week she was hooked, so into him that when he told her how many children he wanted, she couldn't bring herself to tell him that two doctors had pronounced her infertile.

She should have told him. But he was all she'd ever wanted. Their love was so new, she'd been terrified of losing him. After the Lord saved her soul, she'd thought that if she charted her fertile periods and prayed . . .

"Mrs. Morris?"

Sniffling, Deidre wiped the tears from her face. "I-I'm sorry, Jamal. I'll be out in a second." She blew her nose, took the pad out of her purse, and lined her underwear with it. Flushing the toilet, she adjusted her clothes before opening the stall.

As if he were talking a lunatic down from a ledge, he asked, "Do you need me to get you anything?"

Washing and drying her hands, Deidre shook her head.

"When I'm sad, Mama holds my hand. That always makes me feel better." He stretched out his hand. "Do you want to try it?"

Deidre's heart swelled with love for this little boy who reached out to her when she needed it most. She grabbed his hand as they walked back to her office.

He squeezed her hand. "Feel better?"

A tear trickled down her cheek. "Much. Thank you, Jamal."

Back in her office, Deidre put her files in her briefcase. "If you don't mind, Jamal, I'd like to go home. I'll call your mom and give her my telephone number and address."

"That's fine with me. Just as long as you let her know where I'll be. I wouldn't want her to worry."

Deidre almost told him that she was sure his mother wasn't all that concerned. If she were, she wouldn't have forgotten to pick him up. That was the other beef she had with God. She and Johnson would be great parents. They'd never leave their children to fend for themselves. But alas, the babies were gifted to the unfit, while she, Deidre Clark-Morris, babysat.

2

Memories, like demons, kicked Kenisha around as she lay down on that hospital bed while this X-ray-looking machine sent radiation through the cancerous parts of her body. She felt weak and beaten as the ghosts of yesterday reclaimed her soul.

"Dynasty, girl, you ain't right."

"Ah, stop your crying," she told Kenisha as she raked the cards off the table. "We won fair and square, and you know it."

Kenisha sat back and huffed. "Just deal the cards." They were playing Spades. Terrell, Kenisha's boyfriend, was her partner. And Clyde was Dynasty's partner. Although the stiff way Dynasty was treating Clyde made Kenisha wonder if he was still her live-in boyfriend. She turned to Clyde. "You need to stop letting your bad habits rub off on my sister. She was a nice girl before she started messing around with you."

Laughter escaped the mouth of three of the card players. But Kenisha noticed something akin to regret dancing around her sister's eyes. Dynasty's silence changed the mood.

Clyde either didn't notice that Dynasty wasn't on his team anymore, or he was playing dumb. He put his hand over Dynasty's and said, "Ain't nothing wrong with my baby. She knows how the game is played. You're the one who needs to keep up."

Dynasty pulled her hand from Clyde's as she smirked at Kenisha. "That's right, baby sis, you need to keep up."

"It's like that? All right then." Kenisha turned to Terrell and said, "You heard 'em, right? So I need you to help me show these knuckleheads how the game is played for real."

Terrell kissed the deck of cards and then dealt them. He turned over the first round of cards so that everyone could see what the other player was dealt. Clyde got the three of diamonds, Kenisha got the ace of spades, Dynasty got the king of hearts, and Terrell got the little joker.

"It's on now," Kenisha said with glee. She thought for sure that she and Terrell would win this hand, but the rest of the cards didn't go in their favor and they lost that hand also.

Terrell stood and stretched his long, athletic body. "Guess it's time to go. I got people to see."

Kenisha frowned as she cleared the table. "Thought you said you were going to let that mess alone?"

He walked around the table, bent down, and kissed her forehead. "Girl, your man has gotta handle his business. How would it look if I let them thugs get away with creeping on my turf?"

Kenisha awkwardly pushed her big-bellied body out of her chair and stood. "It would look like you had finally gotten your senses together. Like you were ready to grow up and be a father to our child."

Palming her belly, Terrell told her, "Girl, I'm gon' always take care of mine. Believe that."

Gently rubbing the side of his face, she tried again. "I just don't want you to get hurt, Terrell. Every thug on them streets is not gon' back down just 'cause you're mean and mad."

He moved her hand from his face. "Just have my steak ready when I get back here. Come on, Clyde, let's go handle our business."

"I'll be out there in a minute," Clyde said.

Terrell walked out and got into the truck.

Clyde turned to Dynasty. "Can I talk to you for a minute?"

Eyes downcast, Dynasty told him, "Nothing left to say."

"Don't be like this, Dy."

"It's over, Clyde. Just let me go, okay?"

He picked up a chair and threw it across Kenisha's living room. Dynasty jumped up and ran behind the couch.

Kenisha yelled outside, "Terrell, come get your boy!"

"You're not just gon' dismiss me like this, Dy. I've done too much for you."

With the couch between them and Terrell on his way back in the house, Dynasty let loose. "Yeah, you've done a lot for me. But you've done a lot more to me. Don't you get it, Clyde? You ruined everything we had when you made me lose our baby."

"Why you gotta start with her? We've got things to do," Terrell called from the door.

"This ain't over, Dy," he told her as he walked out the door.

Dynasty came from behind the couch and yelled at Clyde as he jumped in Terrell's truck. "Oh, it's over, all right. So stop coming over to my sister's house. I don't want to play cards with you. I don't want to talk to you. I don't even want to know you exist. Do you hear me, Clyde?" She slammed the door, locked it, then sat down and cried.

Kenisha went to her sister and softly rubbed her back. "It'll be okay, Dy."

She looked up. "When? I haven't seen an okay day since your crazy mama birthed me."

"She was your crazy mama first."

They both laughed, then Dynasty asked, "You got any Kool-Aid?"

Kenisha went to the kitchen, poured two glasses of orange Kool-Aid, walked back into the living room, and handed her sister a glass. "I had no idea, Dy. You told us that you lost the baby because of some kind of accident."

Dynasty took a couple of gulps, then set the glass down. "Yeah, Clyde accidentally kicked it out of me."

Kenisha flopped down on the couch next to her sister. "I didn't know, Dy. Dawg. What made him do it?"

Sniffling and wiping the tears from her face, Dynasty asked, "Besides being crazy?"

Trying not to laugh, Kenisha nudged her sister. "What happened?"

"We were at MJ's drinking and having a good time when Carlton walked in."

"Your ex-boyfriend Carlton?"

"Exactly. Well, Carlton spoke to me, and I stupidly spoke back. Clyde snatched me out of that club, took me home, and proceeded to beat me from one room to the next. He said that my baby probably belonged to Carlton. That's when he kicked me. Over and over again."

"If I'd known, Dynasty, there's no way I would have let Terrell bring that dog in here."

"Don't worry about it. The sad part is, I think I still love him."

"How you gon' love somebody that did some mess like that to you?"

"I never said I wanted to love him, Kenisha. I'm all messed up, torn up inside. I just can't stop my heart from loving his no-good behind."

They sat there in silence for a while, both recognizing the irrational desires of the heart, the longings that just couldn't be denied, even when danger signs glared in their faces. Kenisha was still in love with James, her first love, but he was in prison, so she was try-

ing to make things work with Terrell. "Well, if you really love him, have you thought about giving him a second chance?"

Why, why, why did she think Clyde could change? Not a day went by that Kenisha didn't long to talk to her sister, her best friend, again. But her sister was dead, and she had sent her back into the arms of the man who had murdered her—this was her greatest sin. Cancer was her atonement.

A nurse stepped into the room, causing Kenisha to lock her memory back into the past.

"All right, we're done for today. You can put your clothes back on, and I'll see you tomorrow."

"Same time, same place," Kenisha said with false cheer.

The nurse walked over to her bed and put a hand on her shoulder. With sympathetic eyes, the older woman said, "I know this isn't easy for you, but I'm going to try to make you as comfortable as possible every day you have to come to radiation. Okay?"

Compassion wasn't something Kenisha was used to receiving. It made her uncomfortable. She cleared her throat and asked, "Do you know how much longer I need to come here? I have kids. I can't keep dropping everything to be at the hospital."

"You don't have any other options. You need this radiation so we can get that tumor small enough to operate."

"What's your name?"

"I'm sorry, I thought I told you my name. It's Lori Myers."

"Well, Lori, do you have kids?" The woman looked to be in her thirties and so thin that Kenisha doubted she had ever carried any children.

"I'm not married yet," Lori said.

Why did these professional types always think you had to be married before having kids? Kenisha didn't understand them at all. "Well, I'm not married, and I have three." She stood up and put her clothes on, then turned back to Lori and said, "I don't have a reliable babysitter, so I don't know how I'm going to be able to come here every day."

"One thing I've learned in life is that if you've got the will, you'll find a way."

Easy for her to say, Kenisha thought. This middle-class woman was probably living in the suburbs. She had no clue about Kenisha's life. But Kenisha didn't try to enlighten her. She just grabbed her purse and left the room. Before leaving the hospital, she found a pay phone and called Aisha. "Hey, I'm on my way home. Can you bring the kids to me?"

"Well, it took you long enough. My God, Kenisha, it's almost six o'clock."

"I know, I know. It couldn't be helped. Did Jamal have any homework?"

"How would I know? I thought Jamal was with you."

Screaming into the phone, Kenisha asked, "Are you telling me you didn't pick my son up? I called you this morning and asked you to get him for me."

Snapping her fingers. "My bad, Kenisha. I forgot."

Still screaming, Kenisha told her, "You better borrow John's car and bring yourself to Good Samaritan Hospital and pick me up so I can find my son."

"What are you doing at the hospital?"

"Don't waste time asking me stupid questions. Get yourself over here now."

"All right, Kenisha, calm down. I'll be there in a few minutes. Sorry."

"Well, that just makes it all better, doesn't it?" Kenisha slammed the phone down without waiting for a reply.

3

Oreo ice cream and pepperoni-and-ham pizza was a combination for pregnant women. But Deidre sat defiantly on her family-room sectional, with no baby in her stomach, wolfing down ice cream and pizza anyway. She pointed at a video on the coffee table. "Put that in the DVD player," she told Jamal.

Jamal read the movie title as he picked it up. "You like this old stuff?"

"Old stuff? You mean *classic*, right?"

He popped the movie in and then punched play. "Call it whatever you like. All I'm saying is, if it's a black and white, it's old."

In between a mouthful of ice cream and pizza, Deidre laughed. The sound was almost foreign to her. Laughter had been missing in her life since guilt about not being able to produce Johnson's child took hold of her and her "good" job became an evil nightmare.

Since she could do nothing about the child issue, Deidre tried desperately to push Johnson out of her mind. She knew she should have emailed him back at work, or telephoned him so he would know that she wasn't pregnant. But it was too hard to let the words slip out of her mouth. Too hard to hear

Johnson's not-again sigh. So, as she sat back and pretended to watch *It's a Wonderful Life* with Jamal, Deidre thought about the problems at work.

Frank Thomas was the superintendent over the City of Dayton schools. He'd given Deidre a hard time ever since he took the position two years ago. His lack of trust in her ability to run her school effectively was taking its toll on her performance, which was another blow to Deidre's self-esteem and her faith in God. As a Christian, performing well was important to Deidre. She felt that she worked not only for Frank Thomas, but also for God. And when Frank belittled her efforts, she pictured God looking down on her and shaking his finger.

Deidre put her bucket of ice cream on the coffee table as a thought ran through her mind. Maybe she couldn't get pregnant because of all the stress on her job.

"Do you think this getting your wings stuff is for real?"

Remembering that she had company, Deidre turned to Jamal. "What?"

"The angel in this movie. Do you think that's true?"

"Do I think what's true?"

Jamal rolled his eyes and pointed at the TV. Clarence the angel was telling a bartender that he needed to help someone in order to get his wings. "Do you think that's true?"

She turned her face toward the TV. "Oh. I'm not sure."

"What about angels? Do you think they're real?"

Sometimes I wonder. "Yes, of course angels are real."

"Turn left here." When Aisha missed the turn, Kenisha jumped up and down in the front seat of the car. "Where are you going? I told you to turn left back there."

"I was going too fast to turn. Calm down, Kenisha, I'm turning around."

"I'll calm down when I get to my son. How could you forget about him, Aisha? You ain't right."

Making a U-turn in the street, Aisha said, "I already said I was sorry about that. You told me that he's over at his principal's house, right? So he's safe."

Kenisha rolled her eyes as she sat back in her seat and glared at her sister. She just didn't get it. It's a wonder that Children's Services didn't visit her more than once a year. *The annual check-up*, Aisha jokingly referred to the visits she received from social workers. Kenisha would be mortified if some social worker came to her house accusing her of being an unfit mother.

While waiting for her sister to pick her up, Kenisha called the school but only got the voicemail. She called her mother to see if Jamal had called, but her mother was drunk and couldn't remember. Then Kenisha tried her home voicemail, hoping that Jamal had left her a message. That's when relief swept over her as she wrote down the address that Jamal's principal had left for her.

"You might be mad at me right now, but I have something to tell you and since you're in my car, you're stuck listening."

"What is it, Aisha?"

"I turned in my video to the *For the Love of Ray J* show."

Kenisha rolled her eyes again. Her sister was a reality show diva wannabe. Aisha had no talent whatsoever and four kids, so there was no way she was getting on one of those shows. But then again, most of the women on those shows didn't have any talent either. They just brought the drama, and people with nothing better to do tuned in. "What makes you think Ray J wants to become an instant daddy to four kids?"

Aisha shook her head. "Kenisha, you just don't get it. It doesn't matter if Ray J picks me or not. It's the exposure that I'm after. What if I get on that show and some producers see how talented I am . . . maybe I'll get a recording contract or something."

"Didn't they already boo you off of *American Idol*?"

"My sinuses had been acting up that day, and you know it."

Kenisha started laughing. She couldn't help it. Aisha cracked her up. Aisha had big dreams for a project chick who couldn't even manage to get out of bed before noon.

"Laugh all you want, Kenisha. When I'm a big star, we'll see how much you laugh then."

Kenisha waved her hand in the air, dismissing her sister. "Do whatever you want, Aisha. I've got my own problems. I don't have time to worry about you."

"Why were you at the hospital, anyway?"

"Turn right here, she lives on this street."

"Don't ignore me," Aisha said as she turned the corner. "Why were you at the hospital?"

"Slow down, look for 6280. And it's none of your business."

"Oh, so I can play taxi, but I don't get to know nothing."

Kenisha pointed at a red-brick house. "Pull over, Aisha. This is it."

Aisha leaned her head against the windowsill. "Wow. Jamal sure knows who to go home with. Leave it to him to pick some rich white lady."

"Jamal's principal isn't white. She's a sistah." She got out of the car and walked across hunter-green grass, smelling the fragrance of the fresh pine mulch that surrounded the trees. Knocking on the door, Kenisha put a smile on her face and tried to forget that all she wanted to do was to find a bed and lie down.

"So what did you think of the movie?" Deidre asked Jamal as Clarence got his wings.

He got up and took the disc out of the DVD player. As he returned to his seat, he told her, "My mom acted like that guy for a while."

"Which guy?"

"The one who thought everybody would have been better off if he'd never been born."

Cautiously, Deidre asked. "Why does your mom think that?"

"She doesn't now. But after my aunt died, I would hear her crying and saying stuff about it all being her fault." He looked down at his hands. Realized he was still holding the disc and set it on the coffee table. "I watch these old movies a lot with my mom." He pointed at the slices of pizza on the table. "My mom likes pepperoni and ham pizza too."

Deidre recognized the change in subject and let it happen.

"You know what?" Jamal asked. "You remind me of my mom."

"Like how?"

"Well, you're nice, and you like kids."

Deidre smiled at Jamal. "How do you know I like kids?"

"Ah, come on, Mrs. Morris. All the kids at school know that you're fair. You don't just ignore us because we're kids. You listen."

Hearing that from Jamal made Deidre feel much better about the strides she'd made at Jane Adams. Lately, with how her boss had been treating her, she'd started feeling like a failure. Like maybe somebody else could take over as principal and do a much better job. "Thanks, Jamal. I appreciate your saying that."

"It's true. All the kids talk about how cool you are." Jamal's eyes turned sad as he shook his head. "It's too bad you weren't pregnant today. You'd make a great mom."

The smile left Deidre's lips as sadness invaded her eyes. She stood and began clearing the food off the coffee table. *Lord, please make the pain go away*. But the pain would not move. Tears trickled down her face as she walked into the kitchen.

Jamal followed her and sat on the stool behind the counter. "I'm sorry. I didn't mean to make you sad again."

She grabbed a napkin off the counter and wiped the tears from her face, then blew her nose. "I'm all right, don't worry abou—"

The doorbell rang.

Jamal jumped. "That's my mom."

Throwing the napkin in the wastebasket, Deidre told Jamal, "Well, let's go let her in."

Kenisha had few dreams. But the one that stuck with her was about moving her children into a nice home in a nice neighborhood where they could go outside and play without ducking gunfire. Every Sunday when Mr. Hadley, her elderly next-door neighbor was finished reading his newspaper, he would knock on her door and give her the Home section. Kenisha pored over the pages, taking in the square footage and the acreage of the homes. Once, she even took the bus to a home tour event. She walked through three- and four-hundred-thousand dollar homes, asking questions about the structure and feeling the etching in the columns as if she could be an interested buyer. She knew what a quality home looked like. That's why her mouth hung open and she couldn't even say hello when Mrs. Morris opened the door and she stepped into the foyer.

"It's nice, isn't it, mama? Like those houses you look at on Sunday."

"You ain't lied about that, Jamal." Stepping past Deidre, Kenisha looked at the spacious open-floor plan. The winding staircase. "This house is off the chain."

Deidre cleared her throat.

Kenisha turned toward her. "Oh, hey. Gurl, I was 'bout to take a tour of this mug. Thought I was in one of them show homes for a minute. How you doing?"

"I'm fine," Deidre told her, then added, "Thanks for picking Jamal up."

Kenisha caught the college-girl attitude Miss Thang was throwing at her. She was about to go there with her, but after the day she'd had, she just didn't have the energy. So she simply told her, "You don't have to thank me. That's my job."

Deidre turned to Jamal. "Go get your things." She turned back to Kenisha once Jamal was out of sight. "It looks like you forgot your job today."

"Look, lady. I don't know what your problem is, but my son has never been left at your school before. I pick him up on time every day."

"Not today."

"Once, okay. One time out of a year."

"Once is too many."

Kenisha gave Deidre the hand. "Whatever."

"How can you be so nonchalant?" Deidre kept her voice to a whisper as she told Kenisha off. "Jamal is your son. He should be precious, and far more important than any errand you had to run."

Kenisha continued to roll her eyes with the five-finger disconnect still in Deidre's face.

"If you think I'm going to let you ruin Jamal's life, you can think again. I'm calling Children's Services first thing in the morning. We'll see how smug you are then."

Kenisha's hand came down. "Look, lady, you've got it all wrong."

Tears flowed from Deidre's face as she pointed into the family room where Jamal was gathering his stuff. "I'm not going to let you hurt him. A mother should love and care for her child. Not put him in harm's way."

Kenisha pointed in the direction Jamal took off in. "That's my heart. Jamal knows he's my heart. I'd never do anything to hurt him."

Deidre wiped at the tears. "Tell it to Children's Services."

"W-w-wait." No social worker was going to call her unfit. Before Kenisha could stop herself, she blurted out, "I have cancer, okay? I was at the hospital getting a radiation treatment."

"What a terrible thing to say."

"It's more like a terrible thing to have. But it's true. You can call my doctor if you want." She dug in her purse and produced a small white business card. "Here. Call Dr. Lawson if you don't believe me."

Jamal walked back in the room looking from his mom to Mrs. Morris. His mom had this angry look on her face, and Mrs. Morris was standing there with her mouth hanging open. "Is something wrong?"

"No, baby. Let's just go. I need to get out of here," Kenisha told him as she grabbed his hand and swung open the front door.

"Wait," Deidre yelled.

Kenisha turned around to face her accuser. "What else do you have to say, lady?"

"Look, I'm sorry that I accused you of neglecting Jamal. I've seen him around in school, and I've always thought he was well taken cared of."

Kenisha scoffed. "Then why'd you say that stuff about Children's Services?"

Deidre put her hands to her head and massaged her temple. "I've been going through some things lately. But I had no right to take my anger out on you."

"Yeah, Mama," Jamal chimed in. "Mrs. Morris thought she was pregnant, but it turned out she wasn't."

"How do you know?" Kenisha turned to her son.

"Ask her," Jamal said. "She was crying and everything."

Oh, Lord, Deidre thought. If Dr. Thomas found out that she had shared such personal information with a child, he would write her up for sure. She looked from Jamal to Kenisha and then said, "I was in the bathroom crying. Jamal walked in trying to see if I was okay. I'm sorry about blurting such a thing out. But I was in a bit of distress when he walked in on me."

Kenisha doubled over in laughter. When she pulled herself together, she said, "That's a first for me. The women I know get distressed when they find out they *are* pregnant."

Trying to get off the subject, Deidre said, "Well, look, if you need to talk or need my assistance with anything, you've got my number now, so please give me a call." With that, Deidre walked them to the car without so much as an offered prayer for Kenisha's infirmities.

4

Kenisha made Hamburger Helper as soon as she got home. Fed her kids and then put Diamond and Kennedy to bed. Jamal was like her, a night owl. She let him stay up, but never past eleven. His company usually kept her from feeling so lonely. But tonight, when he looked at her with those sad brown eyes, she wished she'd put him to bed with the girls.

"You got cancer?"

Kenisha got up, went into the kitchen, and started running some dishwater.

Jamal followed her. "Do you have cancer?"

She turned to face him. "What you know about cancer?"

A tear trickled down his young face. "I know that my friend Joey's grandmother just died from it."

Kenisha turned off the dishwater and sat down at the small kitchen table. She patted the seat next to her, and her son joined her. "Now, Jamal, you know that Joey's grandmother was old, right?"

"Right."

"But I'm not old. I'm too young to die, right?"

"Right."

She put his small hand in hers and rubbed up from his hand to his elbow. "So don't think like that, okay?"

Jamal snatched his hand away and stood up. "You've got it, don't you? I heard you tell Mrs. Morris that you had cancer."

Jamal was wise beyond his years, always had been. Kenisha had never been able to hide anything from him. No sense trying now. She lowered her head, twisted her lips. "Yeah, baby. I've got cancer."

He cried. Kenisha held her son. His body jerked back and forth as his tears flowed. He held onto her so tight that Kenisha was afraid to let him go. She wanted to comfort him but didn't know what to say. Tears rushed to her eyes as she said, "Come on, Jamal. Stop all this crying. I'm going to need you to be strong for me. You've always been my little helper. And I'm really going to need you now."

Slowly he released his hold, sat back in his chair, and dried his eyes.

Kenisha wiped her own eyes and silently commanded her chin to stop quivering. She had to be strong for Jamal. "Are you going to help me through this, Jamal?"

"I can do it. I'll take care of you, Mama."

She grabbed him and hugged him tight. "That's my little man." It was hard, but she pulled away from the embrace, patted his hand. "Everything's going to be okay. You'll see."

Jamal gave her a weak smile.

"Off to bed with you. I'm going to finish these dishes and go to bed myself. We can watch a movie tomorrow night. Okay?"

Jamal got up. He didn't argue about going to bed before eleven. He kissed his mother on the cheek and walked away.

Her chin started quivering again as she watched Jamal walk away. Jamal had brought so much joy into her life, but Kenisha still remembered the pain he'd caused her.

Tears of regret sprang into Kenisha's eyes as the doctor shouted, "Push!"

"No. I can't."

"You acted like a grown woman when you spread your legs to make this baby. Act like one now and push him out."

She barely knew this man in the white coat, crouched between her legs, demanding that she push her baby out of a hole that was too small for some grapefruit-size head to get through. She turned to James, pleading her case. "He's too big. I can't get him out."

James wiped away the tears that trickled down Kenisha's ashen face. "You can do this, Ke-Ke. You're a woman now. Remember that."

Smirking, the doctor mumbled, "I've never met a fifteen-year-old woman."

Strength from way down deep grew in Kenisha as she shifted her swollen body to look Dr. Holton in the eye. He was disrespecting her. People got cut for messing with others like that where she came from.

"I've been taking care of myself for more years than I can count," she told him, then stilled herself as an explosion ripped through her body. Pain so sharp and mind-blowing, it made her want to travel back to the beginning of time, snatch Eve up by her nappy roots, and smack the fruit juice out of her mouth.

"You okay, Ke-Ke?"

She wanted to smack James too. All his "baby, baby, pleases" had put her in this predicament. But her desire to wipe that smug, bet-you-wish-you'd-listened-to-your-mama look off Dr. Holton's face directed her energy toward her belly. Panting as the pain subsided, she told them, "This baby is ready to meet his mama."

"Then push," Dr. Holton said.

Grinding down, Kenisha pushed, not once, but three times, before her sweat-drenched body collapsed on the bed.

"I've got the head," Dr. Holton said, as he positioned himself to extract the shoulders. "One more push, Kenisha. Come on. You can do it."

Her insides were exploding, or were they imploding? She really didn't care what the correct term was. She was ready to throw in the towel, scream "Uncle," call for a truce, or beg this big-headed baby for mercy. How on earth was she supposed to push again? She was dying. Couldn't they see that? Dr. Holton was right. The delivery room was no place for a fifteen-going-on-thirty-five-year-old girl. There, she'd admitted it. Now could somebody please get this baby out!

If she died with her baby half in, half out, everyone would know she was a fraud—she couldn't really handle life.

She thought about praying. But she hadn't done much of that since she was nine years old, sneaking out to Sunday school at the church down the street from the Arlington Courts project homes where she'd aged beyond her years. That's where she'd heard that Bible story about a woman who wanted a child more than anything. The woman promised God that if He gave her a child, she would give the baby back to Him. Another pain shot through her and she screamed, "He's Yours, God, just help me through this."

The next few minutes passed like a blur. Her last push was faint, but she felt like Christmas had come when the pain of birth subsided. Then she heard the cry of her child and knew that God had been with her.

James moved a few strands of wet hair from her face. "You did it, Ke-Ke. Our son is here."

Stretching out weary arms, she said, "Hand me my son."

The nurse had just finished cleaning the baby. She looked to Dr. Holton. He nodded his approval.

She couldn't sit up. So when the nurse put her baby in her hands, she brought him to her lips and kissed his forehead. She and James had already picked out a name for their son. As best she could, Kenisha lifted Jamal Anthony Moore and proclaimed, "He's a gift from God."

How could this be happening to her? What was God thinking when he let her get cancer? Didn't he know she had three children to raise?

Getting up, she walked back to the sink and started putting the glasses in the water. Once again, she had found herself in another situation that proved God didn't care about her or her children. She swished a drinking glass around in the water a few times. She pulled it out of the water, but instead of rinsing the bubbles from the glass she threw it against the kitchen door.

"You're not fair," she screamed at God as the shattered glass cascaded down the wall. "What am I supposed to do now?"

The patter of six little feet could be heard as Kenisha's children ran toward the kitchen. "Mommy, what's wrong?" asked Diamond, her second oldest.

Kenisha had been staring at the shattered glass when her children ran into the kitchen. She turned around and looked at them. Jamal was eight and her rock. He was the man of the house. Diamond was five and was the typical middle child, always thinking the world was against her or that nobody cared about her. She'd given up thumb-sucking at the age of three; however, when she was sad or mad, that thumb found its way to her mouth. Kennedy was only two. She was still in diapers and refused to be potty trained—only admitting to doing "the number two" after it was already in her diaper. Her babies were too young to live without a mother.

Kenisha got down on one knee, she opened her arms wide. "Come here," she called to her children. They ran into her arms, and Kenisha hugged them all. "I'm sorry, kids. I didn't mean to wake you up."

"What wong?" Kennedy asked in her two-year-old dialect.

"Nothing's wrong, honey. Mommy's angry, but I shouldn't have been so loud. Now, you guys go back to bed, and I promise to be quiet."

"Are you sure you're okay, Mom?" Jamal asked.

Kenisha wiped away the tears that fell down her face. This was the second time tonight that he'd seen her crying. "Yes, hon, I'm okay. Can you put your sisters back to bed for me?"

Jamal grabbed his two sisters' arms. "Come on, back to bed."

Kenisha sat down on the floor and watched her children walk away as if this was the last time she would ever see them. She put her hand over her mouth, trying to stifle the moans that wanted to escape. But she couldn't stop the tears that came back like a river that forever flowed. Her eyes blurred, but she kept watching Jamal shuffle her little girls down the hall. When she lost sight of them, she stood up and ran to the edge of the kitchen, and with her head popping out of the doorway, she watched them march upstairs.

It's not fair, she thought as she crouched down to pick up the shards of glass off the floor. Her mother had been an alcoholic who never did anything for her children that wouldn't first benefit her, but she had already outlived one child and would probably outlive another. Kenisha really didn't understand how horrible mothers like Martha Carson were able to live long enough to ruin the lives of children, but a mother like herself, who only wanted the best for her children, would probably never see them graduate from high school, go to college, start their first job, get married, or have children of their own.

Three out of five of her mother's children never finished high school. One was a crackhead, two were unwed mothers, and one was murdered by her drug-dealing boyfriend. Her youngest sister, Angelina, was the only one of them who was even trying to make something of herself. She was in her third year of college and didn't have time to babysit, let alone have any rug rats of her own running behind her. Sitting down on the couch in the living room, Kenisha wondered if Angelina would consider taking her kids if Kenisha didn't make it through this.

She picked up the remote, propped her feet up on the couch, and said to herself as she turned the TV on, "Only one way to find out. I need to ask her."

"What's the reason for this family meeting?" Aisha asked impatiently.

"Yeah, and I want to know why you think you're grown enough to schedule a family meeting, when that's my job," Martha, Kenisha's mother called out from the couch where she lay with her head propped on a pillow.

Kenisha had called her brother and two sisters and asked them to meet her at her mother's apartment. Actually, Kevin was already at her mother's. His girlfriend had kicked him out two years ago, and he hadn't been able to find another woman with low enough self-esteem to offer him another free place to stay.

Clearing her throat, Kenisha stood in front of her family and said, "I asked you all to meet me here, because I have something important to say. As soon as Angelina gets here, I'll tell everyone what I need you to know."

"What are we supposed to do? Sit here and wait for Angelina? That girl will be late to her own funeral," Aisha said as she glanced at the clock on the wall as if she had some important job to get to.

As if on cue, Angelina opened the front door and ran in. "Sorry I'm late. The traffic getting over here was awful."

"Oh, so it was the traffic today, huh?"

"Shut up, Aisha," Angelina spat in her sister's direction.

"Okay, okay, no picking fights today," Kenisha said as she tried to take charge of the meeting again. "Angelina showed up, and that's good enough for me." Clearing her throat again, she began, "I'm not going to beat around the bush here. I've got cancer, and the doctors don't know if I'm going to make it."

The room became so silent that Kenisha was afraid to say another word. She had sent her and Aisha's kids upstairs to play while she talked to the adults, but she couldn't even hear any sound or movement upstairs. That worried her, so she ran upstairs to check on the kids. All seven children were seated in front of the television watching the Disney channel. She turned around and ran back downstairs.

Her mother was no longer lounging on the couch, she was sitting up, watching Kenisha walk back into the living room. "Did you just say what I think you said?" Martha asked.

Taking a deep breath, Kenisha responded, "Yes, I have cancer." It was getting easier to say now. When she was first told, Kenisha couldn't form her mouth around the words.

"I need a drink." Martha stood up and walked into the kitchen.

"Are you sure, sis?" Kevin asked as he tried to focus his glazed eyes on the real world.

Kenisha nodded.

"Doctors give misdiagnoses all the time. Did you get a second opinion?" Angelina asked.

Kenisha sat down in the chair she had placed in the center of the room. "I wish they were wrong. But I've had two other doctors confirm, so I'm taking radiation treatments now, and I'm going to need help with my kids."

Martha came back into the living room with a bottle of Jack Daniels in one hand, a Miller Light in the other, and a glass cradled between the two bottles. She set the glass on her coffee table and poured the Jack into her glass. After taking a few drinks, she asked Kenisha, "Why'd you wait so long to tell us this wonderful news?"

Was Martha really upset, or was she just using this as an excuse to drink? "I didn't want to talk about it," Kenisha admitted.

"So why you talking about it now?" Martha asked as she leaned her head back and took a swig from her glass. She slammed the glass back on the table and then said, "Let me answer that. You need something from us, so now you want to share with your family."

Was this Martha's first drink today? Her voice was beginning to slur, and Kenisha didn't think that even Jack could work that fast. "Yes, mother, I need your help." She looked around the room at her brother and two sisters, and then added, "I need everybody's help. I'm taking radiation treatments right now, and I need someone to watch my kids."

"If you had listened to me and kept your legs closed, you wouldn't need no babysitter, probably wouldn't have cancer now, either," Martha said, voice still slurring as she twisted off the cap of her beer.

Aisha, who hadn't said a word since Kenisha announced that she had cancer, stood up and shouted, "Leave her alone!" Aisha ran toward Kenisha and enveloped her sister in her arms.

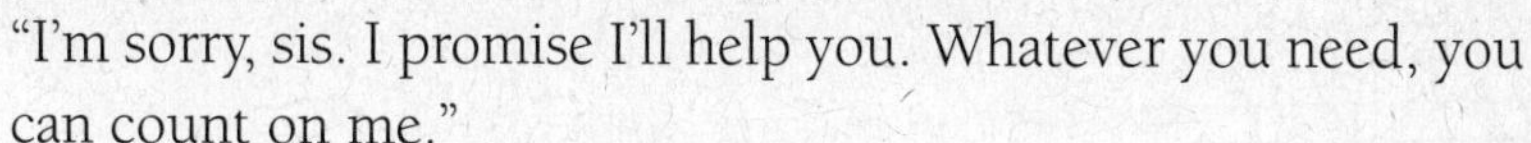

"I'm sorry, sis. I promise I'll help you. Whatever you need, you can count on me."

Kenisha hugged Aisha back. A tear rolled down Kenisha's face. Her sister was irresponsible and a dreamer, but Kenisha was truly touched by Aisha's response to her illness. "Thank you, Isha, I'm going to need a lot of help."

They broke their embrace. Aisha wiped the tears that were rolling down her face. She put her arm around Kenisha's shoulders and said, "That's why we need a star in this family. If I was a movie star, I could do a telethon for cancer research or something."

"Just your being here is good enough for me," Kenisha told her.

"You know that girl is looking for any excuse she can find to get on television. One day she is going to embarrass us all," Martha said.

"Maybe you and I can do a show together, Martha," Aisha said with a smirk on her face.

"Like that Frankie and Neffe show? You can forget it," Martha said. "You're not getting me on television so you can cry about what a drunk your mother is, just to boost your nonexistent career." Martha lifted the glass to her lips and swallowed the contents.

"You just don't want to help nobody," Aisha accused her mother.

How did this meeting turn into the Aisha's "Got Dreams" hour? Kenisha lifted her hand like she did in high school, and said, "I have to get some more radiation treatments before they can operate, so I'm going to need a ride to and from radiation."

As if remembering that this meeting wasn't about her, Aisha turned back to Kenisha and said, "I can do that. You'll see, little sis, I'm going to be there for you."

"I also need someone to watch my kids during radiation and while I'm in the hospital for the surgery." Kenisha looked around the room hoping to find someone just as eager about watching her kids as Aisha had been about taking her to radiation. But no one volunteered. As Kenisha looked around the room, she began to wonder if she even wanted any of them to watch her children. Her mother was a drunk, Kevin was a crackhead, and Aisha was highly irresponsible. Angelina was only twenty and was trying to get through college, but if Kenisha had to leave her kids with anyone, it would be Angelina. She turned to Angelina and said, "I know you've got your own life, Angie, and you were the one who did the right thing by not having any kids, so you shouldn't have to watch mine, but I need you."

"You said one thing right," Martha said as she tried to position herself in an upright position. "Angelina ain't got no kids, and she ain't gon' be watching yours."

"That ain't right. Angelina don't never have to do nothing for this family," Kevin complained.

"And she ain't gon' never do nothing for y'all. Angelina is gon' make something of herself, and I'm not about to let y'all pull her down," Martha said.

"Then who is going to watch the kids while I'm taking Kenisha back and forth to her radiation treatments?" Aisha asked.

"She can bring them babies over here. I'll watch them," Martha said.

"Are you going to be drinking?" Kenisha asked.

Martha put her hands on her hips. "I drank when you were a kid, and I guess you turned out all right."

"No, I didn't," Kenisha responded with fire in her voice. "You were just too drunk to notice the things that happened to me." After that comment, the room erupted. Kevin and Aisha were on Kenisha's side. Angelina, as always, thought they were being too hard on Martha. But the arguments stopped when Martha passed out on the couch.

Aisha took out her camera as she stood over Martha. She turned on the video part of her digital camera and began filming Martha snoring.

"What are you doing?" Kenisha asked.

"I'm getting some footage. Producers love dysfunctional family stories. If I sent them all the footage I have on Martha, I would be in for sure. And then, bam . . . cancer research telethon, here we come."

5

Monday morning couldn't come fast enough for Deidre. She felt trapped in the house with Johnson all weekend long. Every time she looked at him, she saw pity in his eyes, and she didn't want his pity. She wanted his child. But God didn't appear to be interested in what she wanted.

So on Sunday she only half listened to her pastor's message. Oh, she still loved God and was committed to the cause of Christ, but if she was being truthful with herself, Deidre had to admit that a part of her had tuned out. She had wanted to curl up in bed and do nothing but lie under her comforter and watch HGTV all day. But Johnson got up raring to go, as if God had done so much for him that he couldn't wait to get to church and thank Him for it. But Deidre got out of bed out of obligation. Years ago she had read in the Bible that Christians should assemble together even more as "that day" approached. She had always been taught that "that day" was the rapture, but maybe "that day" was also when Christians have just plain ole tuned out.

They made it to church in time for praise and worship. Deidre thought she was doing a good job of hiding her feelings as she lifted her hands in praise and sang just as loud as the rest of the congregants. When it was offering time, she'd walked up to the offering baskets and put her tithes in with a cheerful heart. Deidre had even danced back to her seat. When Pastor Monroe preached his sermon, she leaned in a few times as if she were truly interested in what he was talking about. But in truth, she couldn't replay one word of his sermon.

When the service was over, Deidre stood up, grabbed Johnson's arm, and told anyone who asked that she was blessed of the Lord as she made her way out of the church. Deidre smiled as they neared the exit; she had done it again. She had not let on that she was sick inside. But before they could walk through the exit doors, Mother Barrow tapped Johnson on the shoulder and asked to speak with them for a moment in the prayer room.

Why do we have to go to the prayer room? Deidre wanted to scream.

Johnson said, "Sure thing, Mother Barrow." He turned Deidre away from the exit without asking her if it was okay and walked her back through the church into the prayer room.

Mother Barrow closed the door behind them. "Sit down," she instructed as she pointed to the couch. "From all that shouting and dancing Deidre was doing, I'm sure she's worn out by now."

Deidre didn't see a smirk or anything on Mother Barrow's face, but she was sure that Mother Barrow knew that she hadn't really been praising the Lord, but putting up a front. Deidre's first thought had been to ask the elderly woman to mind her own business. But she had known Mother Barrow for six years, and in that time, the woman had been nothing but kind to her. Deidre couldn't see repaying that with rudeness, so she sat down on the couch with Johnson and said nothing.

"Now, don't go catatonic on me, Deidre. I'm sure no one else noticed that you weren't really in the mood for church today. I wouldn't have noticed it, either, but God gave me a word for you. After receiving His word, I knew it must have taken all the strength you could muster to get out of bed and come to church today."

Deidre felt a tear roll down her cheek. How Mother Barrow could possibly know exactly what she'd been feeling was beyond her, but she had gotten it right. And it was taking all the strength Deidre had not to break down in front of Mother Barrow and Johnson.

"The Lord told me that your heart is broken over not being able to conceive," Mother Barrow said.

Yeah, right, the Lord told her. Deidre had told Mother Barrow herself that she was having trouble conceiving and had asked for prayer. Now the old woman was trying to act like she had some hotline to God. Deidre had half a mind to get up and walk out of the prayer room without so much as a goodbye; then Mother Barrow said something that made her put her whole mind into leaving the room.

"The Lord wanted me to tell you that the struggle is over. Your home will be filled with laughs, love, and children."

Johnson started grinning. He stood up and hugged Mother Barrow. "Thank you, thank you so much for saying that."

But Deidre wasn't smiling. She stood up and pulled Johnson away from Mother Barrow. "Let's go."

Johnson picked Deidre up and swung her around. "Did you hear what she said, honey? Isn't God awesome?"

"Put me down, Johnson."

He put her down.

"Let's go. I've got some papers to grade before school tomorrow."

The light went out of Johnson's eyes as he turned to Mother Barrow. "We've got to go, but I really appreciate that you would tell us what God showed you."

Deidre felt as if the walls were closing in on her, and if she didn't get out of this room right now, she would be crushed. She opened the door and left that prayer room fast. She kept walking until she made it to Johnson's car. She got in on the passenger's side, and it was at that moment she noticed how hard she was breathing. She needed an inhaler, and she didn't even have asthma.

Johnson got in the car. "Why'd you leave like that?"

Deidre couldn't answer him. She was too busy trying to calm her breathing before her heart exploded.

"Are you having a panic attack?" Johnson grabbed her head and pressed it between her legs. "Sit like this for a few minutes, and try to calm down."

How could she calm down? Johnson had just been guaranteed that he would have a house full of children, but Deidre knew that wasn't true. It would never be true, unless Johnson married another woman with a functional uterus.

Rubbing her back, Johnson spoke in a slow, soothing tone. "Take slower breaths, honey. It's all right. Everything is okay."

Counting backward—10-9-8-7-6—Deidre felt her body begin to relax. Her breathing slowed down as she sat back up in the passenger's seat. She couldn't look at Johnson. Couldn't bring herself to witness the longing in his eyes.

"What happened back there? Mother Barrow just gave us some great news, and you acted as if she gave you a death sentence."

"Not now, Johnson. Please, just take me home." Deidre leaned back in the passenger's seat and stared out the window while Johnson stared at her.

Most of the people had already cleared out of the parking lot, but Deidre spotted Sister Winslow holding her three-month-old baby girl as she walked to her car. She was cooing to the baby, so lost in her love that she wasn't paying attention as she walked through the parking lot. She stepped in front of Brother Andrew's car as he pulled out of his spot, and he pressed on the brake. Sister Winslow looked up with an apologetic smile. Brother Andrew rolled down his window and said good-naturedly, "You new mothers are all alike. Too in love to watch where you're going."

Deidre almost started crying again. Why couldn't that be her? Why couldn't she give Johnson what he wanted? But she knew the answer to that, and no prophecy from Mother Barrow was going to change her situation. Johnson finally got the hint, stopped staring at her, and turned on the car.

"We're going to finish this when we get home," he said as they drove off.

But Deidre made sure that they didn't finish anything. After dinner she had suddenly gotten so sick that she had to lie down for the rest of the evening. She told Johnson that she felt too ill to talk, like she might throw up if she opened her mouth too many times. And that was true; the stress of the day had caused Deidre's stomach to flutter.

Miraculously, though, she jumped out of bed bright and early Monday morning, got ready for work, and left the house before Johnson had a chance to grill her about her strange behavior on Sunday.

Walking through the halls of Jane Adams, Deidre watched her kids go from one class to the next. They chatted with friends, laughed, and goofed around in the halls, most of it good-natured fun. But there were a few children who tried Deidre's patience on a daily basis. Ronny Nickels was at the head of her list. And as usual, when Deidre turned the corner over by the third-graders' hallway, she found Ronny shoving a kid against the lockers. Deidre grabbed Ronny and moved him away from his latest victim. "Go straight to my office, Ronny.

I'll be there in a minute," Deidre said as she extended her index finger in the direction of the principal's office.

"I wasn't doing nothing," Ronny said as he pulled away from Deidre.

"You've done your last bit of *nothing* around here for a while." Deidre continued pointing toward her office as Ronny stomped off. She then turned to the little boy who had been shoved against the locker and asked, "Are you okay?"

"Yes, ma'am. Thank you."

Deidre watched the little boy run off to his next class as if nothing had happened. Kids were like that, able to turn the other cheek and move on. But adults held onto bitterness until it ate them alive. But maybe that's because by the time children grow into adulthood, they've turned so many cheeks that they're just plum worn out.

She continued her stroll down the hall, saying hello to children and teachers as they made their way to class. Back in her office, Deidre stopped at the desk of her administrative assistant, Christina Michael. "Call Ms. Nickels and let her know that Ronny is being suspended so she'll need to come pick him up."

"Can't we just let him stay until the end of the day, and then we can send him home with a note?" Christina asked timidly.

Deidre's heart went out to Christina. None of her staff wanted to talk to Shameka Nickels. She was a hateful woman who cursed out the staff of Jane Adams Elementary School on a regular basis. Most of the staff gave Ronny a pass on a lot of his antics just so they wouldn't have to deal with his mother. But the way Deidre was feeling today, she'd willingly take on that woman. "Don't worry about it, Christina. I'll call her myself."

"Are you sure about that, boss? I mean, you shouldn't have to handle my responsibilities."

"It's not a problem." Deidre turned to Ronny, who'd been sitting in one of the chairs against the wall. "Go on into my office," she said and then turned back to Christina. "Call her and then send it through to my line."

In her office, Deidre looked at Ronny, the third-grade bully. She saw nothing but prison in his future and didn't know how to turn him around. The boy had three strikes against him already. His father was in prison, his brother in juvie, and his mother wasn't fit to raise a dog, let alone five willful boys. "Do you understand why I'm suspending you today?" Deidre asked Ronny.

"No." He crossed his arms and stuck out his lips, trying to pretend that he was some real tough thug.

Deidre didn't see it like that. Ronny was a pretender. His entire family was rotten to the core, so he was trying to follow in their path. But Ronny was smart. He had a real aptitude for science and math. Although the family didn't have much money, if Ronny kept his grades up, Deidre could easily see him going to college on scholarship. The problem Ronny had was his mother.

Deidre's phone rang, and she picked it up. "This is Mrs. Morris."

"And this is *Ms. Nickels*. What do you want now?"

"Well, Ms. Nickels, I needed to let you know that Ronny is being suspended, and you need to pick him up."

"How long is he suspended for this time?"

"It will be three days."

"Three days! I can't spend my whole day watching him. What am I supposed to do with him for three days?"

Same thing we do, suffer through, Deidre wanted to say, but she silently prayed that the Lord would help her stay saved during this phone conversation. She sighed and then asked, "What time can you be here to pick Ronny up?"

"I'm not getting out of bed to come pick his bad behind up. Send him home on the bus."

Deidre looked over at Ronny and gave a half smile. She didn't want to argue with his mother about taking time out for her own son right in front of him, so she simply said, "I'll do that," and then hung up the phone before she had to go to the altar and repent.

Juvenile delinquents and prison inmates came from mothers like Shameka Nickels. Too lazy to get out of bed and do the right thing by the very children they had brought into this world. God knew this wasn't right, but with so much free love and so many unplanned pregnancies in the world, neglected and abused children were bound to be the end result. Again, Deidre wanted to question God, because she knew in her heart that she and Johnson would be good and loving parents, but here she was childless, while Shameka Nickels had five children. "I'm going to let you do in-school suspension today. But you'll be home for two days with your mother, okay?" Her tone was more tolerant now, almost as if she were asking his permission to send him home to his mother.

He nodded.

"You know your way to the detention center, so go on. I'll have Ms. Christina bring your suspension papers to you there."

Ronny got up without saying a word and walked toward the door.

Before he could put his hands on the knob, Deidre stopped him. "Can I ask you something, Ronny?"

He turned around and looked at her.

"Your math and science teachers tell me that you're the smartest kid in their class. Your social studies teacher says you know your stuff in his class also. So I just don't understand why you stay in so much trouble when you have a real chance at making something out of yourself. Don't you want to go to college and do something with your life?"

"I don't know nothing about college and all that. All I know is that my mom says I'm just like my daddy, and he don't seem so smart to me."

How could Shameka compare Ronny to a father who was a repeat offender and in prison more than he was out? Maybe she should call Children's Services. Maybe Ronny would be better off with a foster family than with a mother like Shameka Nickels. But each time she thought of picking up that phone and advocating for the rights of children, news reports of other children who'd been hurt in the system made her leave well enough alone. Deidre just prayed that something would happen to turn these kids around.

The rest of Deidre's day was just as busy as the morning. She didn't mind at all. The busyness of her day gave her an excuse not to think about Mother Barrow and her so-called prophecy. Johnson was practically giddy about the older woman's words. His happiness was so apparent that Deidre knew the truth of the matter would break his heart and probably destroy their marriage.

When Deidre and Johnson were first married, she couldn't wait for the final bell to ring so she could rush home to her man. But through the years and because of all this baby talk, she'd started dreading that final bell. Now she grabbed her purse and a stack of files she had already gone through. She needed to take them home in case Johnson wanted to talk about Mother Barrow's prophecy. That way she could point to the files and say that she had too much work to do and needed to talk later.

She put the files in her briefcase and walked out into the hallway. Children were running from their classrooms, through the hallway, and out to the waiting buses. At least some people were anxious to get home. As Deidre headed out the door, a kid dropped his books and his papers scattered across the hall. He bent down, trying to recover his stuff while the other kids stepped on his papers and books, single-mindedly trying to get out of the school building. Deidre put down her briefcase and purse, and began picking up some of the papers. When she turned to hand the paper to the boy who was still on the floor searching for more papers, she noticed that it was Jamal.

She had meant to seek Jamal out today in order to see how he was doing, but with the issues she was dealing with, she'd completely forgotten about him. Sometimes Deidre wondered if God really tolerated self-pity among His believers, or if He just shook His head in shame. She handed him his papers and then asked, "How are you doing, Jamal?"

"I'm all right," he said as he gathered the rest of his papers and then stood up.

But he didn't look all right. Jamal was normally well groomed, with his clothes cleaned and ironed, and his mini Afro combed and neat. But today his clothes were wrinkled, and it looked as if his hair hadn't seen a comb and brush in days.

Now she knew why she had wanted to check on Jamal first thing this morning. He needed her help, but she had been too wrapped up in self-pity to seek him out. Deidre took hold of Jamal's arm and pulled him off to the side. "You don't look like everything is all right. Please tell me what's wrong."

He snatched his arm away from her. "What do you care?"

"I care, Jamal, that's why I'm asking. Is your mom okay?"

He looked away, didn't answer.

"Jamal, please tell me, is something wrong with your mother?"

Deidre saw the tears as they creased the corners of Jamal's eyes.

He wiped the tears away as he said, "Nobody cares about my mother but me."

"Why do you say that?"

"Nobody will help her."

Again, Deidre felt the sting of her selfish behavior. Why hadn't she thought to ask Kenisha if she needed anything? "I'd like to help, Jamal. Can you take me to see your mother?"

6

Jamal jumped out of the car and ran up to his door as if he thought something terrible might happen if he didn't get inside his apartment that very minute. Deidre realized that she was partially to blame for Jamal's panic. If she hadn't laid into Kenisha the day she came to pick Jamal up from her house, then Kenisha wouldn't have blurted out the fact that she had cancer. And Jamal would probably still be blissfully in the dark about the whole situation.

Deidre followed Jamal, noting the trash that had been strewn on the next door neighbor's lawn. From the smell of it, the trash had been exposed like that for several hours, if not more. When Deidre reached Kenisha's front door, she noticed that a small flower garden had been planted near the door. The fragrance that rose from those colorful flowers contrasted with the smell of rotted garbage next door. As she stepped inside the small apartment, a new smell wafted into her nostrils—Pine-sol.

"Wake up, Mama, I'm home," Jamal said as he shook Kenisha's shoulder.

She was lying on the couch in the living room. She opened her eyes and then sat up. She looked at the clock on her wall.

"I didn't know it was this late. I'm sorry I didn't meet you at school. I got so tired after I mopped the floor that I lay down for a minute." She looked at the clock again. "At least, I thought I was only going to lie down for a minute."

"Mrs. Morris drove me home. She wanted to talk to you."

In slow motion, as if drugged, Kenisha looked around the room. When her eyes locked on Deidre, she said, "I wasn't neglecting my son. I normally pick him up and we walk home together. I just wasn't feeling well today."

"I didn't think you were neglecting Jamal. That's not why I stopped by." Deidre motioned toward the chair across from the couch that Kenisha was sitting on. "May I sit down?"

"You didn't ask if you could take my son off the school grounds, or come into my house. So why should you ask to sit down? Just go on and do it."

This is not going to be easy, Deidre thought as she sat down.

"Mrs. Morris wanted to know how you're doing," Jamal said as he sat down next to Kenisha.

"Everything is wonderful," Kenisha said as she looked toward Deidre, lifted her arm, and made a sweeping motion around the living room. "Can't you tell? We're living high off the hog and loving every minute of it."

What Deidre could tell was that although the furniture was probably a decade old, it was in good condition and the house was spotless. For a woman with three children, that was a remarkable feat. Deidre had visited mothers who had maids and hadn't found their homes to be as spotless as Kenisha's. "It appears that your children are doing well with you."

"You don't have to say that. I know that we are just poor folk, living in the projects. I saw that beautiful house you have, so don't tell me you think what I have is any comparison."

"I didn't say that, but I can tell that you keep your children and your home clean. And it looks to me as if you care about the things you have."

Kenisha turned to Jamal while pointing in Deidre's direction. "Is this the same woman who threatened to call Children's Services on me?"

There was an embarrassed expression on Jamal's face as he said, "Yeah, Mom, but I think she wants to help now."

Deidre noticed that it was very quiet in Kenisha's apartment. Too quiet for a place where three children lived. She looked around and then asked, "Where are your other children?"

Kenisha laughed, but it was bittersweet. "If I tell you that, you really will call Children's Services on me."

Raising her hands in surrender, Deidre said, "I know we got off on the wrong foot, but I didn't come here to judge you or to spy on you. I really just want to know if there is anything you need. I'd like to help."

Kenisha was silent for a moment. She looked at Jamal and then back at Deidre. "You'll have to forgive me. I'm not used to people asking to help me out. Mostly everyone I know runs in the opposite direction if I ask for a favor."

"Well, I'm not running. I really want to help."

Just then, Kenisha's back door opened and two little girls ran into the living room. A woman stepped inside the house and then leaned her head out the door and screamed. "No, don't you get your bad self out the car. Sit there until I come back."

The little girls ran to Kenisha and wrapped their arms around her. One of them said, "I missed you, Mommy."

"I missed the both of you too," Kenisha said.

"Well, you won't be missing them no more," the woman said as she stepped farther into the living room. "Look, Kenisha, I'm sorry, girl. I really tried to help, but I can't keep watching your kids and mine too." She lifted her arms and pointed outside. "I've got a new boyfriend, Kenisha. Those four little demons I got are bad enough, and Reggie said he can't handle any more kids at the house."

"What would Ray J say about you taking up with Reggie?" Kenisha asked, trying to hide her smirk.

"Real funny, Kenisha. But the way I see it is—what Ray J don't know won't hurt him."

"Until you get your guest spot on the Maury show, that is."

"Whatever, Kenisha. I'm not having any more kids. So I don't have to worry about that," Aisha said defiantly, then asked, "Are you mad at me?"

Kenisha gave Deidre a look that displayed everything she was feeling . . . good help was hard to find. She then turned back to her sister and said, "I'm not mad at you, Isha. You did the best you could."

Receiving her reprieve, Aisha smiled and then a look of concern etched across her face. "How was your radiation treatment?"

"The same. I'm still a little tired from it." Trying to get off the subject, Kenisha turned to Deidre and said, "This is my sister Aisha." She turned back to Aisha and said, "This is Mrs. Morris. She's Jamal's principal."

"Hello," Deidre said.

"Hey," was Aisha's response, and then she said, "Let me get to the car before Reggie drives off with my kids." She turned and left.

Kenisha told her children, "Y'all go wash your hands and change into some play clothes. I'll have dinner ready in a little bit."

The children didn't talk back or complain; they just ran toward the stairs as if they were eager to do what their mother requested of them.

Kenisha turned back to Deidre and said, "Thanks for coming over here to see about us, but to be perfectly honest, the only thing I need right now is a babysitter."

"She asked me to babysit."

"And what was so wrong with that? You did go over there to help her out, right?" Johnson asked while he and Deidre sat on the living room sofa discussing their day.

Deidre put her feet up on the sofa and hugged her knees to her chest. "Yeah, but I was thinking more along the lines of grocery shopping, housecleaning, or cooking something for her or the kids."

"You don't even like to cook. I do most of the cooking at our house."

"That's not true. We split the cooking and you know it."

"Yeah, but on your days, you normally order pizza or bring home takeout." Johnson leaned back in his seat and shook his head. He tried to understand Deidre, but sometimes she put the *P* in puzzle. "Why couldn't you just do what the girl asked you to do? It's not as if we don't have the space here; we could watch her children for a few days. And besides, watching her children would give us some practice for when we get our own."

Deidre sat up and put her feet back on the floor as she exploded, "I knew it! You just want those kids over here because you're tired of being with me."

Totally confused, Johnson said, "What?"

"You think I don't know how you feel about me?"

Johnson stood and held up his hands in an attempt to ward off whatever storm was brewing inside Deidre. "I love you,

De, that's how I feel about you. Whatever else you're thinking, you've got it all wrong."

Tears had formed in her eyes as she said, "Then why were you jumping all over yourself with joy when Mother Barrow promised you some kids?"

He sat back down and put Deidre's hand in his. "De, it shouldn't be a surprise to you that the news Mother Barrow gave us yesterday would make me happy. You and I have wanted kids since the day we got married. It's not our fault that the process has taken so long."

She snatched her hand away from him and glared. "You mean, it's not your fault. Because we both know that the fault rests on my shoulders."

He wished that he'd never told her about the physical he'd taken in which the doctor informed him that there was nothing preventing him from having a baby. Before he received that news, he and Deidre had been in this thing together—both wanting a child, and both working toward that end. Now Deidre acted like the whole matter was up to her and that if they didn't have a baby, then she had failed him. He'd never said that, had never felt that way. But that didn't stop her from crying herself to sleep. "We are in this together, De. Remember that. That's how we started this marriage, and I won't let you blame yourself for our not having a baby." He pulled her into his arms, kissed her forehead, and whispered in her ear, "It's not your fault, De. It's not your fault."

She pounded on his chest. "That's not true, Johnson. It's just not true."

Johnson looked to heaven as he tried to figure out how he and Deidre had gotten here. When they first got married they were in tune with each other's wants and needs. And it seemed like things only got better after they committed their life to the Lord. But these last few years, when it became obvious that Deidre couldn't conceive a child, it had changed them. Johnson didn't like what was happening, but he didn't know what to do to turn things around.

Deidre knew that it was her fault, and nothing Johnson said would change the facts. When she was a teenager, she'd started having acne problems, gained fifty pounds in a year, and her menstrual cycle would come two months and then skip a month. Her mother had been worried about her, so they'd had several tests run on Deidre. When the doctor had informed her that she had polycystic ovary syndrome, Deidre had given him a blank stare and said, "Huh?"

Dr. Clayton had then informed her that polycystic ovary syndrome, or PCOS as it is normally called, is a condition in which a woman's hormones are out of balance. He had further informed her that this syndrome could cause problems with monthly periods and make it difficult to get pregnant.

Deidre might have only been sixteen at the time, but she had always known that she wanted four children, two sets of twins, so that she would only have to go through labor twice. So she had turned to Dr. Clayton and said, "That can't be right. I'm going to have lots of children. My husband and I will be awesome parents."

What Deidre remembered most about that office visit is that Dr. Clayton, who was normally a cheerful and fun-loving kind of doctor, had this sad expression on his face as he said, "You may still be able to have children, but I have to be honest with you, Deidre, it will be difficult."

After that doctor's visit, Deidre's mom and dad had loved on her a little bit more and helped her realize that she was okay just the way she was—hairy back, acne, extra weight, and all. But as she left high school and headed to college, Deidre developed a hunger for salads and seafood; she started exercising and using dermatology cream for her acne. She still had the hairy back, but Deidre considered herself lucky, because according to Dr. Clayton, she could have grown a mustache or heavy sideburns. All in all, a hairy back wasn't such a big deal.

She was a senior in college when she met Johnson, and thankfully she had dropped all the excess weight by then. For the first time in Deidre's life, a man was actually interested in her. She had considered telling Johnson when they first started dating about her condition and the possibility that she might have a hard time conceiving a child. But who springs news like that on a first date? As the months rolled by and Johnson confided in her that he wanted a houseful of children, Deidre knew she should have told him about her PCOS then, but she had fallen in love with Johnson and didn't want to risk losing him. And anyway, she had been watching the food she ate and exercising regularly like Dr. Clayton had advised her to do. He'd told her that doing those things would make it easier for her to conceive when the time came. So she kept her mouth shut and hoped that things would turn out the way she'd always planned. Except for the twin thing. She no longer cared whether she had twins, she just wanted a child.

She had been married seven years now, and each childless day that passed ate at Deidre. The guilt of her silence was sending her into a depression. Deidre had stopped monitoring the foods she ate, had stopped exercising. She'd put on thirty pounds, and Johnson hadn't said a word. But one day he would figure things out, and that's when she would finally see the truth in his eyes.

7

Kevin went with Kenisha to her next radiation treatment. He sat in the waiting room with Diamond and Kennedy while she lay in the back undergoing her treatment. When she was done, they caught the bus home so that she would be there when Jamal got home from school. Kenisha had promised Kevin dinner if he sat with her children long enough for her to get the radiation treatment. So, even though she was tired, she was in the kitchen making good on her promise. "Is spaghetti okay?"

"I'm not picky," Kevin said as he made his way to the refrigerator. "You got any salad?"

Kenisha put a pot of water on the stove and a skillet for the hamburger. "Everything you need to fix the salad is in there. Wash your hands and make it."

"Oh, so I get to fix the salad, huh? Just like I used to do when we were kids. Remember?"

Yeah, Kenisha remembered. She remembered a lot of things that Kevin used to do before crack took over his mind. Kevin, Kenisha, and Dynasty had been the three musketeers. Aisha had always been so hard to get along with that none of them wanted anything to do with her, and Angelina was too young to kick it with them, so the three of them hung out as if they were best friends rather than sisters and brother. Now that Kenisha thought about it, Kevin's drug abuse hadn't started until after Dynasty's death. So now Kenisha had more guilt to carry around with her. If she hadn't talked Dynasty into going back with Clyde, Dynasty wouldn't be dead and Kevin wouldn't be such a loser.

Kenisha crumbled up the hamburger in the iron skillet and then turned to face her brother. He was happily putting the vegetables in a strainer. He walked over to the sink and rinsed them off and then set them out on the counter and began cutting them up into the salad bowl. "Kevin, can I ask you something?"

"What's up, lil' sis?" he asked as he started slicing a tomato.

"Have you ever thought about checking yourself into rehab?"

He put the knife down, turned toward his sister, and then answered honestly, "I thought about it. But when I'm high, I don't remember as much." Hunching his shoulders, he continued, "Guess I just like it that way."

"What are you trying to forget that's worth what you're doing to yourself? Look at yourself, Kevin. You're skin and bones. You have no place to live, and I know you've started stealing to keep up with your habit. What if someone kills you?"

Kevin turned back to the counter and became one with his vegetables again.

"Answer me," Kenisha demanded.

"Trust me, lil' sis, you don't want to know."

Stirring the hamburger in the skillet, Kenisha said, "I need to know, Kevin. At one point in our lives, I would have trusted you completely with my children. But now . . . if something happens to me, I wouldn't want you around them."

"Nothing's going to happen to you, Ke-Ke. Don't say that."

She smiled; Kevin used to call her Ke-Ke when they were younger and before crack took over his mind. James had begun calling her Ke-Ke after hearing Kevin say it. He'd told her the name fit her better. She had a ton of memories, just none that ever turned out the way they should have. "What are you trying to forget?"

He put down his knife and turned toward Kenisha again. "You really want to know? All right, I'll tell you. But have a seat, because you just had radiation treatment, and I know you're weak from that. What I have to say just might knock you over."

Kenisha took the skillet off the burner, then walked to the stairs in the front of the house to check on Diamond and Kennedy. They were upstairs changing, but she didn't want them to run downstairs in the middle of her talk with Kevin. "Y'all lie down and take a nap until your brother gets home," she yelled up the stairs.

"Aw, Mom, we don't need no nap. We're playing dolls," Diamond protested.

"Okay, then, just play quietly, and I'll let you know when dinner is ready." She went back into the kitchen and sat down at the kitchen table that had been propped against the wall because the fourth leg was wobbly. "I'm ready, so spill it."

Kevin sat down across from Kenisha and opened his mouth to speak but then closed it. He looked down at the table, not meeting her gaze. "Look, let's just drop it, okay?"

"No. Not this time, Kevin. You used to have dreams. I want to know why you never became an architect. Remember those skyscrapers you were always bragging you'd build?"

He still didn't look at her, but he said in a low and bitter voice, "People kept stealing my dreams from me."

"Who, Kevin? Who stole your dreams?"

Silence filled the kitchen, but Kenisha was determined that she wouldn't let Kevin run from his demons anymore. He was going to face them right here and now. She grabbed his face and made him look at her as she gently asked again, "Who?"

"Jimmy Davis."

Kenisha let go of Kevin's face as she stood up. She walked over to the sink, needing a little bit of distance. That name sent fire through her soul, because she instantly knew what was wrong with Kevin. It was the same thing that had done her in. Angelina's father, Jimmy Davis, had raped Kenisha when she was just six years old. He'd told her that if she told anyone, she'd have to go live in foster care. At six, Kenisha had been so afraid of living with strangers. But looking back, she wished she had taken him up on that. Anyone would have been better than a drunken mother who was too passed out to know what was going on in her house at night.

Kenisha put her hands to her mouth. Even now she was afraid to let his name pass her lips. The nightmare hadn't ended until Kenisha was nine years old, when Martha woke up one night and stumbled upon Jimmy and Kenisha. Martha cursed Kenisha for being a "little trollop," and threw Jimmy out. Kenisha didn't care what her mother thought of her, just as long as she didn't have to put up with Jimmy Davis anymore. She brought her hands down from her mouth as she looked directly at Kevin and asked, "He raped you, too?"

Kevin lowered his head as he nodded.

"I could kill him!" Kenisha exploded as the front door opened.

Jamal walked into the kitchen with a playful grin on his face. He discarded his book bag on the floor as he asked, "Who do you want to kill now?"

"Boy, grown folks are in here talking," Kevin told his nephew jokingly. "Take yourself up them stairs with your sisters and leave us alone."

"You ain't grown. You still live with your mama just like I do," Jamal retorted.

"Okay, smart mouth," Kenisha said, "go upstairs with your sisters like your uncle told you. Dinner will be ready in a minute."

"But who you want to kill, Mama?"

Shaking her head, Kenisha said, "Nobody, Jamal. Just go on upstairs so I can finish talking to Kevin."

As Jamal left the kitchen, the fire returned to Kenisha's eyes. She sat back down. "Did you tell Martha?" She desperately needed to know if she had been the only one too scared to speak up.

"Not until a couple of years ago. She had been riding me about being a dopehead, and I told her that the drugs helped me forget what her boyfriend did to me."

"What did she say? Did she accuse you of trying to steal her man like she did me?"

Kevin shook his head. Kenisha could tell that the subject was hard for him to talk about. She was about to tell him that she didn't mean to pry any further into the situation and let him off the hook, when he answered her.

"She said that God would take care of Jimmy, like that was supposed to comfort me."

"Yeah, God be taking too long. And I want folk to get what's coming to them right when they ought to get it."

"Amen to that," Kevin said in agreement.

Shaking her head, Kenisha got up and put the spaghetti in the pot of boiling water. She wanted to bust some heads, but since Jimmy and Martha weren't around, she took her anger out on the spaghetti as she broke it into pieces and then flung them in the pot. She then turned back to Kevin and said, "Martha shouldn't have been allowed to have pets, let alone raise unsuspecting children."

"I'm with you on that. Not a one of us turned out to be worth anything."

"I think Angelina's going to make it. Jimmy might have been a perv, but at least he instilled something in Angelina that the rest of us didn't get. And he's paying the tuition that her scholarship doesn't cover," Kenisha said.

"He should be paying me and you. So I don't want to hear anything about what a good father Jimmy Davis is. I get sick of hearing that mess from Martha. That man owes me and you, and until he pays that debt, he hasn't paid enough as far as I'm concerned," Kevin said with venom in his voice.

Trying to move the subject away from the boogey man, Kenisha said, "I always thought you started smoking because of Dynasty."

Sorrow etched across Kevin's face as he said, "I took my first hit the night of Dynasty's funeral. But it would've happened even if Dynasty had lived. I just had so many images in my mind that I've been trying to forget. I thought drugs could do it for me."

After that, Kenisha didn't know what to say to Kevin, so she called the kids down and they ate dinner together. Kevin hung around after dinner. He and Jamal played tic-tac-toe, and the girls cheered for the winner no matter whether it was their brother or their uncle. As it got darker outside, Kenisha could tell that Kevin was getting antsy.

He finally jumped up and said, "Got to go."

"Why don't you stay here with us tonight?" Kenisha asked.

"Naw, I got things to do. But thanks for the offer. I'll let you know if I need to crash."

Kenisha got up and walked Kevin to the door. As they stepped onto the porch, he told her, "And don't worry about nothing but getting better. If you need a babysitter, I can watch the kids."

Kenisha wanted to tell Kevin that she wouldn't allow him to watch her children because she worried that he might sell them while on a crack high. But after what she'd learned today, she didn't want to cut a deeper wound into his soul. So she simply grabbed his arm and said, "I need you to promise me something."

"Anything, lil' sis. Name it."

"I-if I don't survive, I want you to promise me that you'll get off drugs so my kids can be proud of you. And you won't become an embarrassment to them. I don't want them to hide when they see you coming."

A sad smile played on Kevin's face as he said, "Like we used to do with Cousin Joey."

Cousin Joey was Martha's first cousin. The entire family had been proud of him after he passed the realtor's exam and became a high-powered realtor making a six-figure income. Then Joey found cocaine. After his business took a nosedive, he downgraded to whatever was available on the street. He had always been a sharp dresser, but once the drugs took over, Joey stopped bathing, and wore rags with holes in his pants and in his shoes. His full-time occupation now consisted of begging for spare change. "Yeah, just like Cousin Joey. Don't make my kids ashamed of you like that, okay?"

"Ain't nothing gon' happen to you, anyway, Kenisha."

"We don't know the future, so I need you to promise me that you'll do better."

"Yeah, all right, whatever," he said and then walked away.

Kenisha had two more radiation treatments before Dr. Lawson scheduled an appointment with her. She nervously sat in his office waiting for the lifeline that she desperately needed him to give her. After keeping her waiting for twenty minutes, Kenisha thought he would at least show up with a smile on his face, but Dr. Lawson looked just as grim as he always did, making Kenisha wonder why she hadn't found herself a happier doctor.

"Hello, Ms. Smalls," he said as he sat down behind his desk. "Sorry to keep you waiting."

"Not a problem as long as you're bringing good news. If not, I might have to cut you for keeping me waiting so long." She said it in a joking manner, but she said it to test the waters also. If Dr. Lawson laughed, then she could relax, because she would then be convinced that he had good news. But he didn't laugh. At best he gave her a grudging half smile for her attempt at humor. Kenisha's stomach churned, and she felt like she needed to throw up.

Dr. Lawson put the folder he was carrying down on his desk and opened it. "Well, the news isn't all bad," he said as he lifted his head to finally look at her.

Again Kenisha wished that she had found a more cheerful doctor. Who says "The news isn't all bad?" when they could just as easily say, "I have some news for you. Some of it is good." She couldn't hold her peace any longer. She glared at Dr. Lawson as she said, "You know what? If I'm dying, I'd rather you tell me with a smile on your face. I can't take this gloom-and-doom attitude of yours."

Clearing his throat, Dr. Lawson said, "Well, Ms. Smalls—"

"Call me Kenisha. If you're getting ready to ruin my day, you can at least act like you know me."

"Okay," he said slowly, as if he were talking to someone who was emotionally unstable. "Here's the deal, Kenisha. The tumor has shrunk enough for us to be able to operate."

She had been holding her breath, but once she heard Dr. Lawson's news, she let out a sigh of relief as she jumped out of her seat. "What's wrong with you? You had me so scared. That's good news, and you should have said that when you walked through the door."

"Please sit back down, Kenisha."

"Why?" Kenisha said as she put her hands on her hips. "So you can rain on my parade? No, thank you. Just tell me what else you have to say."

"Look, Kenisha, I'm not trying to be all gloom-and-doom like you said. I just feel an obligation to let you know exactly where we stand. So will you please sit down so we can discuss this?"

Kenisha sat back down. She took a deep breath and said, "Let me have it. What's the bad news?"

"Our biggest problem is the late detection."

"I'm only twenty-three years old, Doc. I didn't think I needed to run to the hospital for every ache and pain," Kenisha interrupted.

Dr. Lawson steepled his hands in front of his mouth. When he moved his hands, he said, "I understand that, Kenisha. And most people your age would be perfectly fine not going to a doctor, but you had cancer, and even though the tumor has shrunk, I'm not sure that we got to it in time."

The look on Kenisha's face displayed the bewilderment she was feeling. "I don't understand what the problem is. You said the tumor shrunk, so you can operate, right?"

"Yes, we can operate. I'd like to schedule you as soon as possible. You'll be in the hospital for a few days after the operation, so you'll need to find someone to keep your children. Will that be a problem?"

With the family she had, yeah, that was going to be a problem. Kenisha wanted to ask Dr. Lawson if he'd like to watch three well-behaved children while she had a couple of tumors pulled out of her. But then she thought about something Kevin had said about Jimmy Davis owing them a debt. Although she would never in a lifetime ask that man for anything, she had no problem with making Angelina pay her father's debt.

Angelina had spent her life being pampered by that perv and worrying about nothing but studying and getting good grades. Angelina was Martha's pride and joy. Mommy dearest had always favored Angelina just because her father had a good job. But if Martha had been any kind of mother, Jimmy wouldn't have had a job at all, because he would have been in jail. So as far as Kenisha was concerned, today was payday, and Martha could scream to high heaven if she wanted to, but the princess was going to be babysitting. "Yes, I do have someone to keep my kids while I'm in the hospital. It won't be a problem."

"Good, then I'll get you scheduled for next week."

"All right, then, I'll make arrangements for my kids." Kenisha stood up, preparing to leave.

Dr. Lawson closed the file as he said, "I don't want to get your hopes up, Kenisha. We'll do the surgery and then some chemo. But there are no guarantees."

"Doc, hope is all I've got. So when you open me up, I need you to be full of hope that day too, okay?"

He nodded. "Okay, Kenisha. I'll do what I can."

"I've got three kids, Doc. You're going to have to do better than that," she said as she opened his office door and walked out. She raced out of the hospital as fast as she could, tears streaming down her face. She was suddenly claustrophobic and needed air like a fish needed water.

As Kenisha walked to the bus stop, she called Angelina and told her all about how her father had raped her when she was a child. She then told Angelina that she owed her a favor, because somebody had to pay for what Jimmy Davis did. By the time Kenisha hung up the phone, Angelina was in tears, but she had agreed to keep Kenisha's children while she was in the hospital, and that was all Kenisha cared about.

8

Deidre and Johnson sat down in the family room for their normal Saturday morning scripture reading and prayer time. They'd been married for seven years but hadn't dedicated their lives to Christ until the third year of their marriage. Since that time, as long as Johnson wasn't deployed, they made Saturday morning the time they sat down as a family with God.

"So what have you been reading this week?" Johnson asked Deidre.

This was normally how their family time with God began: they would discuss the chapters or verses in the Bible that they'd read individually that week and then talk about what stuck out for them. Deidre thoroughly enjoyed reading the word of God, because each time she read a particular book of the Bible, she found something new that she hadn't seen the last time she read it. But lately she hadn't felt much like delving into her Bible, so she admitted, "I didn't have time to read anything this week."

Johnson hesitated for a moment, started to say something, shook his head, and then said, "I've been reading in 1 Corinthians this week. I came across some verses in the second chapter that really stuck with me. Would you like to hear them?"

Deidre hated herself for being so fickle with God, but she really didn't want to listen to Johnson quote scriptures this morning. She wanted to crawl back into her bed and throw the covers over her head and stay there until the morning passed by. But the look on Johnson's face made her feel bad about her sour mood. So she said, "Yes, Johnson, please tell me about the scriptures that impacted you this week."

Johnson opened his Bible and flipped to 1 Corinthians. When he reached the second chapter, he pointed at the fifth verse and read, "*Your faith should not stand in the wisdom of men, but in the power of God.*" He then pointed at verse 9 in chapter 2 and read, "*But as it is written, 'Eye hath not seen, nor ear heard, neither have entered into the heart of man, the things which God hath prepared for them that love him.'*"

Deidre was trying to get involved in Johnson's scripture reading, but it was so hard to be optimistic. Because even though she knew in her heart that the promises of God were *yea, yea, and Amen,* it felt more like *no, no, and no way* where she was concerned.

"Those scriptures spoke so clearly to me this week," Johnson was saying. "Because I truly believe that God hasn't forgotten us and that He has our best interests at heart, no matter what it looks like right now."

She leaned her head back against the couch and said, "I wish I had your faith. Honestly, Johnson, I just really don't know what God is thinking concerning my heart's desire." She put her hand against her heart as she continued, "Having a baby with you would mean everything to me, but God doesn't seem to care."

"Don't say that, honey."

A tear rolled down her face. She wiped it away. "I don't want to say things like that, but I'm thinking it, Johnson. So why shouldn't I say it?"

He pulled his wife into his arms and wet her face with loving kisses. "I don't like to see you hurting like this, De. Tell me what I can do to help you, and I swear I'll move heaven and earth to make it happen."

She knew Johnson meant every word he said, but he still couldn't help her. He wanted a child, and she desperately wanted to give one to him, but nothing they had tried so far had made any difference. And Deidre knew with everything in her that one day soon she would have to pay for how she had deceived Johnson.

"Can we just go on and pray?" Deidre was trying to move things along faster than their normal relaxed Saturday morning pace. They usually fixed breakfast together, and then sat down in the living room and discussed the scriptures and the way each of them felt the scriptures had impacted their lives that particular week. And depending on what they were dealing with—impending deployment, mistreatment by a bad boss, financial situations, or whatever the case might be that week—Johnson and Deidre had always been able to come together and discuss it. But things had changed, or more precisely, the one thing that Deidre desperately wanted to change hadn't. And now she just wanted to get on with the ritual so she could get to the rest of her day.

"Okay," Johnson said as he gently put Deidre's hands in his. And then Johnson went before God in prayer. He thanked God for all His many blessings, praised Him for being a great and wondrous God. Once he was done with his prayers of thanksgiving and adoration, Johnson began praying for the many people he and Deidre had added to their prayer list. Before he finished, Johnson brought Deidre and himself to God's remembrance. He thanked God for providing the answer to their situation, and for helping them see and understand which way God was leading them.

Deidre had been enjoying the prayer until Johnson started talking to God about their situation. It was the same thing with no results each week, except for this new thing Johnson had added about God helping them see which direction He was leading them in. She wanted to question Johnson about his motives for saying something like that. Did he no longer believe that God was going to give them a child? What direction did he believe God was leading them in? But she didn't say anything. Any question she had would just expose her failure as a woman.

Ready to have this time of sharing over and done with, Deidre stood up and asked, "So what are you planning to do today?"

He stood with her and put a smile on his face. "I was just about to ask you that. What about it, woman? Do you want to spend the day with a soldier?"

She started to reject him, but then she remembered that she needed to pick up a few things at the commissary. Whenever she went on base, she liked to go with Johnson, so she said, "Yeah, let's shop on base today. I have a few things I'd like to pick up."

"All right, let me take a quick shower, and I'm all yours."

As Johnson walked away, Deidre silently prayed, asking God to lift her out of this depressing mood that she was in. She told herself that she was going to put a smile on her face and go out and enjoy the day with her husband.

Johnson made it easy for Deidre to find things to smile about. He held her hand as they walked through the flower shop. He bought her a red rose, but he didn't just hand it over, he bowed down, got on one knee, and presented it to her as if he was making a presentation to a queen. Deidre took the rose and inhaled the fragrance. "Thank you, Johnson," she said as they continued to stroll through the BX.

Numerous vendor tables lined the halls. Deidre liked to shop at the vendor tables before going into the actual BX because she knew that the people who rented the vendor tables were small businesspeople, surviving from day to day. At one of the tables, she found a butterfly necklace. At another she picked up a T-shirt of President Obama and his family. At the third and final table they stopped at, Johnson found some African American artwork that he wanted to hang in the family room. But Deidre wasn't so sure if she wanted to look at another couple lounging on canvas in her family room; she was more into abstract art, so she politely pulled Johnson away from the table and walked him into the BX.

They spent hours on base, and Deidre was actually enjoying herself. When they had purchased everything they wanted at the BX, Deidre and Johnson headed over to the commissary, and that's when the smile left her face. Marissa Thompson, the woman Johnson worked with at Wright-Patterson, pushed her cart next to Deidre's. Johnson and Marissa had first worked together when they were both privates and stationed at Andrews Air Force Base. Deidre always wondered how Johnson and Marissa ended up at Wright-Patt together after all these years. Johnson said it had just been sheer coincidence. But as Deidre looked at Marissa's protruding stomach, she wondered if that had actually been the truth.

"Hey, girl, so you hanging out with your military geek today?" Marissa lightheartedly joked with Deidre.

"Yeah," Deidre answered, emotionless. She couldn't concentrate on anything but Marissa's stomach. Marissa wasn't married, so Deidre had no clue who the father was. And then she wondered why Johnson had never even mentioned that Marissa was pregnant.

Marissa patted her stomach and said, "I've got two months to go. I can't wait to deliver. This little one is kicking my butt."

Johnson came back down the aisle carrying a box of Fruity Pebbles cereal with a childlike grin on his face. However, by the time he stood in front of Deidre and Marissa and saw the look on Deidre's face, his smile evaporated.

"I didn't know you were expecting," Deidre said, while looking from Marissa to Johnson.

A puzzled look crossed Marissa's face. "Really? I thought Johnson told you."

Johnson cleared his throat as he playfully punched Marissa's shoulder. "Deidre and I have better things to do than talk about you."

"Oh, it's like that, huh?" Marissa fired back. "Then maybe I'll just take that godfather thing back. What do you think about that?"

Deidre was speechless. Johnson was being named godfather to a baby that she knew nothing about. She turned toward Johnson. He looked nervous, but why would he be nervous if he wasn't guilty of anything? No longer in the mood to grocery shop, Deidre released her shopping cart and started walking out of the commissary without saying another word to Johnson or Marissa.

"Hey, hon, where are you going? We haven't finished shopping," Johnson said, trying to get Deidre to come back.

Deidre kept walking. She didn't trust herself around Johnson and Marissa on a military base. Both of them were enlisted, so if a fight broke out, Deidre was sure she would be the one who would go to jail. When she stepped outside, Deidre remembered that the truck doors were locked and Johnson had the key. It was August so it was hot outside, but Deidre didn't care.

She'd fry before going back into that store with Johnson and Marissa. She sat down on the bench outside and tried to come up with plausible reasons why Johnson had hidden Marissa's pregnancy from her. But the only thought that kept rearing its ugly head was that Johnson was the father; that had to be the reason he hadn't told her.

So many thoughts were running through Deidre's mind right now that she couldn't think straight. Had Johnson planned this little meeting between the three of them? Was he going to tell her about his baby right there at the end of the cereal aisle? Deidre looked around, wondering if everyone on this base knew what a fool Johnson had made of her. She wanted to run, just get out of there. But the one thing that kept her on the bench waiting for Johnson was that her heart didn't believe that the man she married could do something like that. She was just being emotional. There had to be some other explanation as to why Johnson had never mentioned that the woman he worked side by side with every day was expecting a baby.

"Hey, why'd you run out of the store like that?" Johnson asked as he walked over to her.

"Let's just get in the truck and go, please." Deidre got up and walked to Johnson's Ford pickup and stood there waiting for him to unlock the door.

Once in the truck, Johnson turned to Deidre again, and asked, "Am I missing something, Deidre? What just happened?"

She wouldn't look at him and didn't open her mouth to answer. She just leaned her head against the headrest and stared out the window.

Johnson waited a moment trying to give her time to speak, but when it was clear that she wasn't talking to him, he turned on the engine and drove home. When they walked in the house, he tried again. "Do you want to talk about what you're upset about?"

At the base, Deidre had felt so consumed with her thoughts that she couldn't open her mouth to form words. But in the safety of her home, Deidre's tongue began to loosen. "Why didn't you tell me that Marissa was pregnant?"

Johnson shrugged. "I don't know. I guess it must have slipped my mind or something."

Deidre folded her arms across her chest and twisted her lip. "Mmph. Well, did you forget to tell me about a wedding also?"

"What wedding?" Johnson's eyebrow rose.

"Does Marissa have a husband or not?"

"Oh, no, she's still not married."

Unfolding her arms as if she was preparing to use them, Deidre asked, "Is it your baby, Johnson? Is that why you didn't tell me that Marissa is pregnant?"

"What!" Johnson said, clearly taken aback by the accusation. "Did I miss something here? Because you seem to be on a page that I didn't even know was in the book. What's going on?"

Deidre rolled her eyes and walked away from Johnson without saying another word.

He grabbed her arm. "Deidre, don't shut me out like this. What is going on with you?"

She pulled her arm from his grasp. "Nothing is going on with me. I just want you to answer my question. Is Marissa carrying your baby or not?"

"Of course not. I don't even know why you would think such a thing."

Deidre saw the look of hurt on Johnson's face and was immediately sorry that she had put him through this inquisition. Of course the baby wasn't Johnson's. He was a good and upstanding, God-fearing man. Johnson would never hurt her like that. But sometimes it was hard for Deidre not to think that everyone had secrets, since she knew she had one. "Look, Johnson, I'm sorry for accusing you of something like that. It just seemed odd that you didn't tell me that Marissa was pregnant."

"I didn't tell you because I didn't want you to get upset. But I never thought you would assume the baby was mine."

Deidre raised her hands, wanting to put an end to the conversation. "Okay, Johnson, I really don't feel like talking about this anymore. I'm going to bed."

He looked at his watch. "It's only six in the evening. We haven't even had dinner yet."

"I don't feel like eating right now. Can you just find yourself something in the kitchen? I really need to lie down."

"All right, go ahead. I'll be in the room in a little while."

Deidre went off to her room and lay down for the rest of the night. It was all too much for her to deal with. Everyone seemed to be able to get pregnant but her. Even women with no husband were able to find someone to get the deed done, but here Deidre was with a husband who wanted so desperately to be a father, and she couldn't give him what he wanted. The guilt was eating away at her, and she didn't know how much more she would be able to take before she just exploded. How she wished she had been honest with Johnson when they first met. Maybe if she had told him back then that she probably wouldn't be able to have children, he wouldn't have married her and she wouldn't be in such torment now.

Like many nights gone by, Deidre cried herself to sleep. When Sunday morning rolled in, she crawled out of bed and got dressed for church as a duty-bound servant of God. She sat in the service and listened to the message. However, she didn't really hear a word Pastor Monroe said. But when the altar call was made, the Holy Spirit tugged at her heart. She stood up and walked down to the altar, but instead of telling one of the altar workers her prayer request, Deidre fell on her knees at the steps of the pulpit and began crying out to God.

"I'm so sorry, Lord. I'm so sorry," was all she said for a long while. Deidre cried out to God as the barren woman in the Old Testament did after being tormented by her husband's other wife about not being able to have children. The woman begged God for a child and promised to give that child back to God if He would hear her cries. Now Deidre did the same. She told God that she would gladly raise her child in the fear of the Lord, if He would just forgive her for what she'd done to Johnson and heal her womb.

When Deidre finished praying, she looked around and noticed that the sanctuary was empty, all except for Johnson, who sat on the front pew with his head bowed, praying as well. She walked over to him and nudged him. "You ready?"

As he stood up, he said, "I think we should adopt."

9

Kenisha hated hospitals. She had been in a hospital only three times, for the birth of her three children, and that had been plenty enough for her. Hospitals were cold and impersonal. But the thing she hated most was that there were no locks on the doors. Anyone could sneak into her room late at night and violate her and then ease right back out. That's why, even being heavily medicated, Kenisha was having a hard time sleeping. She would nod off, and then hear a noise and her eyes would flutter open and she would watch the door until she drifted off to sleep again. The surgery had left her in a lot of pain, but Kenisha was afraid to ask the nurse for more pain medicine that might put her in a deep sleep. And if she was in a deep sleep, she wouldn't be able to defend herself from anyone sneaking into her room for some late-night fun. No, she would just wait until morning to ask for some more pain medication.

But by morning, Kenisha's body was so racked with pain that she was sweating and shaking.

"Good morning," the nurse said as she entered the room to check Kenisha's vital signs. "How's our patient today?"

"Terrible," Kenisha said through gritted teeth to the woman in the navy blue smock and matching pants.

"Terrible?" the nurse repeated and then asked, "Were you able to sleep last night?"

Kenisha shook her head.

"Look at you," the nurse said as she stood next to Kenisha. "You're drenched with sweat. Let me get some towels and wipe away all that sweat."

Before she could move, Kenisha grabbed the woman's arm and pleaded, "Pain medicine. Please."

"I'm sorry, I figured you might be in pain by morning, I just didn't realize how much pain." She picked up a small white cup from her tray and handed it to Kenisha with a glass of water. "I brought some pain medicine in with me. So just swallow those pills, and that should take care of the pain in a few minutes."

"Thanks," Kenisha said as she swallowed the pills and then drank the water like a man dying of thirst.

The nurse walked over to the chalkboard and wrote her name. "I'm Linda," she said as she turned back to Kenisha. "So if you need anything today, just call me or hit the nurse button." Linda wiped the sweat from Kenisha's face and neck, then checked her vitals and left the room.

Kenisha eased her head back onto her pillow and before she knew it, she was in dreamland. And in her dream, she was with Dynasty again. Dynasty was getting ready for her first date with Clyde. She came over to Kenisha's house and asked to borrow a sweater.

"I don't know about loaning out my clothes to you, Dy. The last time I let you borrow something, one of your friends stole it."

"Girl, give me that sweater. I'm going out with Clyde, and I want to look cute."

"Terrell's cousin Clyde?"

Dynasty nodded, dancing around the room, enjoying life.

"You didn't tell me you were interested in Clyde. When did you start seeing him?"

"This is our first date. And I didn't tell you because I know you don't like him."

Kenisha took hold of Dynasty's arm and stopped her from dancing around the room. She looked her in the eyes and said, "I don't have a problem with Clyde, Dynasty. What I don't like is the way he treats women. I saw him beat on his last girlfriend."

Dynasty brushed that comment off. "He told me all about it. The girl was cheating on him."

Kenisha shook her head. "I don't think you should go out with him, Dy. Just leave him alone. All right?"

"Kenisha, Kenisha. Girl, wake up."

"I know she can hear us. This just don't make no sense. The girl slept all night, now she wants to sleep the day away too."

Kenisha heard the rude voices around her that were interrupting her conversation with Dynasty. They sounded like her mother and her sister Aisha.

"Get up, girl. Stop being so lazy."

That was definitely her mother. That woman never had a kind word for her. But why was she bothering her while she was trying to warn Dynasty about Clyde. All she needed was a few more minutes with Dynasty and . . . somebody shoved her; she tried to hold onto Dynasty. Kenisha's eyes opened, and she saw her mother and sister standing over her. She rubbed her eyes and looked around the room, trying to figure out where Dynasty had gone. Then it hit her. She wasn't with Dynasty. She was in a hospital room recovering from surgery.

"So you just gon' sleep all day, huh?" Martha asked.

"What time is it?" Kenisha asked while rubbing her eyes.

"Girl, it's one o'clock. Even I don't sleep that late," Aisha said.

Kenisha lifted her eyes to stare at the ceiling as she wondered why the last two people she wanted to see right now would be the first and probably the only people to come to the hospital to see about her. Just some more of her rotten luck, Kenisha supposed. "The pain pills they gave me this morning must have knocked me out."

"Don't take too many of them things," Martha warned. "The last thing you need is a habit."

Kenisha couldn't believe the audacity of her mother, to come in here and criticize her about pain pills when she was a falling-down drunk. Kenisha hoped that her surgery had gone well, and she didn't want to jinx herself by telling Martha off, so she clamped her mouth shut and hoped that they would leave soon.

"This room is so small you can hardly turn around in it." Martha was determined to find something to complain about.

"Why don't you sit down, Martha? Then you won't have to worry about turning around," Kenisha said as she scarcely avoided rolling her eyes.

"Don't get snippy with me, missy. I didn't have to come all the way down here to check on you, but I did, didn't I?"

"Most people wouldn't need a pat on the back for seeing about their own child. Especially when that child is sick," Kenisha said, losing the battle with showing respect for her mother.

"Can the two of you ever be in the same room together without griping at each other?" Aisha asked while shaking her head.

Martha sat down in the chair next to Kenisha's bed and waved her hand in the air as if swatting a fly. "I'm not worried about Kenisha. She's just trying to make me feel guilty like she did Angelina, and I'm not having it." Martha took a flask out of her purse, opened it, took a swig, and then recapped it.

"Martha," Kenisha admonished. "You can't drink in here."

"Hush, girl. You might be able to stop me from keeping my grandbabies, but you can't stop me from drinking if that's what I want to do."

"This is the exact reason you're not allowed to watch my kids. If you're drunk and passed out somewhere, who is going to protect my children when one of your perverted boyfriends tries to touch them?"

Before Martha could respond, Aisha said, "I'm tired of listening to y'all argue when I have good news."

"What is it now, Isha?" Kenisha asked.

"Guess who got a call back from *The Bad Girls* show? They want me to interview for next season's show."

Kenisha's mouth hung open, her eyes widened.

"I know," Aisha said excitedly. "Isn't that great?"

"Isha, girl, you can't fight. You got beat up on a weekly basis when we were in school. You don't need to be on that show with those girls."

"You can't tell your sister nothing," Martha said. "I told you that she was going to find a way to embarrass us all, and getting beat up on that *Bad Girls* show will do it. I won't be able to hold my head up in this town after one of those girls wipes the floor with Aisha's skinny behind."

"Don't hate," Aisha said as she got out of her seat and started boxing around the room. "I'm not afraid of those girls. I can handle myself."

There was a knock on the door. The door opened, and Deidre Morris walked in, carrying a basket of flowers as Aisha sat back down.

"Hey, Kenisha, I just stopped by to see how you're doing."

"Finally," Kenisha said, flinging her hands in the air and pointedly glaring at her mother. "Somebody wants to know how I'm doing."

"Don't start with me, girl," Martha said. "Like I said, I didn't have to come down here, and I didn't have to let Angelina watch them kids of yours so that you could get operated on." Martha opened her flask and took another drink.

"Am I interrupting something?" Deidre asked, still holding the flowers in her hand.

"No, my sister was just showing us how she's going to get herself beat up on that *Bad Girls* show," Kenisha said.

A look of confusion crossed Deidre's face. "The *Bad Girl* what?"

"Don't worry about it. It's some crazy reality show that Aisha is trying to get cast on." She then pointed to an empty table behind her bed. "You can put those flowers on that table if you want."

"All right," Deidre said cautiously, as she walked over to the table and set the flowers down.

Martha told Kenisha, "You need to buy Angelina some flowers when you get out of the hospital. That girl has had to put her life on hold in order to watch your kids. And you didn't even say thanks, just made demands about her father not being able to visit while your kids are there."

"Her father doesn't need to be anywhere near my kids, and you know why. So don't sit there and act like I'm being unreasonable," Kenisha said in a huff.

Martha stood up and held out her hand to Deidre. "My daughter is too rude to introduce us, so let me do it myself. I'm Martha." She gestured toward Aisha and said, "And that's my oldest daughter, Aisha."

Deidre shook Martha's hand and then turned to Aisha. "Nice to see you again."

"You're that schoolteacher, right?" Aisha asked.

"I'm the principal at the school Jamal attends," Deidre said as she looked around the room.

"Grab that stool over by Martha and have a seat. We're all friendly here," Aisha said, and then looked at Kenisha and corrected herself. "Most of us, anyway."

Deidre sat down and smiled at the group. "So how is everyone doing?"

"Kenisha is in a bad mood as usual," Aisha said as if she didn't have a care in the world. "Martha's drinking, and I'm being my wonderful self." Then she told Deidre, "Why don't you and I talk, so we don't have to listen to Kenisha and Martha argue?"

"Okay, what do you want to talk about?"

"For one thing, do you think a reality show about teachers would work, and if so, how can I become a teacher?" Aisha said.

Kenisha broke out in laughter. "Girl, stop bothering Deidre. You know you don't want to be in a room full of bad kids. You don't even want to keep your own kids."

"Yeah, but I made you laugh, didn't I?" Aisha said with a mischievous grin on her face.

10

When Deidre left the hospital, she felt a little melancholy. Although she had laughed and joked with Aisha, one fact kept running through her mind: she had not been there for Kenisha when the girl needed her. All Kenisha had wanted was for her children to be in a safe place while she was in the hospital, but Deidre hadn't offered shelter to three wonderful children who needed it. She also hadn't offered any comfort to Johnson in his quest to become a parent. Her behavior sickened her, and she was tired of it.

Deidre picked up the phone and dialed her mother. Loretta Clark was a God-fearing woman who loved her children and treated them and others with respect. She was a far cry from Kenisha's mother, and for that, Deidre was thankful. When Loretta answered the phone, Deidre said, "I need you to pray for me, Mama."

"What's wrong, honey? What's happened?" Loretta asked with concern in her voice.

"I've done some things that aren't right. I need to change, but I don't know what to do."

"I'm on my way over there."

"No, I didn't call so that you would rush over here. You live an hour away. Just pray for me. I'll be okay," Deidre said.

"Put on a pot of coffee. I'm on my way. We can pray together once I get there." Loretta hung up the phone.

Deidre did as she was told and put the pot of coffee on. She then sat down at the kitchen counter and waited on her mother. True to her word, Loretta Clark was knocking on Deidre's door in a little less than an hour. "How'd you get here so fast? Are the cops on your trail again?"

"Naw, I shook them off on I-75," Loretta said with a giggle as she walked straight to the kitchen and poured herself a cup of coffee.

"Mother, you have got to stop speeding. That isn't funny. I don't want anything to happen to you, okay?"

Loretta put two spoonfuls of sugar in her coffee and then raised her hand as if she were in court. "Okay, I promise." She set her mug on the kitchen counter and pulled up a chair. "Where's Johnson?"

"He's still on base. I don't think he'll be home until about seven."

"That gives us enough time for some girl talk. Now come here and sit down with me."

Deidre sat down next to her mother. She tried to smile but her heart wasn't in it.

"Ah, honey." Loretta hugged her daughter. "I heard the distress in your voice over the phone. What's got you so upset?"

"It's the same thing it's always been—my inability to have children. Now Johnson wants to adopt, and I'm just not sure how I feel about that."

"Wouldn't adoption be the answer to your prayers? I mean, you and Johnson would be parents just like you both have always dreamed about."

Deidre shook her head. "My having a child would be the dream Johnson and I have had. Adopting would be like admitting that we have no faith in God."

Loretta patted her child on the shoulder. "God has all sorts of ways to solve the problems we encounter," Loretta said, then added, "Why don't you just admit what's really bothering you? Do you think that Johnson will finally figure out that you can't have children if you agree to adopt?"

Deidre didn't respond, but the sadness in her eyes said it all.

"Don't you think Johnson has already figured that out?"

"I think he knows that I'm the reason that we haven't had any children. But he doesn't know that I've known I'm the reason all along. And I feel so guilty for not telling him the truth from the beginning."

"Honey, now, I've always told you that deception has a price. Aren't you tired of paying for your deception?"

Tears fell on Deidre's lap as she lowered her head. "I'm tired of it, Mom. But I just don't know what to do to fix it."

"Talk to your husband, Deidre. He is a better man than you give him credit for."

"You make it sound so easy," Deidre said. "I've been lying to him for years. How can I expect him to forgive me just like that?"

"Johnson loves you, honey. Give him a chance."

Deidre raised her head. She was silent for a moment, and then she told her mother, "I met this twenty-three-year-old woman who is battling cancer."

"That's awful. When did you meet her?"

"Her son is one of the students at my school. I kept him while she was getting a radiation treatment one day."

"That was nice of you," Loretta said.

"It really wasn't. I was mad about having to watch him. And then before she went into the hospital for surgery, she was trying to find someone to watch her children and even though I knew Johnson would have loved to do it, I didn't volunteer."

"So how do you feel about your decision?"

"I feel awful, because I know the only reason I didn't help her is because of my own issues about having children."

Loretta sipped on her coffee as she said, "I think you're being too hard on yourself. But I also think you need to let go and move on with your life."

"That sounds real good when you say it, Mom, but how do I move on when I don't know what to do? What do you tell your clients?" Loretta was a crisis counselor for Alcoholics Anonymous. She talked with people who had to deal with guilt and regrets all the time.

"I'm not always allowed to tell them everything I want to." She held out her hands for Deidre. When Deidre took her mother's hands, Loretta said, "Let's pray."

Deidre bowed her head and listened as her mother went to the throne room of God on her behalf. Deidre couldn't say what was different about this prayer, for she had prayed about this same issue a number of times. But this time, she felt that God was taking a heavy burden away from her.

When they finished praying, Loretta said, "Let's move this little chitchat into your computer room. I've got an idea."

Deidre took her mother into the computer room and then turned on the computer. "Now what?" Deidre asked as she turned toward Loretta.

"Go to Google."

Deidre opened her Internet browser, went to Google, and then turned back to Loretta, waiting on further instructions.

"Look up adoption services in Ohio," Loretta said.

Deidre shook her head. "I don't think I'm ready for something like this. What if I'm right, and adopting a child shows a lack of faith on our part?"

"And what if adopting a child brings unspeakable joy into your home?"

Deidre was still shaking her head, so Loretta became a bit more forceful with her. "Now you listen to me, Deidre Clark-Morris. That husband of yours is a good man, and he wants to raise a child with you. Johnson doesn't care if that child is birthed through you or comes through adoption. He'll love it just the same. So you stop being foolish and give that man what he wants."

Without saying anything, Deidre stopped shaking her head and began typing into the Google search bar. Deidre and Loretta spent the next hour researching adoption services.

But the kicker as far as Deidre was concerned was that the final decree of adoption wouldn't even be issued until the child had lived with the adoptive parents for at least six months. So, therefore, the courts could come into the adoptive parents' home at any time within those six months and remove a child whom they had grown to love as if he or she was their very own. Deidre didn't like that at all.

When she was done looking up the process, she started looking for agencies that she and Johnson could visit in order to get more information. The first agency that looked good to her was one called Action Adoption. The information on their website really touched Deidre. They talked about making *forever families*. And something else caught her attention about the Action Adoption agency. The website stated that they believed all children had a right to a loving, caring, and supportive family to aid their growth as moral, functional members of society. That simple statement made her think about Ronny.

How she wished he had the Action Adoption Agency on his side rather than that poor excuse for a mother he had.

Two other agencies looked like they might be able to help her and Johnson, so she wrote their names down on her notepad with the addresses and telephone numbers also. By the time Johnson arrived home, she was well equipped to talk to him about his heart's desire.

When Johnson came into the house, Loretta kissed him on the check and then left.

"Was it something I said?" Johnson joked. "Why wouldn't my mother-in-law want to stay and visit with me?" he asked Deidre.

"I need to talk to you, so she wanted to give us some privacy." Deidre grabbed Johnson's hand and then walked him over to the couch and sat down. She then handed him the papers about adoption that she had printed off the computer.

"What's this?" he asked, before looking at the papers.

"You have been very patient with me, Johnson. And for that, I really want to thank you. But my mom helped me see that it's time for us to move forward and for me to stop clinging to something that might never happen for us."

As he read the information on the papers, he turned back to Deidre and said, "But I thought you were against adoption. Every time I brought it up, you refused to even discuss it."

"That was selfish of me, Johnson. I've been praying about this, and"—she swallowed hard on her pride, wishes, hopes, and dreams in order to give Johnson his wishes, hopes, and dreams—"I think we should give this adoption thing a try."

Cautiously, he asked, "Do you really mean it, Deidre? Do you really think we could do this?"

To Deidre's surprise, she really did want to check out those adoption agencies. In her heart, she knew that she was now ready to be a mother any way God saw fit. At that moment,

Deidre imagined her mother speeding up I-75, praying to God on her behalf. *Keep on praying, Mom. Just keep on praying.* "I mean it, Johnson. I think this will be good for us."

Johnson jumped out of his seat, picked Deidre up, and twirled her around the room in a manner he hadn't done since the first year of their marriage. "Thank you, Deidre. Thank you for doing this."

Deidre put her hand on her husband's cheek. "Thank you, Johnson, for loving me in spite of everything."

The next day, when she and Johnson went shopping at the BX, Deidre stopped at one of the vendor tables to look at some jewelry that had caught her eye. After she selected the pieces she wanted, she set off in search of her husband. She checked the electronics department, the auto parts department, and the shoes, all the normal places where Johnson hung out when they came to the BX. Her final stop was in the baby department. Deidre didn't even know why she walked over there, except that she had a feeling that she might find Johnson snooping around. When she saw him standing over a crib with that wide-eyed expression he got when something truly brought him joy, her spirit leaped within her.

She had misunderstood her husband and cost them years of unnecessary pain. For now she knew that Johnson's heart was so big it could even make room for another man's child. At that moment, Deidre decided that she wouldn't look back. She, too, could love a child that wasn't pulled from her belly. She walked over to Johnson and poked him. "Hey."

"Hey, yourself," he said as he turned to her.

Deidre pointed at the crib, "So I take it you want a newborn?"

"Wouldn't it be great if we could get a baby? That way we could raise her as our own."

"Oh, so you want a girl too, huh?"

Johnson pulled Deidre into his arms as he said, "Yeah, a girl who would be just as beautiful as her mother, and give me a hard time and drive me up a wall."

"Hey, you better watch it. Me and my daughter may just double-team you."

Johnson kissed Deidre. "I'm just joking. How could the woman I love drive me up a wall?" He put his arm around Deidre as they walked around the store.

Deidre enjoyed spending time with her husband, and she especially enjoyed seeing him in such a good mood. But she was still bothered by the fact that she hadn't told him the truth. She had deceived Johnson. She'd strung him along for all these years, letting him get his hopes up about a child that had never come.

Later that night, Deidre got on her knees and begged God to forgive her for the mess she'd made of her life. She prayed for the newborn that Johnson wanted. "Give him his heart's desire, Lord." She also prayed that God would help Johnson forgive her when she finally told him the truth, for she knew that she couldn't live with this lie much longer.

11

Monday morning came well before Deidre was ready to face another day of work. But this was the day that she would also make appointments with the adoption agencies, so she jumped out of bed excited to see what the day would bring.

She and Johnson sat down for a quick breakfast of instant grits with toast and jelly. As they were cleaning off the table and preparing to leave, Johnson said, “So you’ll call me when you know something, right?”

Deidre laughed. “It’s not as if they’re going to give me a kid after one phone call, Johnson. I’m just setting up appointments today.”

“I know, but I want to know what they say. How long a wait we might have and all of that.”

“Okay, Johnson, I promise to call you right after I’ve made the appointments.” With that, they parted ways.

When Deidre arrived at school, Christina Michael, her administrative assistant, ran over to her before she entered the school office and said, “It’s not my fault. I tried to tell that woman that you had a busy schedule today, but she doesn’t listen.”

“What woman? What are you talking about?”

Christina opened the door to the school office. The sight of Ronny and Shameka Nickels seated outside her office explained everything.

"What's up, Ms. Nickels?" Deidre asked as she unlocked her office door.

"You know what's up." Shameka stood up and put her hands on her hips. "I want you to stop suspending my son every time the sun shines, or I'm going to keep coming down here and getting in your face about it."

"All right," Deidre said in the calmest voice she could muster. "Follow me into my office."

Shameka rolled her eyes as she turned to Ronny and said. "Get up boy, we got to go talk to this heifer."

Jesus, keep me near the cross. Deidre sat down behind her desk and tried her best to comport herself in a professional manner. But it was really hard to deal with Shameka Nickels. The woman was an awful mother who had five other kids besides Ronny the terrorist. The boy was sure to grow up and rob a bank, stab his best friend to death, or do something equally horrible that would guarantee him a life sentence in prison. "Why did you want to see me today, Shameka?"

"You know why. You suspended Ronny again, like I've got all day to sit around and watch him. Your teachers get paid to watch Ronny during the day, and I think it's high time that they do their own job."

Right now, Deidre really needed to have a little chat with Jesus because she just didn't understand why she was childless, but Shameka Nickels was allowed to raise all the juvenile delinquents she wanted. "My teachers are not babysitters, Ms. Nickels. They are not here to watch your son. They teach, and they can't do that if there are unnecessary disruptions in the classroom."

Huffing, Shameka said, "When Ronny acts up, your stupid teachers need to paddle him. I'm okay with that."

"We're not allowed to discipline children in that manner anymore."

"Well, then, why can't y'all just put him in detention or take away his lunch or something? Anything but send him home with me. I've got things to do."

Taking a deep breath, Deidre turned to Ronny and said, "Can you wait outside so I can speak with your mother?"

Ronny folded his arms and leaned back in his seat like a gangster. Shameka popped him in the head with her fist and said, "Get out of here. You heard the principal."

Distressed by Shameka's manner of discipline, Deidre turned to her after Ronny closed the door behind him and said, "If you do that in my presence again, I will have you arrested."

"How you gon' have me arrested for disciplining my own child? Y'all don't want to do it, so don't complain when I do it myself."

Shaking her head, Deidre told Shameka, "I'm going to be blunt here. I think you need parenting classes, and Ronny needs to see a therapist about his behavioral issues before they get any worse."

Shameka exploded out of her seat. "How you gon' tell me that I need parenting classes when you don't know the first thing about being a parent? You've got nerve, lady. I suggest you mind your own business and stop suspending my son before I report you to the superintendent."

"Your son is a bully and an extortionist," Deidre said, thinking that news might convince the woman that her son needed counseling.

"If these kids can't fight, that's their problem, not mine." Shameka swung her purse onto her shoulder and strutted out of Deidre's office.

After Shameka left, Deidre was unable to move from behind her desk. She had become paralyzed by the thought that she and Johnson might end up adopting a kid who'd had a mother like Shameka Nickels. The thought terrified her. How would she and Johnson deal with a juvenile delinquent? She could see it now. She'd have to lock her bedroom door when Johnson was deployed so their kid couldn't come into her room and kill her. While she was picturing herself cowering in her bedroom, the phone rang.

Grateful for the distraction, Deidre picked the phone up on the first ring. "This is Deidre Morris."

Johnson's voice boomed from across the line. "I'm not trying to be a pest about this adoption thing. I just wanted to thank you again for being willing to check into this."

He must have felt her chickening out from miles away. "Honey, I was thinking about something."

"What's up?" Johnson asked.

"Well, when you're deployed, I will be all by myself with this child. I'm just wondering if I'm ready for that."

She heard the disappointment in his silence and instantly wanted to pull those words back into her mouth.

"Don't back down now, Deidre. We've waited a long time to get here. Why don't we just trust God and keep moving forward?"

"I'm sorry, Johnson. I guess I let this situation at work freak me out." She held out her hands as if steadying herself. "Everything will be fine. I'm just going to pray that we don't end up with a juvenile delinquent or a serial killer or something."

"What?"

"Nothing, Johnson. Just ignore me. I'll call you after I talk with the adoption agencies." Deidre hung up as she tried to regain her confidence.

But Deidre knew that if she put off calling the adoption agencies, she was just going to freak out again. So she picked up the phone and dialed the Action Adoption Agency. She picked them first because she really liked their slogan about making *forever families*. Patricia who answered the phone informed her that her name was Patricia Nelly. Deidre found the woman to be very personable. Patricia made it easy for Deidre to say what was on her mind. "My husband would like to adopt a child, but we don't know the first thing about the process."

"Well, that's why I'm here," Patricia said in the most reassuring voice Deidre had heard in a long time. "I can walk you through the process and set you up with an appointment."

"That would be wonderful," Deidre said as she felt herself begin to relax.

"I can fit you in tomorrow afternoon around three, if your husband is available at that time," Patricia said.

"That quick?"

"It's a slow week for me. And we don't like to keep our prospective parents waiting."

"All right, then, Johnson and I will be there. Do we need to bring anything with us?"

"Just bring identification. And since this is our first meeting, I'll be asking about your social and medical history. I'll also want to know what type of child you and your husband are looking for."

A non–serial-killer type. "My husband wants a newborn. Is that possible?"

"In this day and age, I never say never. But if a newborn is what you're looking for, just be prepared to wait a little longer."

12

"How can you call yourself a convenience store if you don't even have milk?" Kenisha screamed at the clerk behind the counter of the store that was a few blocks away from her apartment.

"Ma'am, I'm sorry, the manager forgot to order the milk. But we should have some next week," the clerk told her.

The man behind the counter spoke with a Middle Eastern accent, so some of his words didn't come out as he intended them to. But Kenisha never made fun of him for the way he spoke as she had witnessed so many other customers doing. The way Kenisha saw it, her people had been disparaged and mistreated simply because of stereotypes or misconceptions, so she would never do that to anyone else. But that didn't stop Kenisha from going smack off about this milk situation. Her anger had nothing to do with this man's ethnicity or his dialect. She wanted milk, and they didn't have it.

"My kids want milk this morning. What am I supposed to tell them? Eat your cereal dry today, and then next week, when y'all decide to get off your lazy behinds and order some milk, they can drink the milk in a glass, because the cereal will be gone by next week."

"Why don't you just go get them some milk at the grocery store?" the clerk asked.

"How am I supposed to get there?" Kenisha screamed at the man.

Jamal pulled on her shirt sleeve as he looked around at the other customers in the store. "Come on, Mama, let's go."

"No," Kenisha said as she snatched her shirtsleeve out of Jamal's grip. "You stand against the wall and hold your sisters' hands while I finish telling this man how I feel." Kenisha turned back to the clerk and said, "I bet your kids have milk. You probably took the last gallon out of this store just so my kids would have to do without."

"Come on, lady, there's no conspiracy against you. They just don't have any milk," a customer in the store yelled out.

Kenisha turned in his direction. "How do you know there's no conspiracy against me? People have been conspiring to do me wrong all my life, and today is no different."

"I'm going to call the police if you don't leave," the clerk finally said.

"Call the police," Kenisha said as she became more and more irrational. "Tell them to bring backup, because the way I feel right now, I just might go down in a blaze of glory."

Kennedy and Diamond started crying. Jamal tried again. "Come on, Mama, we don't need the milk. Let's just get out of here."

The tears Kenisha saw on her little girls' faces was the only thing that stopped her tirade. She turned back to the clerk and said, "You better be glad that my kids don't want your old sour milk, or else I would stay here and tear this place down and then sit outside and wait for the police to show up." For good measure, Kenisha pushed over a rack of Lay's potato chips as she grabbed Kennedy's hand.

"Yeah, yeah, we get it. You're bad. Just don't bring your bad self into this store anymore," the clerk said as Kenisha walked out of the store with her three children.

"Why did you do that?" Jamal asked as they walked home.

They were crossing the street in the middle of oncoming traffic, so Kenisha had to concentrate on getting her children to the other side of the street safely. Once they were across the street, she looked at Jamal. Kenisha could tell that she had embarrassed him. That hadn't been her intention when they left for the store. But when there was no milk in a place that should have had milk, something broke inside Kenisha. "I don't know, Jamal. I just got so angry. I'm sorry if I embarrassed you, but I don't think I need to be around the general public right now. So y'all are just going to have to make do with the food we have in the apartment. Okay?"

"Yeah, that's fine," Jamal said, and then he turned to his sisters and said, "Did y'all hear that? No complaining—we eat what we have, and that's that."

"But, Jamal, what if I don't like what we have?" Diamond asked.

"That's just too bad. I don't like a lot of things either, but ain't nobody giving me no choices," Kenisha said as she opened the door and let the kids into the apartment.

She took to her bed after helping Kennedy out of her coat. Jamal fixed breakfast, then lunch, and finally dinner. Kenisha hadn't been able to get out of bed. Aisha came over and helped Jamal the following day. She'd made macaroni and cheese, green beans, and meatloaf for dinner. There had even been enough leftovers for the next day, which was a good thing, because Kenisha had become despondent as she continued to lie in her bed.

When Kenisha was a kid she had watched a movie called *Sparkle*. There were three sisters in the movie—the ugly sister, the plain sister, and the pretty sister. The pretty sister thought she was going to live the fabulous life after hooking up with this big-time drug dealer. But her life just went down the toilet. Before the pretty sister died, she sang a real pretty but sorrowful song about how giving up was so hard to do. Kenisha remembered feeling the girl's agony and her pain as she sang that song. For weeks after seeing the movie, Kenisha, Aisha, and Dynasty walked around the house, using sticks as microphones and singing, "Giving up is so hard to do." But now, as she lay in her bed, not wanting to even get up and bathe herself, Kenisha realized that the song had been wrong. Giving up wasn't hard to do at all. Living was the hard thing. Especially when all the odds were stacked against you.

She had done everything her doctor asked her to do. She'd taken radiation, she'd let them cut on her, and she'd even done chemotherapy. But it was all for nothing, as she found out last week while sitting in Dr. Lawson's office.

"We've done everything we can do, Kenisha. But the cancer hasn't let up. It has spread through your body."

"What does that mean?"

"It means there's nothing left to do." He hunched his shoulders and then said, "We can continue chemotherapy, but . . ."

"But what?" Kenisha demanded.

"But I don't think it's going to work."

Kenisha closed her eyes. She put her head in her hand as she thought about her children. Pictures of their beautiful faces at different stages of their lives flashed through her mind. But as she realized that this doctor was condemning her children to a future without her, she raised her head, looked him square in the face, and asked, "So what's the final verdict? What are you telling me?"

Dr. Lawson was silent as sorrow etched across his face.

"Spit it out, Dr. Lawson. How much time do I have left?"

He opened his mouth and hesitantly said, "Six months, tops."

"So, I'm twenty-three, and you're telling me that I'm going to die at twenty-four? Is that right, Dr. Lawson?" Kenisha stood up, not waiting for an answer, because she already knew. "That ain't right," she said as she walked out of his office and slammed the door.

She had denied the truth of Dr. Lawson's statement that day, but as the days wore on and he didn't call to tell her that some terrible mistake had been made, she became angry and just wanted to lash out at someone. That's why she had found herself in that convenience store going off about a gallon of milk.

But now as she lay in her bed, collecting bedsores, she faced the awful truth. Her doctor had given her a death sentence. Facing the truth herself was one thing, but what Kenisha needed to figure out was how she was going to tell her children. She had promised them that she would be completely healed after the surgery.

How could she tell them this awful truth? More important than that, who would be here to protect her children from men like Jimmy Davis? Would Jamal have a similar fate as Kevin had as a child and then end up on drugs? What about her little girls? Tears streamed down Kenisha's face as she imagined someone violating her children. It just wasn't fair. How could a loving God let things like this happen to innocent children? And why was she expected to worship a God who would allow a mother to die and leave her children unprotected?

She covered her head with her pillow and moaned out her sorrow. It seemed to Kenisha that she'd been moaning for a lifetime.

"I brought you something to eat, Mama," Jamal said as he opened her bedroom door.

Kenisha turned to face her son with a frown on her face. "I thought I told you to go to school?"

"I'll go when you're feeling better."

"No, Jamal. You've missed two days already. You don't need to be here taking care of me. You need an education. Do you hear me?"

"Well, I'm not going back to school until you get out of that bed." He put the bowl of ham-and-bean soup on the nightstand next to Kenisha's bed and stood there waiting for her to lift herself up.

"Jamal, you know I don't like all that back talk. Don't make me whup your behind."

"You'd have to get out of bed to do it. So go right ahead; please whup me."

The sound of her son pleading for a whupping tore at her heart. She didn't want him worrying about her or being willing to put himself in harm's way just to pull her out of this abyss she had fallen into. "Just go to school, okay, Jamal? I promise I'll get out of this bed tomorrow."

"What's wrong with you?" he asked in a tone that displayed all the fear he was feeling. "All you did was throw a few potato chips on the ground, and I'm sure that clerk has been yelled at before."

Jamal always looked out for his mother. This boy had truly been a gift from God. If God even gave out gifts. She had always imagined that she would be there for the important moments in his life. Like when he tried out for sports. Jamal wanted to play both basketball and football. Kenisha just knew he would be a star on the field and on the court. So she would have to be there to chase away all the gold diggers. Kenisha could foresee all the skirts chasing after her handsome son now. If she wasn't alive, who was going to be there to say, "Get away from my Heisman-Trophy-winning, Super-Bowl-ring-wearing, multimillion-dollar son"? The thought of not being there to steer her son away from so many of the wrong influences that were sure to come his way caused Kenisha to ache all over, and she began to cry. "I'm so sorry, Jamal. I'm so sorry."

"What's wrong, Mama?" Jamal asked as he rushed to his mother's side.

Kenisha couldn't stop crying. She wanted to, because she saw how her mood was scaring Jamal. But she was powerless to do anything about it. "M-mommy just needs some rest. Leave me alone for a l-little while. Okay, Jamal?"

"I'm going to get you some help," Jamal said as he ran out of his mother's room, down the stairs, and to the telephone. He dialed his Aunt Aisha. She picked up on the fifth ring. "My mom needs help. Can you please come see about her?" Jamal begged.

Aisha's voice was groggy from sleep as she asked, "Is she hurt?"

"She won't stop crying," Jamal answered.

"Okay, tell her I'll be over there this evening."

"No, Auntie Isha, she needs you now." Jamal's voice was frantic.

"Calm down, Jamal, your mama is all right. I was up all night practicing for this reality show interview, so I need a little extra sleep. I'll be over there as soon as I get up," she said and then hung up the phone.

Jamal sat staring blankly at the walls as the dial tone blared in his ear. Then an idea struck him. He hung up the phone and pulled a piece of paper off the refrigerator. His mom kept telephone numbers of schools, hospitals, and such attached to a magnet on the refrigerator. Jamal scanned the list and found the number for his school. He dialed and after hitting several options, he was connected with the school secretary. "May I please speak with Mrs. Morris?" Jamal asked.

"She's in her office. Who's calling?" the woman asked.

"My name is Jamal Moore. I'm a student there, and I really need to speak with Mrs. Morris because I'm in trouble."

"The assistant principal handles most of the student issues. I can transfer you to Mr. Landers right now if you like."

"No!" Jamal shouted. "Please just tell Mrs. Morris that I'm on the phone. I know she'll help me if you just let her know that it's me."

There was hesitation on the line; then the woman said, "Hold one moment, please."

Holding his breath, Jamal silently prayed to God: *please let Mrs. Morris pick up the phone, please let Mrs. Morris pick up the phone.*

"Jamal? Jamal, what's wrong?" Deidre asked as she picked up the phone.

"Please come over here, Mrs. Morris." The words gushed out of Jamal's mouth.

"What's going on, Jamal?"

"It's my mom. She hasn't come out of her bedroom in days, and now she's crying and I can't get her to stop. Please help us, Mrs. Morris." Now tears were running down Jamal's face, and his voice cracked as he finished his sentence.

"I'm on my way, Jamal. Go sit with your mom until I get there."

"Okay. Thank you," Jamal said as he wiped the tears from his face and hung up the phone. He then ran back up the stairs and into Kenisha's room. She was still crying. Jamal went over to his mother and put his arms around her. "I don't want you to be sad, Mama."

"I'm sorry, Jamal. I just can't stop crying," Kenisha said as she brought her pillowcase to her face and wiped the tears.

Jamal ran to the bathroom, tore some tissue off the roll, and ran back to his mother. He tore the tissue in half and wiped

Kenisha's face with one half and handed the other half of the tissue to her and said, "Here, blow your nose."

Kenisha took the tissue and blew her nose. She sat up. "You take such good care of your mama. I couldn't have asked for a better son."

13

When Deidre hung up the phone, she pushed the intercom and then asked the school secretary, "Can you cancel my appointment with Dr. Thomas? I need to take care of something, and I'm not sure how long I'll be gone." She stood up, grabbed her coat and car keys, and left the building.

She wasn't sure why, but she felt connected to this family. The sound of Jamal's sorrowful voice had almost broken her heart. She wanted to do whatever she could to help him.

Deidre wasn't sure what had happened to cause Kenisha's depression, but she knew for sure that Kenisha had definitely spiraled into a depression, because she had been there herself. All these years of not being able to conceive a child and not being able to tell Johnson the awful truth had caused Deidre so much pain, that even knowing Jesus hadn't stopped her from spiraling into the grips of depression every now and then.

Deidre's deep depressions had caused her to wonder if she had truly given her life to Christ when she'd uttered the sinner's prayer, or if she had just been saying words that meant nothing and went nowhere? But then she would remind herself of the biblical heroes in the Old Testament, like Elijah. The prophet Elijah was almost supernatural in his zeal for the things of God, but this same man fled to Mount Horeb, sat under a juniper tree, and asked God to let him die. For Deidre, the most memorable part of that story was found in 1 Kings 19:7: "*And the angel of the LORD came again the second time, and touched him, and said, Arise and eat; because the journey is too great for thee.*"

Deidre had certainly learned that some of life's journeys were simply too great for her, and she needed to lean on the Lord to get through them. Just as God had sent an angel to strengthen Elijah, Deidre knew that Johnson had been her angel, sent from heaven above. He had helped her move past the pain, and now she wanted to do the same for Kenisha. So she prayed for God's healing power to touch Kenisha and end her depression.

When Deidre arrived at Kenisha's apartment, she jumped out of her car and rushed to the door. She knocked and then turned the knob, hoping that the door would open. It was locked, so she knocked again, or rather, she pounded on the door this time. "Jamal, it's me."

The door swung open and Kenisha was standing there holding a bunch of soggy tissue in her hand. "The way you were banging on my door, I thought you were the police."

Kenisha looked disheveled, with her hair standing on top of her head. She smelled as if she hadn't seen a shower in days, but Deidre didn't say a word about her appearance. "I was worried about you," Deidre said as she walked into the apartment. "Jamal sounded frantic when he called the school."

"Oh, don't worry. Jamal will be back in school tomorrow. I already let him know that he can't stay here with me."

"That's not why I'm here, Kenisha. I was really concerned about you." She pointed at the wet tissue in Kenisha's hand. "Jamal said that you couldn't stop crying. What's going on?"

"Trust me," Kenisha said, "you don't even want to know my horror story."

"Jamal also said that you hadn't been out of your bed in several days."

Kenisha lifted her arms and twirled around before plopping down on the couch in the living room. "I'm out of bed now. So you can go on back to work. Don't worry, I'm not going to neglect my children."

"Why do you act so defensive all the time?" Deidre asked.

"How am I supposed to act? You did threaten to call Children's Services on me. And now you want to keep coming over here acting like you're concerned. But how do I know that you're not just trying to build a case against me with the truant officer?"

"Mrs. Morris isn't here because I skipped school today, Mama. I called her and asked her to come," Jamal interjected.

"Why didn't you tell me that you called her?" Kenisha asked.

"I called Auntie Aisha first, but she was tired from being up all night. So I called Mrs. Morris and asked if she would come help you." He hunched his shoulders and then added, "Nothing I was doing seemed to work."

"Jamal, I'm sorry I scared you, but you can't go calling everybody in the world, telling them our business. Some things are best left in your own home. Okay?"

Jamal looked down at his feet as he said, "Okay, Mama, but you're not acting like yourself. You need help."

"Talk to me, Kenisha. What's wrong?" Deidre tried again as she took a seat on the chair next to the couch.

Kenisha looked at Deidre for a moment, shook her head in frustration, and then stood up. She turned to Jamal and said, "Fix yourself some lunch. I'm going to sit outside for a minute and talk to Mrs. Deidre."

Jamal nodded and went to the kitchen.

Kenisha put on a pair of house shoes and then opened the front door and walked out.

Deidre got up and followed her out. She unlocked her car doors, and she and Kenisha sat down in the front seats.

"Talk to me, Kenisha. Is there anything I can do to help?" Deidre had dealt with numerous parents in her years as a teacher and principal. Once in a great while she ran into a mother who made her want to reach out and help. Kenisha was such a mother. Deidre saw so much potential in this young woman. Kenisha might be a young mother with too many kids and too many baby daddies, but she really cared about her children. And because of that, Deidre found herself wanting the best for all of them.

"The cancer has spread," Kenisha said matter-of-factly.

A look of shock and dread crossed Deidre's face before she could pull it back. "What do you mean, the cancer has spread? They operated on you, and you did the chemo."

"Same thing I've been saying ever since I got the news. But to be truthful, Dr. Lawson didn't make any promises to me. He said all along that the surgery might not work because of the late detection." Kenisha leaned back on the headrest and exhaled. "What I don't understand is how I was supposed to know that I needed to get checked out. I'm only twenty-three. People my age don't get cancer. Right?"

"That's what I would have thought. I'm so sorry, Kenisha."

"Me too. Dr. Lawson thinks I have less than six more months left to live." Kenisha shook her head. "If I make it the full six months, I'll be twenty-four, but that's still too young to die."

Deidre was speechless. She'd driven over here thinking that Kenisha's mother had hurt herself or that the chemotherapy was affecting her, but never in her wildest imagination had she thought that Kenisha was dying. It was just as Kenisha had said—she was too young to die.

"You're awfully quiet for someone who wanted to talk," Kenisha said with a smirk on her face.

"To tell you the truth, I don't know what to say."

Kenisha must not have known what to say either, because the car became deathly silent. Then something came to Deidre. In truth, Deidre didn't know why she hadn't thought of this first. She turned to Kenisha and asked, "Have you prayed?"

Scoffing at the thought, Kenisha said, "I gave up on that when Dr. Lawson told me that I had cancer. If God wanted to help me, He could have just made sure none of this happened to me, but He didn't. So you can save the prayer for the next sucker."

But Deidre wasn't going to let it end like that. She felt bad that she had been too wrapped up in her own misery to offer prayer the first day Kenisha had told her about the cancer. But Deidre firmly believed that being late was better than never showing up at all, so she said, "Prayer works, Kenisha. I've seen lives changed through prayer."

Kenisha turned cold, unyielding eyes on Deidre. "Yeah? Well, tell that to my children when I'm dead." She opened the car door and got out.

Deidre rolled her window down. "Wait, Kenisha, don't leave. I want to help you."

Waving goodbye, Kenisha said, "Sorry, Deidre, I don't have time to pray. I need to clean my house and fix dinner for my children. But don't worry. I promise that Jamal will be in school tomorrow."

"Okay. Well then, I'll come back over here on my lunch break tomorrow so we can talk." Deidre rolled up her window as Kenisha walked back into her apartment.

Driving down the street, tears streamed down Deidre's face as she kept picturing Kenisha waving goodbye to her. "How could that young girl be dying?"

Her heart ached for Kenisha and the children. She couldn't imagine how it would be to bring children into the world and find out that she would not be able to raise them to adulthood. That would be almost as bad as never being able to have children. Deidre smashed her hand against the steering wheel as anger gripped her so tightly that she needed to lash out at somebody or something.

When she got back to work, Christina handed her a note from Dr. Thomas. "He seemed upset, so I would call him right away."

"Okay, thanks," Deidre said, dreading picking up the phone to call Dr. Thomas. He was never pleasant to her, but now she had ticked him off by canceling their meeting. She dialed the phone anyway. When Dr. Thomas was on the line, Deidre said, "Sorry about missing our meeting. Something urgent came up."

"I just bet it did," Dr. Thomas said. "But your little stunt of running out of the office today isn't going to help you."

With a look of confusion on her face, Deidre asked, "Did I do something wrong, Dr. Thomas?"

"You tell me. Shameka Nickels filed a complaint against you. She says that you have singled her son out, and that you have suspended him numerous times for small infractions that other kids would have just received detention for."

"That is simply not true. I have tried to work with that woman. But she doesn't seem to care that her son terrorizes the kids in his class. My teachers can't perform if they constantly have to stop what they are doing to discipline Ronny Nickels."

"Well, I will be conducting a full investigation, and if it appears that you have singled this boy out, you'll be looking for a new assignment."

Did this man just threaten to fire her? Deidre didn't know how much more of Dr. Thomas she was going to be able to tolerate. The man never gave her the benefit of the doubt on anything. But she wasn't about to stand idly by and lose her job over false allegations. "I welcome your investigation, Dr. Thomas. Maybe once you're finished reviewing our files and talking with Ronny's teachers, you can give me a little guidance. Because Ronny is a very bright kid, with a good future ahead of him, if he gets steered in the right direction."

"I'll look at everything and let you know what I find," Dr. Thomas said before hanging up the phone.

For the rest of the day, Deidre tried her best to forget about Shameka Nickels, but she felt so bad for Ronny that she couldn't get him off her mind. And then, every time she thought about Ronny living with that awful mother of his, her thoughts strayed over to Jamal, and she feared for his future—a future without his mother.

That night when Deidre went home she told Johnson about the horrible day she'd had—about Kenisha's doctor telling her she had six months to live and about her suspicions that Ronny Nickels would end up serving a life sentence in prison. Then she asked if he would pray with her.

"Let's do this," was all Johnson said before he and Deidre bombarded heaven on behalf of Kenisha and her children. When they were finished praying for Kenisha and her children, Deidre and Johnson then bombarded heaven on behalf of Ronny Nickels.

14

True to her word, Deidre went back over to Kenisha's house on her lunch break the next day. She knew that Jamal was at school because she had seen him. Deidre just hoped that Kennedy and Diamond were out of the house as well. She had the feeling that Kenisha hadn't told them anything yet, so she didn't want anything to hinder their conversation.

When Kenisha opened her front door, Deidre noted with pleasure that Kenisha had combed her hair and located the shower. She was dressed neatly and appeared to be in better spirits. "Don't tell *me* that prayer doesn't work," Deidre said as she walked into Kenisha's place and sat down. "I prayed for you all night, and look at you. You're practically radiant."

"I don't know if prayer had anything to do with it. I was just tired of letting my kids wander around like lost pups. So I knew I had to pull myself together." Plopping down on the couch beside Deidre, Kenisha added, "I'm not dead yet."

"That's what I wanted to talk to you about." Deidre turned to face Kenisha. "Johnson and I prayed for your healing last night, but then it came to me that you need to participate in this also." Deidre grabbed Kenisha's hands. "I want to pray with you, okay?"

Kenisha appeared to give the suggestion some thought, but in the next moment, she slid her hands away from Deidre. “You can believe what you want, Deidre. But as far as I’m concerned, prayer just gives people false hope. And I have finally come to terms with the fact that I’m dying, so if it’s all the same to you, I’d rather not go backward. I need to move forward and figure out what I’m going to do with my children.”

Deidre wanted to dispute Kenisha’s comment about prayer providing false hope, but a slight nudging in her spirit let her know that this was not the time. So she simply met her where she currently resided. “Okay, so let’s say that if all else fails and you do . . . die”—she hesitated, not wanting to say that word—“is there anyone in your family who would be willing to adopt your children?”

“I wouldn’t want any of them to raise my children. And if I even thought they’d get them after I die, I’d probably put them all in a room and kill ’em. And then I’d stand trial, knowing that I wouldn’t live to serve my time.”

“If I didn’t think you were joking, I’d have to call the police right now.”

Kenisha rolled her eyes. “Okay, I might not kill them. But my kids can’t live with those people. They deserve better than that.”

“Do you have a will?”

Stretching her arms out indicating the items in the living room, Kenisha sarcastically said, “Yeah, I have so many valuables that I meet with my attorney every year to update my will, right after I meet with my financial advisor.”

“You don’t have to be a smart aleck, young lady. I’m just trying to tell you that if you have specific wishes for your children, it’s best to have it written out and notarized.”

“Okay, then, I’ll make sure to write down my wishes.”

"It's not enough to just say what you don't want, Kenisha. We need to determine who might be a good fit for your children. So let's at least start by compiling a list of your immediate family members."

"Well, that will be quick, because I'm going to reject them all."

"You can't just dismiss them so quickly, Kenisha. What about your mother? You really don't think she would step up to the plate and take care of your children if something happened to you?"

"My mother is a drunk. And besides that, she never protected her own children, so how can I expect her to protect mine?"

"Okay, I understand why you don't want your mother. But what about Aisha?"

"Aisha is lazy. She has four illiterate children, and two of them are over the age of seven. No way will Aisha destroy my children's future the way she's doing with her own children. And before you ask, Kevin is a wonderful guy, but he is addicted to drugs and therefore is not stable enough to keep my children."

Deidre felt so sorry for Kenisha, but she tried her best not to let it show. If she knew nothing about the young woman in front of her, she knew that Kenisha couldn't stand to be pitied or looked down upon. "What about your father? Do you have any communications with him?"

Kenisha scoffed. "I don't know if I can call the man who impregnated Martha a father. I know he paid his child support. But he never visited me when I was a kid."

"Did he and your mother not get along?"

"All I know is the man's name is Dwayne Smalls. He owns a chain of fast-food restaurants and has children littered all over this city. But the only ones he claims outright are the ones he had with his wife."

"You've never seen him?" Deidre had been daddy's little girl until the day her father died of a massive heart attack. She remembered crying as if the world had come to an end when her daddy died. But Kenisha spoke of her father with no emotion at all. Deidre just couldn't fathom how her life would have been had she grown up without the love of her father.

"I went to one of his restaurants a few years back." Kenisha's eyes took on a faraway look as if she was picturing the scene all over again. "I dressed my children in their nicest clothes, and we ordered our food and sat down at one of the tables and waited for him to come in. We had been finished with our food for over an hour when he finally walked in the door. He had some files with him, so he walked over to one of the tables and sat down.

"I got up and walked over to him. I put my hand out and said, 'Sir, my name is Kenisha, and I brought my children here today so they could meet you.'

"He ignored my hand as he looked up at me and said, 'If it's money you want, you need to ask your mama for it. I paid my child support, and if she didn't give it to you, I don't have anything to do with that.'"

"That's pretty cold," was all Deidre could say.

"Don't I know it. So, anyway, that was the first and the last time I saw the man."

"But he gave you his last name."

"My mom blackmailed him into doing that. I was child number three, and she was tired of not being able to list the name of the father on her children's birth certificates. So she promised not to tell his wife if he would give me his last name and sign the birth certificate."

Things were looking pretty bleak as far as family members went, but then Deidre remembered something and snapped her finger. "Don't you have another sister? The one who kept your children while you were in the hospital."

Kenisha smiled. "Angelina is smart. That girl is going places. And as much as I hate to agree with my mother, she doesn't need three kids stopping her from achieving her goals." A look of determination overtook Kenisha as she said. "I wouldn't want her to have my children, anyway."

"Why not? You just said she's going places."

"Angelina isn't the problem. It's her father. He's a pervert, and that man will never get his hands on my children. He's ruined enough children in my family."

Again, sadness overtook Deidre at the thought of the life Kenisha must have led, but she didn't pity Kenisha. Rather, she admired the strength in this girl who grew up too soon and, if the doctors were right, would be gone from this earth way too soon. Deidre remembered watching the Michael Jackson memorial and listening as Usher sang "Gone Too Soon." The song was endearing, and it had touched a special place in Deidre's heart. But she hadn't known Michael Jackson. She knew Kenisha, and as she thought of that song while they sat on the couch, discussing possible options in the case of her death, Deidre couldn't hold back any longer, and a tear fell down her cheek, followed by several others.

"I'm sorry," Deidre said, knowing that Kenisha wouldn't want to see her tears.

"I'm sorry too. I wish I had a different family. I wish my mother had never run into Jimmy, the child molester, and I wish I didn't have cancer. But there's no sense wishing the day away when I need help finding a family for my children."

At that moment, Deidre flashed back to her conversations with Johnson about adopting. And then she realized that God did, indeed, work in mysterious ways. Because while she was thinking that Johnson's sudden interest in adopting a child showed a lack of faith in her ability to conceive a child for them, it had been God planting a seed all along. She and Johnson must have had that conversation so that when this moment occurred with Kenisha, Deidre would know exactly what to say. Her eyes lit up as she asked, "Have you thought about checking out some adoption agencies?"

"I don't know," Kenisha said hesitantly. "What if the father is a pervert or the mother is a drunk?"

"These agencies screen the prospective parents pretty thoroughly."

"How do you know?" Kenisha folded her arms across her chest.

"Johnson and I have applied with the Action Adoption agency, and they are running thorough background checks on us. If you'd like, I can do a little more research on the process."

Kenisha unfolded her arms. "You'd do that for me?"

"Of course. All I have to do is Google a few things and then make a few calls. Once I have the information, we can decide what we want to do."

Kenisha looked away as she said, "I'd appreciate it if you'd look that information up for me. I don't have a computer, so I'd have to go to the library to do it, and right now, I don't think I'm suitable company for the general public."

Deidre looked at her watch and then stood up. "It's way past my lunchtime, so I need to get back to work."

"Good thing you don't have classes to teach, or you'd probably have to fire yourself, huh?" Kenisha said with a laugh as she followed Deidre to the door.

"I might not have classes, but I have a superintendent who could give me the boot. But I'm not trying to give him a reason."

"Thanks for stopping by," Kenisha said as she opened the door.

This was the first time Kenisha had ever thanked her for anything. Kenisha had been so defensive about everything from the moment they'd met that Deidre never knew what might set the girl off. But now it seemed as if Kenisha was letting her guard down a bit. That made Deidre feel good. She had misjudged Kenisha when they had first met, and ever since that time she had been trying to make things right. It appeared that she and Kenisha were rounding a new corner, and maybe they were even becoming friends.

"I'll talk to you in a couple of days, once I have some more information on what you need to do." Deidre was all smiles as she left Kenisha's house.

When she got to her car, though, the tears began to fall. Deidre drove down the street and then parked her car. She was so shaken up by the whole thing. No one should have to deal with so much misery in such a short span of time. She wanted to help Kenisha but felt that anything she could do would certainly not make up for the lifetime of suffering this young girl had endured.

Deidre picked up her cell phone and dialed her mother.

The phone rang three times, and then Loretta Clark picked up. "Hey, sweetie, it's so nice to hear from you."

Deidre couldn't stop the tears from flowing as she opened her mouth and blurted out, "Mom, I just want to thank you for being a good mother. You've always looked out for me, and I appreciate it."

"Are you crying?" Loretta asked with concern in her voice.

"Yes."

"Why, honey. What's wrong?"

Deidre wiped the tears from her face and then said, "I have a new friend. Her name is Kenisha."

"Well, that's nothing to cry about," Loretta said, sounding a little baffled.

"She's dying, Mom. She's only twenty-three years old, she has three kids, and she's dying."

"I'm so sorry to hear that, honey."

"Would you pray for her, Mom?"

"Yes, of course I will. Now dry your eyes and trust God—okay, Deidre?"

"All right, Mom. I'll do that."

Deidre had researched adoption agencies. And she had found out how the process would work for her and Johnson, but she didn't know much about what Kenisha would need to do in order to have her children adopted. So she sat back down in front of her computer and began her research. She printed off dozens of pages and jotted down a bunch of notes on her notepad. The entire process seemed pretty straightforward. To get the process started, Kenisha would have to appear before the probate court and relinquish her rights so the adoptive family could petition the court for a decree of adoption. The probate court would have to approve both Kenisha's application and the adoptive parents' petition before a decree of adoption could be ordered by the court.

When she was done, she called Kenisha. "Hey, I've got that information we talked about," Deidre said as soon as Kenisha picked up the phone.

"That quick?"

"The Internet is a wonderful thing."

"So what do we do now?"

"In order to have the children adopted, you'll need to apply with the probate court. Before doing that, I would suggest having someone in mind, so the courts don't pick someone for you."

"I wouldn't want the courts to pick my children's parents," Kenisha said in a whisper.

"Are the kids in the room with you?" Deidre asked.

"I'm in the kitchen, but they're in the living room watching a movie, so I don't want to talk too loud."

"When do you plan on telling them what's going on?"

"I haven't got that far yet. I don't know."

"Okay, we can talk about that later, but my recommendation is that we check out a few of these adoption agencies and see if any of them are able to help you."

"When can we do that?"

"I'll make a few calls tomorrow and see if we can make some appointments."

"Okay." Kenisha hesitated and then said, "Thanks, Deidre."

15

The first place Kenisha and Deidre had an appointment was a social services adoption organization. It was there that reality slapped Kenisha in the face hard. The woman who sat behind the desk appeared to be in her mid-fifties, with salt-and-pepper hair that was neatly swirled into a bun on top of her head. Her name was Leann Banks, and she was the kind of woman someone was always shushing, because she told it like it was with no sugar on top.

"It is unfortunate that you have three children in need of adoption. I could probably place the two-year-old within six to nine months, but the other two might take years."

Kenisha held up her hand, halting the conversation. "Are you saying that my children wouldn't be placed with the same family?"

"Most of my adoptive parents only want one child, two at the most. It is a rare adoptive parent who will take three children at one time. I'm sorry, Ms. Smalls, because I realize that you don't have the kind of time I would need to place your children with suitable parents."

The story was the same at the other agencies. No one could guarantee that Kenisha's children would all be raised together, not even the *forever families*–slogan place.

Kenisha then talked with Children's Services to find out what would happen to her children if she died before finding someone to adopt them.

The social worker, Mr. Nater, told her, "If your children do not already have a guardian at the time of your death, they would be placed into the system and would live with foster parents until someone adopts one or all of them."

"Would you be able to ensure that my children stay together?" Kenisha asked with her fingers crossed.

"No. I'm sorry, I would not be able to guarantee such a thing."

Kenisha was distraught, but Deidre admonished her not to give up. Then about a week after the visits to various adoption agencies, Kenisha received a packet from one of the agencies with information on four couples that were either interested in adopting Kennedy alone or both Kennedy and Diamond together, but not Jamal. As she and Deidre sat down at her kitchen table to review the information on these people, Kenisha was at the point of tears over the fact that none of the couples wanted her son. "What is Jamal supposed to do? He's a good kid, but he needs guidance just like anybody else."

"I know, I was thinking the same thing myself," Deidre admitted.

"How can these people think that eight is too old? If they're willing to take the two- and five-year-old, why not their older brother? Those girls should have someone to look out for them."

Trying to cheer Kenisha up, Deidre said, "All of this won't even matter when God heals you."

"In the meantime, what am I supposed to do about this?" Kenisha held up the papers they had been reviewing on potential parents.

"I've been thinking about this, and I really believe that your children should stay together. So let's throw all of these people back where they came from and wait and see what happens next."

Kenisha threw the papers back on the table. "I agree. If they don't want my son, then they can't be very nice people, anyway. Let's go sit down in the living room and get away from these papers."

They got up and walked into the living room. It was Columbus Day, so school was out. The kids were over at Aisha's playing with her children, so Kenisha could review the information from the adoption agency without prying eyes.

"How are the kids doing?" Deidre asked when they were seated.

"They're doing good. I think Jamal knows something is up, but he hasn't asked me yet. That boy is just too smart for his own good."

"Yeah, I realized that the first time I met him. He was only seven at the time, but he spoke with so much wisdom that I was instantly impressed."

Kenisha saw a gleam in Deidre's eyes every time she spoke about Jamal. So she knew that Deidre cared about him. And it seemed to Kenisha that Deidre would be a good mother, but she wondered why Deidre hadn't asked about adopting her children. "When we met, I remember that you were upset because you thought you were pregnant, but it turned out that you weren't."

The look on Deidre's face told Kenisha that she had touched on a taboo subject. Kenisha lifted her hand and said, "Look, if it's none of my business, don't worry about it . . . forget I said anything."

"It's okay. I don't mind telling you," Deidre said. She took a deep breath and then said, "I can't have children. When I was a teenager my doctor discovered that I had polycystic ovary syndrome."

"Poly what?"

"It's a condition that can cause problems with a woman's menstrual cycle and make it difficult to get pregnant."

"Just because it's difficult doesn't mean it won't happen, right? Isn't that what all that prayer stuff you're always talking about should take care of?"

"Well, it hasn't happened yet, and Johnson and I have been trying for several years."

"Is that why you and Johnson applied with that adoption agency?"

"Yeah, Johnson wants to be a father in the worst way."

"Would my death count?"

It was the first of the month, so Kenisha sat patiently waiting for Chico to knock on her door. She knew he would be there soon. This was the day he always visited Kennedy and just before leaving, Chico always seemed to find a reason to ask to borrow a few dollars. Kenisha normally didn't give him a dime, but today she had a twenty on the kitchen table, right next to the form for relinquishing parental rights that she needed him to sign.

Kenisha stood at the sink washing the breakfast dishes when she heard Chico pounding on the back door. "Here we go," she said to herself as she opened the door.

"Hey, girl, what's been shaking?" he said as he strutted into her apartment.

"Nothing much, Chico. How about you?"

"Oh, you know how I do it. I'm always gon' find a way to get to the top."

Chico used to say that to her when they first started dating. She used to believe him. But that was when he had a real job and wasn't ninety pounds of human waste. "I'm glad you stopped by, Chico. I need to talk with you about something."

"Oh, you're actually going to be nice to me today?"

"I don't have any more fight in me, Chico. Can you sit down at the kitchen table so I can talk to you?"

"Do I get breakfast?" he asked with hopeful eyes.

"Sure, sit down and I'll get you a muffin." Kenisha took the twenty off the table and put it in her pocket before she grabbed the blueberry muffins out of the cabinet. She handed two muffins to Chico and then sat down. As he devoured the food, she told him, "I'm dying, Chico."

"What?" he said as he stuffed one of the muffins down his throat.

"I have cancer. My doctor doesn't think I'm going to live very much longer."

He laughed. "Is this some kind of trick? You're too young to have cancer."

"That's what I thought too. But it's true, Chico. And I've got the aches and pains in my body that prove something is definitely wrong."

"Your brother tried to tell me that you were sick, but I didn't believe him. I thought he was tripping off of some bad crack or something."

"It's true." Sometimes Kenisha amazed herself at how calm she had become with the news of her impending death. She was able to talk with Deidre about it without bursting into tears, and now she was having a rational conversation with Chico—telling him about her death as if she were telling him about Kennedy visiting the zoo for the first time.

Chico leaned back in his seat and stared at her for a moment. "Well, I'll be," was all he said when he'd found his voice again.

Kenisha turned over the piece of paper that had been lying on the table. She put an ink pen on top of the paper as she looked at Chico and said, "I need to find someone to adopt the kids."

Chico scratched his head. "Ah, man, Kenisha, I really wish I could do this for you, but I don't even have a place to lay my head on the regular."

Kenisha put her hand on Chico's shoulder and tried her best to empathize with him. "I know you'd do it if you could, Chico. But you're not in the position right now, and Kennedy needs a mother and father who can take care of her." She pushed the paper closer to him and then asked, "Would you please sign this form relinquishing your parental rights to Kennedy so I can find her an adoptive family?"

"You want me to give up my rights to my daughter?" Chico asked in a tone that indicated he thought he should be getting the father-of-the-year award, rather than being booted out of the club.

"It's the best thing for Kennedy, Chico. She doesn't need to go into the foster care system. She needs to be with a loving family who will protect her and help her to grow into the woman she is meant to be."

"Why can't your mother take them?"

"You know why."

Chico stood up. "You can't do this. I've got rights just like anybody else. You can't just take my child away from me."

Kenisha took the twenty out of her pocket and put it back on the table. "Look, Chico, I really don't want to take Kennedy away from you. But if I die and Kennedy doesn't have adoptive parents waiting to take her, she'll go into the foster care system, and you know they will never let you have her. She'll be all alone, without her sister and brother, and without you, anyway. Is that what you want?"

"Well, no, but . . ." His eyes were on the twenty as he sat back down and pointed at the money. "Are you trying to bribe me with that?"

"No," Kenisha said. "I figured you might need a little money, so I wanted to help you out."

"If I don't sign these papers, are you still going to give me that twenty?"

Kenisha put her hands in her pocket and pulled out another twenty. "Tell you what, Chico, why don't I just give you forty dollars? But that's as high as I can go, because I'm trying to save as much money as I can for my children's future."

"You want me to take that money so you can say I sold my child for forty dollars."

"No, I want you to do the right thing and give up your rights to Kennedy, and then I'm going to give you forty dollars. Two very separate things."

"How do you know I won't get myself together so that I can take care of my own kid?"

"I wish that were true, Chico. But I can't take the chance. I won't be around to take Kennedy off your hands if things become too much for you to handle. Think about your daughter, Chico. Do the unselfish thing for her."

"And you promise not to tell Kennedy about the forty bucks?"

Kenisha lifted her hand in the air as if swearing on a Bible in court. "I promise."

He grabbed the paper, signed it, and then snatched the money off the table and stood up. "There, are you happy? I've just given up the only thing that ever mattered to me on this earth."

"I know you care about Kennedy, Chico, but you did the right thing."

"Whatever," Chico said as he turned and stormed out of Kenisha's apartment.

Kenisha could tell that Chico was upset by what had just happened, but she couldn't afford to feel bad for him. Chico had destroyed his relationship with his child the moment he decided crack was more important. And if he would sign those papers so quickly, in order to get forty dollars, what would he do to his child when push came to shove? No, Kennedy would be better off if she forgot about Chico altogether.

Now came the hard part. Kenisha picked up the same pen Chico had used to sign his rights away and began writing a letter to James, Jamal's father. James had been Kenisha's first love. Even after Kenisha had two other children while he was locked up, James had forgiven her. He'd told her to do her thing while he was behind bars, but when he got out, they were going to be a family again. They had made so many plans for the future that Kenisha hated to write a letter that would cause him to stop dreaming of a better tomorrow. She only hoped that James wouldn't do something stupid that would add more time onto his sentence. He had eight more years to go as it was already. *Please, James, please be reasonable*, Kenisha spoke those words to the four winds as she put pen to paper.

Hey Baby,

I hope things are going well for you. I know you were scheduled to take your GED test a couple weeks ago. How did that go? I saw your cousin Joey a couple of weeks ago. He's been staying clean. He wanted me to let you know that he's got a job and his own place now.

Well, I wish I could tell you that I'm still counting down the days until you get released, but the truth of the matter is that I have some bad news.

I really hate to burden you with this, James. Especially since I know that you're just trying to do your time and get home. But a couple of months ago I was diagnosed with cervical cancer. I had an operation and did some chemo, but nothing worked. You see, James, I'm dying. So I won't be here when you get out. I'm real sorry about that, because I really was starting to believe some of them dreams of yours. But do me a favor, James. Please don't stop dreaming just because I won't be here to listen. I want you to accomplish everything we talked about. Do it for Jamal, okay?

But here's the thing, James. Jamal is almost nine and by the time you get out he will be sixteen. And you already know the type of trouble we were getting ourselves into at the age of fourteen, so we both know that Jamal needs guidance. Someone who can steer him in the right direction before he starts making bad decisions. I'm asking you to sign this relinquishment of parental rights form that I'm including in this envelope and mail it back to me. It's the best thing for Jamal, so please don't be stubborn about this.

Before I let you go, I just wanted to make sure that you know how much I have loved you. I haven't always done the right thing by our love, but you were the first guy I ever loved, and you will be the last. My heart will break for what could have been from now, until . . .

All My Love,

Kenisha

Kenisha folded the letter and the request form into an envelope, sealed it, and then she put her head on her kitchen table and cried for the things that might have been but never would be. Deidre kept telling her to have faith in God and to pray for healing, but Kenisha was living in this body that was deteriorating more and more each day. She had lived in her body for twenty-three years, and now she was dying in it. The only difference between the two was, instead of all the mental pain she had endured, she was now enduring physical pain. The sad thing was, she'd take all the pain this world had to give if she didn't have to say good-bye to James and her children.

16

Within three days, Kenisha received a collect call from James. He was frantic with worry over her, but Kenisha tried to calm him. "I'm okay, James. I've come to terms with this dying thing. There's nothing I can do about it anyway, so I might as well accept it."

"Have you told the kids?"

"No, I wanted to wait until I found the right adoptive parents for them."

"How much longer do you have?"

"I don't know. Dr. Lawson told me two months ago that I had less than six months. But to tell you the truth, I've been in constant pain since last week, and I'm starting to feel a little weak."

She heard a banging sound as if James' fist had hit something metal. He said, "I don't want to hear this, Kenisha. This isn't what we planned."

She held the phone tighter against her cheek as if the sound of his voice could caress her. "I know, James. If I could change it, I would stay here and wait for you to get out, and then the five of us could be a family. But it just doesn't seem like that is going to happen. So we've got to do what's right for Jamal."

"What's right, Kenisha? You think giving up rights to my son is the right thing to do when you don't even know who would raise him yet?"

"I'm working on that, James."

"Yeah, well you let me know when you've got things all figured out. Because I'm not letting my son go to just anybody. If the people you pick want Jamal bad enough, then they'll come out here and meet me face-to-face."

Kenisha knew this wasn't going to be easy. James was no Chico. Even though both men loved their children, James loved Jamal more than he loved himself. "Baby, I know this is hard. But we have to face facts. If I'm gone with no one to take. care of Jamal and the girls, my mother will get them or they will go into foster care, and I honestly don't know which one is worse."

"How do you know that some miracle cure won't be found before you die? Anything can happen, and you're acting like it's already over."

Kenisha fought back tears, because the truth was, she wished she had the luxury of hoping and dreaming. "If it wasn't for my kids, I would be right with you, James. You think I don't want to hope that a cure is found for me just in the nick of time? But if I don't make plans for my kids, and I should leave this earth, I don't think I would be able to go in peace."

"Let me speak to my son," James demanded.

"All right." Kenisha laid the phone down and hollered upstairs for Jamal to come downstairs and get the phone. When Jamal picked up the phone and started talking to his dad, Kenisha opened the front door and took the mail out of the mailbox. She sat down on the couch and sorted through all the junk mail. A look of disappointment spread across her face until she looked at the last envelope in her stack. It was from one of the adoption agencies she had signed up with. She was holding her breath as she opened the envelope and searched through the papers for what she had been desperately hoping for. And then she saw it. Jamal's name was on the paperwork. Someone was interested in adopting Jamal.

"Johnson, I need to go over to Kenisha's. I'll be back in a little while."

Johnson came out of the kitchen drying his hands on a towel. "I'm almost finished with dinner. Can't you go over there after we eat?"

"Aisha just picked the kids up. Kenisha and I have to go over the new paperwork she received from those adoption agencies before they get back. Just eat a snack so you can wait for me. We can eat together when I get back. Okay?"

"Okay, we can eat dinner later. But before you go, I need to know something."

"What's up?"

"Were you serious the other night when you asked if I wanted to adopt Kenisha's children?"

"I know, I know. You want a newborn. But Johnson, those kids deserve a chance. Kenisha wants us to take them and that touches my heart because I know how protective she is about those kids."

"Just a couple of weeks ago, you were worried that I might get deployed and leave you to take care of one kid, but now you think you can handle three?"

"I don't know. It's a lot to take in. I'm still trying to process it myself," Deidre admitted.

"I really had my heart set on a newborn."

Deidre put her hand on Johnson's cheek. He had captured her heart from the first moment she saw him. All she had known back then was that she wanted Johnson Morris to be hers. She wished that she could give him his heart's desire, but sometimes she just had to let her heart change with the times. "I wanted a newborn too, baby. But will you pray about this? Let's see what God thinks."

"Okay, De, you go and help Kenisha and I promise that I'll pray about this."

Deidre grabbed her coat out of the closet. "All right, we'll talk about this some more when I get home. Okay?"

"Go see about your friend. I'll be here when you get home."

Deidre hadn't wanted to pressure Johnson into adopting three children rather than the baby he had in mind. As far as she was concerned, she had kept Johnson in the dark about issues important to both of them, so she was in no position to throw stones about him for wanting a newborn baby. But the truth of the matter was, Deidre had become attached to the children, especially Jamal. She wanted those kids and could do nothing but pray that God would help Johnson want them also.

Deidre tried to rein in her emotions. Kenisha had enough to worry about; she didn't need to be bothered with Deidre's problems. But the minute she walked into the apartment, Kenisha sensed her mood and asked, "What's wrong?"

"Nothing, don't worry about it. Let's just get down to business before the kids get back."

Kenisha pulled out the papers concerning potential parents for her children. She pointed at the packet on top and said, "This is the one that came for Jamal."

Deidre wanted to scream, "No." She didn't want anyone else to adopt Jamal. She wanted Johnson to want him just as much as she did. But she tried to be supportive. "That's great, Kenisha. Did his father release his parental rights?"

Kenisha picked up a towel and wiped the sweat from her brow as she shook her head. "James wants to meet the people I pick before he decides whether or not he'll sign the papers."

"You can't blame him for that. He just wants to make sure that Jamal ends up with the right people," Deidre said as she took the packet out of Kenisha's hand.

"I know. But I don't have time for James to go all stubborn on me. Chico signed Kennedy's papers with no hassle."

"Didn't you tell me that Chico was on drugs?" Deidre scanned the papers while she and Kenisha talked.

"Yeah, but that doesn't mean he don't love his child. I can tell that he does; he's just got that monkey on his back. I'm just glad I don't have to go through this with Diamond's dad. Not that I'm glad he's dead. I just know that he probably would have refused to sign just to irritate me. It wouldn't have been about what's best for Diamond. I really don't know why I ever started seeing that cat. Maybe Dynasty would still be alive if I hadn't fooled around with Terrell."

"You don't know that, and it's best not to even speculate on the matter." Deidre turned to the paper she was reading. She'd gotten halfway down the page when she looked back up at Kenisha. "It says here that the potential parent is a single man, in his late forties."

"I know." Kenisha's tone displayed the disappointment she felt. "The man had been married for fifteen years to a woman who couldn't have children. She died in a car accident last year, and now I guess he wants an instant family."

Sweat beads were now on Kenisha's neck and running down the front of her shirt. She picked her towel back up and dried herself off.

"Are you okay?" Deidre asked with a look of concern.

"Yeah, it's just hot in here."

"It feels good in here to me."

Kenisha laughed. “On top of everything else, don’t tell me I’m going through menopause too.”

Deidre laughed at that.

“Next, the doctor will tell me I’ve got crow’s feet or I’m growing two heads or something.”

“No, no,” Deidre said, still laughing. “You’re going to go to the doctor, and he’s going to say, ‘Good news, Ms. Smalls. We’ve found a cure for cancer.’”

“And what would that be?” Kenisha asked with a grin on her face.

“Sweating.”

The two women broke out in laughter again. And then, as Kenisha wiped some more sweat from her face, she said, “I need to bottle this stuff. I can probably cure the nation.”

At that moment, Deidre truly admired her friend. Kenisha had been stricken with an incurable disease but still found a way to laugh about it. Most people in Kenisha’s position would be having a pity party, but not Deidre’s friend. She was steadfast and determined to do right by her children until she took her last breath.

Getting them back on track, Kenisha asked, “Okay, so what do you think of this guy?”

Deidre shook her head. “My biggest problem is that he’s single. I mean, what’s his motive for suddenly wanting to adopt a son?”

“Yeah, my first thought when I read that he was single, was that the guy was some type of pervert, trying to get a defenseless little boy to call him Daddy by day and who knows what by night. But then, when I read the part about his wife not being able to have children, that made me think of you and your husband. What if something happened to you and then Johnson wanted to adopt a child as a single guy? Would you want him to be turned down?”

Deidre hoped and prayed that nothing would happen to her anytime soon. She wanted to experience the joy of parenthood with Johnson. But if for some unfortunate reason she died before they adopted or had a child, Deidre wouldn't want Johnson to be denied the opportunity to become a father just because he was single. "I guess you're right. You should at least talk to this man to get a better impression of him."

"Hey, is something wrong? You look sad," Kenisha said.

"No, I was just thinking about Johnson and some of our issues. But I didn't come over here to burden you with my problems, so let's just get back to these packets."

"Is he cheating on you?"

Deidre thought about the day she had irrationally accused Johnson of fathering the child of his co-worker. When her sanity had returned, she had felt bad because she knew the kind of man Johnson was. He had made vows to her, and he would honor them until the day he died. "No, Johnson isn't a cheater."

"Good, because I know people. We could have his arm or leg broken, couple black eyes. You name it."

Laughing, Deidre nudged Kenisha. "Keep your thugs away from my husband."

"All right, all right," Kenisha put her hands in the air as if surrendering. "But he better stop making you so sad, or else I might have to deal with him myself."

Deidre turned back to the packets. "Do you still have the information on those two couples who were interested in taking Diamond and Kennedy?"

"I threw the ones that only wanted one or the other away, but I kept the two who wanted both girls. I hoped I wouldn't need them, because I really want someone who is willing to take all three of them."

"Keep hope alive," Deidre said in her best Jesse Jackson imitation. "You don't know what God has planned."

"Can I ask you something?" Kenisha asked as she pulled the two packets of the potential parents out of the paperwork and set them on the coffee table.

"Sure, what's up?"

"Did you talk to Johnson about my kids?"

Deidre nodded, trying her best not to show the emotions she was fighting against way down deep inside her. "We're discussing it. But I didn't want to get your hopes up until I get a final answer from Johnson."

"I know you want Jamal. Is the problem the girls?"

"Oh, no, Kenisha. It's nothing like that. I wouldn't want to see your children split up. I would take all three of them if Johnson and I decide to do this."

"Then what's the problem. Is it Johnson? Why wouldn't he want my children?"

Deidre held up a hand, trying to halt Kenisha's accusations against her husband. "I have no doubt that if we took your children, Johnson would welcome them with open arms, but after waiting for a child for so long, Johnson has his heart set on a newborn."

"Why can't you convince him that my children are better than some newborn? If it's diapers he wants, Kennedy still wets the bed sometimes. Just put a diaper on her."

How could Deidre explain her reluctance to push Johnson into something he didn't want? She had lied to him for so long, and now that she was finally willing to face the fact that they needed to adopt, Deidre wanted Johnson to get his heart's desire, even if that meant giving up hers—giving up Jamal.

Demanding an answer, Kenisha said, "Why can't you convince Johnson to take my kids?"

Eyes averted, Deidre said, "I can't push him on this. He knows what I want. I'm hoping that he will come to the same conclusion."

"Well, while you're sitting around doing nothing but hoping, my kids will be split up."

"What if God heals you, Kenisha? This whole discussion will all be for nothing, then."

Defiantly, Kenisha shot back, "What if God doesn't heal me? Then what will you do?"

17

Kenisha waited for Deidre to respond to her question. When she didn't, that left Kenisha with thoughts of her own. Like, maybe Deidre really didn't want to adopt her children. Maybe Deidre was worried that little ghetto children couldn't keep their noses wiped. Maybe Deidre thought she was too good to help kids who were in need of families to love and protect them.

When Deidre finally opened her mouth, she asked Kenisha, "Why do you have such little faith?"

"You know what?" Kenisha said as she stood up and moved away from Deidre. "I think this whole faith-and-prayer thing that you're always on is a crock. You're not trying to keep me and my kids together. You just don't want to get stuck with my little ghetto brats."

Raising her hands to fend off Kenisha's words, Deidre said, "I never said anything like that."

"You didn't have to say it. Actions speak louder than words every day of the week. You're dragging your feet on adoption because you're afraid that you might get a project kid. You and your husband probably think that if you adopt a baby, you can pray away all that genetic poorness."

"A project kid? Is that what you think? That I don't want to be bothered with poor children? I hate to break it to you, Kenisha, but I didn't grow up in Beverly Hills, myself. My father worked hard every day of his life, but we couldn't even scrap our way to middle class when I was a child."

"Then why don't you want my children?"

"I do want your children. Who wouldn't want them? They are so very precious. I would be proud to call those kids mine."

"Then why haven't you tried to adopt them? You know they need a mother and a father."

Tears fell down Deidre's cheek as she lowered her head.

"You are a hypocrite! I can't believe I fell for your whole act of wanting to be there for me and the kids. I should have known when you couldn't even babysit for me that you didn't want my kids to be anywhere near your big, pretty house with the manicured lawn and big backyard."

"What are you talking about, Kenisha? Jamal has already been over at my house."

Putting her hands to her ears, Kenisha stormed to the front door and snatched it open. "Get out of my house."

"What's wrong with you, Kenisha? I'm trying to help you."

"I don't need your pity."

"I'm not pitying you. I just want to help." Deidre stood up. "Look, I understand your anger. I would be upset too, but I'm not the enemy. I just need a little more time to make this work."

"I know your type," Kenisha sneered. "You'd gladly adopt a child from Africa or some underprivileged country, because that shows what a humanitarian you are. But ask you to take a child out of the ghetto, and you start having nightmares about getting robbed and murdered while you sleep."

Balling her fist, Deidre protested, "I don't think any such thing about your children."

"Get out of my house!"

"Why won't you let me help you, Kenisha? I know you've been through a lot, but why do you mistrust every shred of kindness that comes your way?"

"Oh, okay, well, if you won't go voluntarily, I'll help you out." Kenisha walked away from the door with every intention of strutting over to Deidre, grabbing her arm, and throwing the woman out of her apartment. But her legs locked on her.

One minute she was walking and seeing red as the anger inside her kept building, and the next she was falling flat on her face and into an abyss that was so dark and so controlling that she couldn't get out.

"Kenisha, Kenisha, what's wrong?" Deidre asked as she ran to her. She turned Kenisha over. As she felt the girl's arms and then her forehead, Deidre realized that Kenisha was burning up with fever. "Wake up. What's going on?" Frantically, Deidre began looking around for the telephone. Finding it, she ran to it and dialed 911.

When the operator picked up, she screamed, "I need an ambulance. My friend has just passed out. I don't know what's wrong with her. She's got a fever."

"We'll get an ambulance to you quickly. What's the address?"

"I don't know," Deidre said, then threw down the phone, ran to the front door and looked at the numbers above the door. She ran back to the phone and gave the woman the address.

"Okay, now, can you tell me what happened?"

"She passed out. She has cancer. Can you just get someone here?" Deidre was screaming into the phone because she didn't understand why these emergency people asked so many questions. Shouldn't they be able to tell where you're calling from? And why did they have to ask a thousand questions? If a person is passed out, they should just get there and figure out what's wrong while they're on the way to the hospital.

"Calm down, ma'am. I'm just trying to help before the paramedics get there."

Before Deidre could respond to the woman, Aisha, Jamal, Diamond, and Kennedy walked through the open door.

"What's going on in here?" Aisha demanded as she knelt down beside Kenisha.

"She passed out. The ambulance is on the way," Deidre told her while still holding the phone.

The kids gathered around Kenisha with worried looks on their small faces. Jamal said, "Wake up, Mama. We're home. Wake up."

At that moment, Kenisha moaned and then shook her head as if trying to clear her mind. "What happened?" she asked while lying on the floor, looking up at everyone.

"You passed out," Deidre said for the third time within the space of ten minutes. Then Deidre told the 911 operator. "She's awake now."

Aisha tried to help Kenisha get up, but Deidre stopped her. "They said we should let her lie there until the paramedics get here."

Aisha let Kenisha go and then grabbed Diamond's and Kennedy's arms. "Come on, let's sit down and wait for the paramedics." As Aisha sat the girls down on the couch, she picked up the papers that were strewn across the coffee table. "What's this?" Aisha asked. "Why is Jamal's name on this adoption request form?"

"I've got to go," Deidre told the operator as she hung up and then grabbed the papers out of Aisha's hand. "This stuff belongs to Kenisha. You'll have to talk to her about it later," Deidre pointedly looked at the kids, hoping Aisha would get the message. But nothing appeared to be sinking in.

"Why did you snatch those papers from me? That is my sister's business, and I have every right to know what's going on."

The paramedics picked the perfect time to rush through the doors. They picked Kenisha up and strapped her onto their bed on wheels. "She looks a little disoriented," said the female paramedic, who couldn't have been more than twenty-one or twenty-two. "Does anyone know her medical history?"

Aisha jumped in. "Of course I know her medical history. I'm her sister."

"Can you come with us, so we can ask a few questions while we get her to the hospital?"

Aisha hesitated for a second, but then she looked at her sister, compassion dancing in her eyes. "Yes, I can come. I just need to call my mother and have her go to my apartment and sit with my kids."

"What about Kenisha's children?" Deidre asked. "Should I drop them off with your mother as well?"

Aisha shook her head. "Kenisha would die before letting Martha watch her kids. You're her friend. Why can't you keep them for a few hours?"

Deidre turned to the girls and then looked at Jamal as he fussed over his mother. They needed someone. She wouldn't turn her back on them at a time like this. "Okay, you go with Kenisha, and I'll take them to my house. My husband should be able to watch them for a little while. And then I'll come to the hospital and see how things are going."

"See you in a bit," Aisha said as she jumped in the ambulance after Kenisha had been rolled inside.

Jamal turned to Deidre. "Can I go to the hospital with you?"

Deidre was still shaken up from all that had happened. She wanted to cry, but she couldn't very well break down in front of the children, not when she wanted them to believe that everything was going to be all right. "Not tonight, Jamal. I'm not sure if children are allowed in the area your mom will be in. Now help me grab a few things for you and the girls so I can get y'all to my house."

As they headed upstairs, Deidre called Johnson from her cell phone. When he answered, she asked, "You aren't getting ready to go anywhere, are you?"

"No, why?"

"Kenisha was just rushed to the hospital, and I need to bring the kids to the house with us. Is that all right?"

"Yes, of course," Johnson said. "I'll warm up dinner for them."

"Thanks, Johnson, I'll be there shortly." She hung up the phone and then grabbed a laundry basket out of Kenisha's bedroom and put pajamas, socks, T-shirts, and extra clothes in it. Jamal put their toothbrushes, lotion, and combs in a bag and then they left.

"Is my mom going to be okay?" Jamal asked as they drove down the street.

How could she answer that question? Was death ever okay? She'd heard family members comfort themselves by saying their dead loved one was finally at peace. But when Deidre's dad had died, she wasn't thinking about his peace, only her own sadness.

But Kenisha had woken up, so Deidre didn't think that she was dying today. And she hoped and prayed that God was listening to her prayers as she said, "I think she's going to be all right. She was conscious when the paramedics took her out."

Kennedy started singing her ABCs and Diamond corrected her on every letter that she missed. Deidre smiled as she remembered how she and her sister used to act. Deidre and Michelle were only a year apart, so they were constantly com peting for their parents' attention. Michelle was the younger, so Deidre had always tried to show her mother that she was smarter than Michelle. Whenever Michelle said or did anything wrong, Deidre had always been quick to correct her.

The problem was, when they got older, Michelle seemed to do everything right. She'd gotten married right after college and then worked in her field for three years, until she had her first baby, which came right on schedule. Michelle and her husband had four children in all, and Deidre was still struggling to have one.

Johnson must have been waiting by the door because as soon as she pulled into the driveway, he came out of the house and helped her with the kids. Jamal grabbed Diamond's hand and walked her to the front door. Deidre went to the trunk to grab the basket with the kids' things. Johnson leaned into the back seat, where Kennedy had fallen asleep. He unbuckled her, and the little girl began to stir. Deidre closed the trunk as Johnson pulled Kennedy into his arms. Kennedy snuggled against Johnson and said, "Daddy," and then fell back to sleep.

Deidre's head popped up. She looked at Johnson, wondering if he hadn't understood Kennedy. But one look at the widening grin on his face and Deidre knew he had felt each syllable of that one word. "Let's get them in the house, so I can go to the hospital and see about Kenisha."

They had four bedrooms in their spacious home. But so far, only two of the rooms had been put to use: the master bedroom where she and Johnson slept, and the room down the hall from their bedroom, which had been turned into a home office. Deidre went upstairs and took clean sheets out of the closet and made the beds in the two empty bedrooms.

She then went back downstairs and told Johnson, "I made the beds. So just put Diamond and Kennedy in one of the bedrooms together, and let Jamal have the other."

"I got this," Johnson said as he took bowls out of the cabinet. "You go on to the hospital. I'm going to feed the kids, then I'll pray for their mom with them. We'll watch a movie, and then I'll put them to bed."

Deidre kissed Johnson and then headed out of the house. But as she drove to the hospital, she realized something that took her by surprise. Since Kenisha had passed out she had been moving on autopilot, but not once had she stopped to pray. Something was wrong with that, because Deidre had been the type of Christian who wouldn't do anything without praying first. Johnson hadn't forgotten. He'd added prayer time to his list of things to do with the kids.

She pulled her car over to a strip-mall parking lot and called Johnson. When he picked up, she said, "I didn't pray the whole time. I called 911, grabbed the kids' clothes, but I didn't pray for Kenisha during this whole episode."

"You can pray now, Deidre. It's never too late to pray."

She closed her eyes, took a deep breath, and then exhaled. "Are the kids eating?"

"Yeah."

"Would you mind if we prayed together?"

"I'd love to pray with you, Deidre," Johnson told her. He walked upstairs to their master bedroom, and then they united in prayer on Kenisha's behalf.

As Deidre entered the emergency room and asked for Kenisha's room, she felt as if she were ten pounds lighter. She wasn't burdened down or worried. After she and Johnson had prayed, Deidre began to believe that God was in control once again. However this turned out, it would all work together for good somehow. God would make it good.

18

How is she doing?" Johnson asked when Deidre came through the door. He was standing in the entryway with a cup of hot cocoa in his hand.

"Are the kids asleep?"

"Yeah, I finally persuaded them to lie down about an hour ago."

Deidre looked at her watch. "They didn't go to bed until eleven o'clock. Two of them have school in the morning."

"Tomorrow's Sunday, babe," Johnson said as he handed her the hot chocolate. "Here. When you called and said you were on your way home, you sounded exhausted. So I thought if you drank this, you'd get to sleep faster."

Deidre gently touched Johnson's face with her hand. "You're a prince. I don't deserve you."

"Aw, shucks, Mrs. Morris. You're making me blush," Johnson said jokingly.

She leaned in closer to him and whispered, "Let's go to our room so I can tell you about Kenisha."

Johnson followed Deidre up the stairs. When they were in bed, he turned back to her. "Is she doing better?"

"They gave her some pain medicine, so she's a little loopy. But to be honest with you, it doesn't look good. The doctors said that her body is starting to shut down." A tear slid down Deidre's face as she continued, "The doctors don't think she'll last much longer."

Johnson pulled Deidre into his arms and held her.

"I don't know what happened, Johnson. I've been praying and believing . . . and then this. I just can't see God in this no matter how I look at it. This woman takes care of her children, and she wants the best for them. But she won't even live to see what becomes of them."

"We've got to stay in faith, Deidre. Keep praying even when it looks bad."

She pulled away from her husband. "You say that, Johnson, and I have tried to believe this whole 'pray until something happens' mantra, but it gets harder and harder every time my prayers go unanswered."

Johnson wiped the tears from Deidre's face. "God is in the prayer-answering business, baby. I believe that with every fiber of my being, but I also know that the Bible talks about the Heroes of Faith and how many of them died without receiving the promise, but still they remained in faith, believing that God was able."

"But why does it matter that God is able, if He won't help us?" Deidre asked, really needing the answer to her question as she lay her head on Johnson's chest.

Johnson leaned back against the headrest. He ran his hand through Deidre's hair, and then he began speaking in a slow, deliberate fashion. "Remember the story of the three Hebrew boys who were thrown in a fire that was meant to consume them, just because they believed in God's ability to deliver them?"

Deidre nodded.

"What did they say, just before being put in the fire?"

In a matter-of-fact tone, Deidre responded, "They told the people that even if God didn't deliver them from the fire, as far as they were concerned, that changed nothing, because they knew that God could do it."

"Exactly!" Johnson exclaimed. "And I believe the things we go through in life give us the opportunity to put our faith in God. Whether he chooses to bring us out of this or that or not, our job as Christians is to believe that He is well able."

"But, Johnson, I do believe that God is able. And I think that is what bothers me the most. Because if He is able, then that means He is choosing not to answer my prayers. And I don't understand that."

"Ah, babe, it is not our job to understand. We are only called to believe. The rest is God's business. Okay?" He bent down and kissed Deidre's forehead.

"I guess you're right. But, Johnson, I'm really getting tired of all this praying with no results. I need God to show me something."

Johnson turned out the light. "Okay, baby, just go to sleep. Things will be better in the morning, I promise."

Deidre tried to go to sleep, but she had too much on her mind. She closed her eyes and let her mind drift in a hundred different directions. She prayed that Johnson was right about tomorrow being better, but in truth she couldn't see how things could get better from here. Kenisha was dying, and her children would be motherless. Each one of them was already fatherless for one reason or another, but now they would also be forced to live without their mother. It just didn't seem right.

Deidre had talked to Aisha while they waited outside Kenisha's room during the doctor's examination. And although it seemed as if Aisha was finally understanding the magnitude of Kenisha's situation, she still wasn't prepared to take on three extra children. "I can barely take care of the four I already have. And Kenisha has her children so spoiled, I would never measure up with them."

"Do you think Kenisha will change her mind about allowing your mother to take the children?"

Aisha adamantly shook her head. "Kenisha has never let Martha watch her kids. She says that Martha doesn't protect children. Ever since Kenisha was a kid, she has always talked about protecting herself, and then when she got older, it was all about protecting her kids."

That knowledge made Deidre appreciate how much trust Kenisha had placed in her, because for Kenisha to ask her to adopt her children meant that Kenisha believed that Deidre would keep her children safe. Kenisha had put a lot of faith in her, and now Deidre wanted to beg Johnson to forget about his dreams of having a newborn. But she knew she had no right to take yet another dream away from him. Getting to sleep that night was one of the hardest things Deidre had done in a long time.

The next morning Deidre and Johnson took the children to church and then went to the hospital to see Kenisha. The girls ran to their mother, jumped on the bed, and hugged her. But Jamal hung back.

"What's wrong?" Deidre asked him when she noticed his hesitancy.

They were in the doorway of Kenisha's room. Jamal pointed at the tubes and monitors.

"That's just an IV tube. They're replenishing Kenisha's system with necessary fluids. And that monitor is just keeping track of her heartbeats. The nurses want to make sure that she's okay, even when they're not in the room."

"Oh," Jamal said as he stepped into the room and walked over to Kenisha.

"Hey, boy, I've been waiting all morning to see y'all," Kenisha said as Jamal gave her a hug.

"We went to church first. Mr. Johnson said that we could ask the kids in the children's church to pray for you. So I did," Jamal told her.

"Yeah," Diamond chimed in. "I prayed that God would stop you from being sick all the time."

"I'd like that too," Kenisha said honestly.

Johnson held out his hand to Kenisha. "I'm Johnson Morris. I've heard an awful lot about you. But it's nice to finally meet you face-to-face."

"Likewise," Kenisha said. Her voice was hollow. Tired.

After that, the kids bombarded Kenisha with questions, one after the other, until Johnson volunteered to take the kids home and feed them.

"Thanks, honey," Deidre said as she stood up and kissed her husband. "I'll call you when I'm ready to leave or I'll catch a cab home."

"Call me. No wife of mine has to ride in a cab." Johnson grabbed up the kids and left.

"You have a good husband. I wish I had met someone like him."

"Yeah, he's all right," Deidre agreed.

"Can I ask you something?" Kenisha turned to face Deidre.

"Ask away. I'm all ears."

"Okay. Why are you here? I mean, I tried to throw you out of my apartment yesterday. If I hadn't passed out, I would have. And now you've got my kids. But when I asked you to watch them for me before, you acted like that was a big problem."

"I'm sorry if you thought I didn't want to help you out with your children. But the truth is, my reasons were even more selfish than you had guessed."

Kenisha gave Deidre an *aha* look. "So you admit it?"

Deidre held up her hand. "Let me explain. This is not going to be easy for me, but I think I at least owe you an explanation."

"I'm listening."

Taking a deep breath, Deidre began her story. "I told you about my condition, which makes it hard if not impossible for me to conceive."

Kenisha nodded.

"But what I didn't tell you is that my husband doesn't know that I have this condition. I've known since we started dating that Johnson wanted lots of kids, but I didn't want to lose him, so I keep my mouth shut. I made my mom and sister stay quiet about it also. They begged me to tell him the truth, but I refused."

"I thought Christians didn't believe in lying," Kenisha said without an ounce of judgment in her voice.

"That's why this whole thing has been so hard on me. Johnson and I got saved a couple years after we got married. My sister, Michelle, called to congratulate us. I remember how excited she was for me. I was excited also. Then she told me that I should tell Johnson about my PCOS so that there would be no secrets between us. And I told her not to ever bring that up to me again.

"I shouldn't have been so mean to her, but I was scared. I've been scared my entire marriage."

"But Johnson is willing to adopt, so if you tell him the truth, he might even be that much more willing," Kenisha said hopefully.

Deidre put her head in her hands and let the tears flow. The guilt of her deception had worn on her for so long that she could no longer contain her emotions. "I'm sorry, I'm sorry. It's just . . . I don't even feel worthy of Johnson's love. He has suffered with me for seven long years, wanting a child as much as I do. I just wanted to be able to give him a child myself. If I could do that, my lie wouldn't matter."

"But he loves you, I could see that."

"I know he does. But now we have another problem. See, ever since we decided to adopt, Johnson has had his heart set on a newborn. And even though I would love nothing more than to adopt your children, I don't know if I can disappoint Johnson one more time." The tears fell harder as she finished. She looked at Kenisha, hoping to glean an answer to a question that had been plaguing her for years. "How do I tell a man who wants children so bad, that I will never be able to give him any? And that he has to give up his dreams for a newborn because I have fallen in love with your children?"

Shaking her head, Kenisha said, "People deceive others all the time. The only reason you're feeling guilty about this is because of your church. It's the church. That's why I don't go. If I want to know what a loser I am, I'll invite my mother over."

"That's not the way it is. The church provides hope."

"You mean false hope."

"No, no, Kenisha, that's not true. The hope that God brings is not false," Deidre told her as she wiped the tears from her face and thought back to the conversation that she and Johnson had had last night. She believed every word Johnson said, so therefore she believed God. Faith was the answer, whether she lived to see the rewards of her faith or not. "I do believe that God answers prayers. Whether he answers mine or not does not change the fact that God is good and that He is well able to do anything we need Him to do."

Without a second thought, Kenisha said, "I can't put my trust in a God that could allow me to die so young and you to yearn for children you'll never have."

19

On Thursday Kenisha found out that she was being released. Her fever was gone, but she still felt tired and nauseated. The doctors felt they could do nothing more for her, and it was best that she spend her remaining time with her children. Martha and Aisha were in her hospital room waiting for her release papers so they could take her home. Martha was complaining, "I am just really upset with you, Kenisha. I don't know why you didn't tell us the final diagnosis you received months ago. I am your mother. Whether you like it or not, I brought you into this world. And I have a right to know if you are dying on me." Martha had a tissue in her hand, and she kept pressing it to her face to halt the tears that were falling from her eyes.

"Martha is right, Kenisha," Aisha chimed in. "Jamal's principal told me about your final diagnosis. I thought you were just depressed because of the chemo. You had no right not to tell us." Aisha's voice broke as tears creased the corners of her eyes.

Kenisha started to feel bad. Her family was not the best, but she shouldn't have shut them out. "I'm sorry. Y'all are right. I should have said something."

"No more secrets," Martha demanded. "I need to know what's going on. That's why I'm taking you straight to my place when we leave this hospital. You and my grandkids are going to stay with me—right where you belong."

"So now you want to be a mother to me. A little late on your job, aren't you, Martha?" Kenisha said without caring how rude she sounded.

"This is no time to start a fight, Kenisha," Aisha admonished. "We love you, whether you believe it or not. And we want to help."

"Where is Kevin? I haven't seen him." Kevin normally stopped by her apartment or called at least once a week. But she hadn't seen or heard from him in two weeks.

"I don't know," Martha confessed. "He hasn't been home, and he hasn't called, either."

Kenisha sat up in her bed and glared at her mother. "And you're not worried? Have you called the police?"

Rolling her eyes, Martha waved the suggestion off. "Why would I call the police when that boy is probably off on a crack binge somewhere?"

"You are really something, Martha. You don't care about nobody but Aisha and Angelina. And the only reason you care about Aisha is because she runs all your errands," Kenisha let out a huff. "What kind of mother wouldn't even go look for her son?"

Martha stood up and turned to Aisha. "I'm not going to sit here while this girl talks to me like a dog. I'll wait downstairs."

"Kenisha, you've hurt Martha's feelings. Apologize. You two need to start getting along. After all, you're going to be staying with Martha from now on."

Rolling her eyes, Kenisha said, "She has lost her mind if she thinks me and my kids are going to stay with her."

"You can't stay alone anymore, Kenisha. Your doctor told us that you're going to need round-the-clock care." Again, Aisha's voice broke off.

"Just take your mother home, Aisha. I've got a place to stay. I don't need y'all to help."

"So now you don't want to be bothered with me either," Aisha said.

"No, Aisha, I'm glad you came. I'm glad you and I are starting to get along better. But I can only take so much of Martha."

Martha pointed a finger at Kenisha. "Don't worry, little girl, you've kicked me around for the last time. But one day, you're going to beg to see me."

"Don't hold your breath," Kenisha said as Martha stormed out of the room.

Aisha stood up and glared at Kenisha. "That woman has been crying her eyes out ever since I told her what's going on."

"She's probably just drunk."

"How can you be so cruel?" Aisha asked.

"I'm dying, Isha. Guess I just don't feel like playing nicey-nice anymore."

Aisha looked as if she felt Kenisha's pain. She walked closer to the bed and hugged her. "I'll talk to you later, little sis. Keep your head up."

Kenisha lay back on her pillow, grateful for the silence. The moment her mother had walked into her room, she knew that things were going to end badly. Ever since Martha had failed to protect her, Kenisha had despised the woman. Having Jamal at fifteen had been a godsend as far as Kenisha had been concerned. It gave her the incentive to get her own apartment at the age of sixteen. She'd only had to pay thirty dollars a month for the place, but Kenisha would have gladly given them her entire welfare check, just to get away from Martha.

Why did the woman come around her now? Did she really think she could make amends for all the mothering she hadn't done when Kenisha was a child? And did she really think that Kenisha was going to let her children sleep in a house where Martha would be too drunk to know what was going on under her own roof? Fat chance. At this point Kenisha didn't know if she would even want her children to have a relationship with that "mommy dearest" after she died. No, it would be better if they stayed far away from Martha. Kenisha would make sure whoever adopted her children knew better than to try to keep her kids connected with Martha.

"Hey, how are you doing today?"

Kenisha turned toward the door and watched Deidre walk in. "Doing okay, just making some plans, that's all."

"Speaking of plans," Deidre said as she took her coat off and sat down, "have you decided whether or not you're going to move in with me and Johnson?"

Kenisha had just told her mother and sister that she already had somewhere to go, but in truth she hadn't accepted Deidre's invitation and wasn't sure she wanted to. "You and Johnson don't need me and my kids running around your house."

"Johnson and I talked about this already. We want to do this for you, Kenisha. So, please let us help you."

"Have you told Johnson the truth yet?"

Before Deidre could answer, a nurse rushed into the room with release papers in her hand. "You're all set, Kenisha. But you need to take it easy. I don't want to see you back in here for a long time."

"I'll try," Kenisha told the woman with a smile.

"Let me get the wheelchair, and we can get you on the road." The nurse left the room.

Kenisha then turned back to Deidre and asked again, "Well, did you tell him?"

Deidre shook her head.

Slamming her fist against the mattress, Kenisha chided Deidre. "I don't have much time left, you know. Maybe if you told Johnson the truth, he'd be willing to take my kids, rather than wait for a newborn."

"I'm hoping that Johnson will come to that conclusion on his own."

"After what you told me the other night, I can understand that," Kenisha said, then added, "But what if you never conceive? My children need someone now. If you let this opportunity go, they are going to be piecemealed from one family to the next, while you and Johnson are still childless."

"Do you really have to be so harsh all the time?"

"I'm not trying to be harsh. I just wish you would face the facts, so we can help each other." Kenisha had thought about their predicament all night. Deidre was childless, but she and her husband desperately wanted children. Kenisha's children were already fatherless and would soon be motherless. So, the way Kenisha saw it, Deidre and Johnson needed children to love, and her children needed parents—it was a perfect fit.

"Johnson is having so much fun with the kids. I just know he'll make the right decision. You just have to give me a little more time."

"I'm running out of time," Kenisha said matter-of-factly.

When Deidre didn't respond, Kenisha said, "Maybe I should move in with you. That way, Johnson might just fall so in love with my kids, that he will forget all about adopting a newborn."

The nurse strolled back into the room with the wheelchair. She looked around the room. "Do you have everything?"

Kenisha pointed to the bag next to her bed. "I put everything in there."

"Well, let's get going," the nurse said as she helped Kenisha off the bed.

When they arrived home, Deidre found Johnson rolling around on the ground in the backyard with Jamal and Diamond. She was taken aback by how childlike he looked, laughing and giggling with the kids. Then Mother Barrow's prophecy ricocheted in her head: *Your house will be filled with laughter, love, and children.* At the time, Deidre had thought the prophesy cruel, because as the years passed and they remained childless, the only prediction that was spot-on was the one that came from her doctor—she would never have children. But as she watched Johnson with Kenisha's children, she wondered if God had shown Mother Barrow a vision of these children. And if the love and laughter in her home would come from them.

Deidre decided to leave Johnson alone with the kids a little longer, to give him some more bonding time. She turned away from them and headed back into the house.

Johnson jumped up and ran after Deidre. "Hey, did you need me?" he asked when he caught up with her.

The look in his eyes was joyful. The joy had been missing in Johnson's eyes for the past few years. Deidre had been praying desperately to get pregnant so that Johnson could get his joy back. "I just came to tell the kids that Kenisha is in the family room."

"They'll want to know that." He turned back to the kids and yelled, "Come on in, your mom is waiting for you two hoodlums in the family room."

Deidre poked him. "Don't call them hoodlums."

"If you had seen the way these two kids hemmed me up, you'd call them hoodlums too," Johnson said good-naturedly.

Deidre could tell he loved every minute of whatever game he, Jamal, and Diamond had been playing. "Where is Kennedy?"

"Napping. She counted to ten, said her ABCs, and spelled a few three-letter words like *cat* and *dog* for me. Then I guess she just got tired, because she told me that she wanted to lie down."

Jamal and Diamond ran past them as they went inside the house.

"She knows how to spell?" Deidre asked in astonishment.

"Yeah. Whatever Kenisha has been doing with her kids, it's been working. They are smart little kids."

"I know Jamal gets good grades, but I had no idea that the two-year-old could spell and count."

Johnson put his arm around Deidre and escorted her back into the house. "Let's go fix dinner for our full house."

Deidre went into the kitchen and scrambled up some Cheeseburger Hamburger Helper. Johnson gathered the kids together, they blessed the food, and then they ate at the dining room table. Deidre went into the family room to check on Kenisha. She was reclining in a La-z-Boy with a warm blanket covering her body. "Do you want me to bring a tray in here so you can eat?"

Kenisha shook her head. "I'm too nauseated to eat, and it hurts when I swallow."

"You have to eat to keep your strength up, Kenisha."

"I know. I'll eat later."

Deidre went back into the dining room and ate her dinner with everyone else. But her mind kept drifting back to Kenisha. The girl had told her that she didn't have much time left, and the way things were going, Deidre was truly starting to believe her. Of course, she would continue to pray for

Kenisha, but if things didn't turn around, Jamal, Diamond, and Kennedy would need someone. She looked at the innocent faces of the children before her, as they chowed down on a simple Hamburger Helper meal. At that moment, she wanted to beg Johnson to give up his dream of a newborn and embrace the kids who were right in front of them.

Kennedy held up her bowl and said, "All gone."

Johnson smiled as he took the bowl from Kennedy. "Yes, princess, it's all gone. You did a good job."

Kennedy stood up in her chair and held out her arms for Johnson. "Pick up."

"All right." Johnson stood up and did what he was told. "I'll take you to the family room to see your mom." He picked Kennedy up and put her on his shoulders, and they happily bounced out of the room.

As Deidre watched them go, she wondered if Johnson and Kennedy got along so well because they both were given the last names of presidents for their first names. Maybe they felt some connection that the rest of the world would never know.

"I'm finished too," Diamond said, pushing her plate back.

"Yeah, me too. I'm full," Jamal said.

"Do you to have any homework?"

"Ah, Mrs. Morris, we don't want to do no homework," Diamond said.

"I'm sure it will only take you a few minutes to do your homework, and then you can go into the family room and watch a movie or something with your mother."

"Okay," Diamond said reluctantly.

"Do you want me to help you clear off the table?" Jamal asked, being his normal helpful self.

"Thanks, Jamal, but I'll do this. You and Diamond just go and get your homework done so you can spend some time with your mom before going to bed."

The two of them got up from the table and went to get their book bags. Deidre started taking the plates off the table and scraping them out so she could wash them. In the middle of her work, she realized that she was humming. She stopped mid-scrape as she recognized the feeling of contentment and joy in her spirit. She hadn't felt this way in a long time. Was this the same type of joy that she saw on Johnson's face?

Deidre's heart was turning somersaults as she washed the dishes. She had wanted her own child for so long that she had never imagined she could find room in her heart for a child who didn't belong to her. But these children had somehow found a place in Deidre's heart, and she wasn't sure if she would be able to let them go.

Johnson came into the kitchen and pulled Deidre into his arms. He kissed her and then said, "I want to talk to you about something later tonight."

"Okay," Deidre said, then watched as Johnson left the kitchen walking as if he were floating. Deidre turned back to the sink to finish the dishes. As she worked, she told herself that she knew what Johnson wanted to talk about tonight, but before she would agree to adopt Kenisha's children, Deidre was going to tell Johnson about her secret. The guilt was eating her alive, and she didn't want to continue living a lie. She only hoped that God would give Johnson the ability to forgive her for what she had done to him.

20

Wringing his hands, Johnson wore out the rug in his bedroom as he walked back and forth working on his spiel. He had made such a big deal about adopting a newborn that he was worried that Deidre might also have her mind set to wait for a newborn. And if that were the case, she might not want them to be parents to Kenisha's wonderful children. Deidre had also worried that adopting an older child might bring problems that she couldn't handle while he was deployed.. But Johnson was willing to give up his military career if he could have these children in his life forever.

Deidre walked into the bedroom smiling, but her smile disappeared as she looked at her husband. "You look serious. What's up?"

"Sit down," he told her as he moved out of the way so she could sit on the lounge chair in their bedroom. When she was seated, Johnson turned to her and said. "I know we talked about adopting a newborn, and I also know that you had expressed reservations about adopting an older kid. But I've made a decision that should ease your worries about that."

"I'm listening."

Rubbing his hands together, Johnson plowed right into it. "Well, as you know, I will have twenty years of service in as of next year, and that makes me eligible for retirement. So," he nodded as if convincing himself, "that's what I plan to do."

Deidre's mouth fell open as she stared at her husband. When she finally found her voice again, she said, "You love being in the military, Johnson."

"I love you and the possibility of having children more. I think we should adopt Kenisha's children. What do you say, Deidre? I'm willing to retire so that I can help you with them. So can we do it?"

Standing up, she turned to Johnson with tears in her eyes. "I can't let you do this."

He grabbed Deidre's hands, brought them to his mouth, and kissed them. "I want to do this—for us."

"Oh, Johnson, what have I done to you?" She snatched her hands away from him as she backed up. Fear was etched across her face.

"What's wrong, Deidre? I thought this was what you wanted."

Shaking her head, Deidre sat down on their bed and turned away from her husband.

"Why won't you look at me, Deidre? What's wrong?"

"I don't know how to tell you this."

"Just tell me what's on your mind. It can't be as bad as you're making it out to be."

"It is, Johnson. I'm so sorry," she sobbed.

"You haven't done anything, babe. Why are you acting like this? I thought you wanted to adopt. Please be okay with this, Deidre. We could be such good parents to Kenisha's children. I know we talked about a newborn, but I'd like to have these children instead."

"Johnson Morris, you are the most unselfish person I know. You have given up so many of your dreams to be with me, I won't let you give up another."

"I haven't given up anything, Deidre. You are my dream. We've made a good life together, and it will only get better with those kids in our lives. What do you say, babe?"

"I'm not letting you quit the military."

"But you were worried about us getting a juvenile delinquent if we adopted an older child. Remember, you told me you didn't want to be left here while I was deployed. It's understandable; some children have attacked their foster parents or adoptive parents."

She put a finger to Johnson's lips. "Kenisha's children aren't like that." She closed her eyes, trying to block out the pain of her deception. "I haven't been honest with you, Johnson. And I can't agree to adopt the kids with you until I tell you everything."

"What's wrong?"

She took a deep breath and then let the words flow from her mouth. "I can't have kids, Johnson."

"I know that, Deidre. That's why we're considering adoption."

"Yes, but I've known I couldn't have children for quite a while." She choked on her words as she said, "I put you through seven years of torture, and I knew."

Holding on to his confusion, Johnson asked, "How long have you known?"

"Since I was a teenager. My mom had some tests run on me when I started having a lot of pain and some other symptoms that we didn't understand. The doctor told us that I have polycystic ovary syndrome."

"What's that?"

She got up from the bed, went into the bathroom to get some tissues, and then wiped her face and blew her nose. "It's a condition that makes it very hard for a woman to conceive. Some women have had children despite this illness, but I just don't appear to be one of them."

Something was wrong with his ears. He couldn't have just heard what he thought he'd heard. There had to be a mistake. So he turned to Deidre for clarification. "Are you telling me that you knew this before we got married?"

Nodding, she lowered her head.

Johnson came off the bed as if being too close to it would defile him. "Do you know how many times I talked to your mother about the children we would have when we first got married? I bet the two of you had a good laugh over that."

"No, Johnson, my mother begged me to tell you the truth. I wouldn't listen to her, but that hasn't stopped her from praying for us every single day."

"That's honorable of you to be willing to take the blame. But where was your honor when you were lying to me for all these years?"

"It wasn't like that, Johnson. I honestly believed that I would be able to have children, so I thought my diagnosis was a nonissue."

"Except you didn't trust me enough to tell me about this nonissue." Johnson threw up his hands. "I've got to get out of here," he said as he flung the bedroom door open and stormed down the stairs.

"Johnson, wait, don't leave. We need to talk about this," Deidre yelled as Johnson descended the stairs.

He grabbed his keys off the entryway table and opened the front door. He then turned back to his wife and said, "You should have talked to me years ago. You chose not to. Well, guess what, Deidre. Now I don't want to talk." With that he walked out of the house and slammed the door.

Johnson got into his truck, gunned the engine, and sped off. Since the day he had met Deidre, his life had been connected to her. All he had ever wanted was to please her. He'd even been willing to give up his military career. But their life had been built on a lie, and Johnson didn't know if he could handle that.

He drove around aimlessly for a while, then turned his car toward Fairborn, Ohio, in the direction of Wright-Patterson Air Force Base as he headed to Marissa's house. Deidre wouldn't appreciate that he'd gone to see Marissa, but Johnson didn't care at this moment. Marissa had always been a good friend, and she always told him the truth. And that's what he needed right now, to be in the presence of someone he could trust.

Marissa lived in a small, one-story brick house just five minutes from the base. Johnson knocked on her door, hoping that she hadn't already gone to bed or that her boyfriend wouldn't throw him out if he was there. When Marissa opened the front door, the first thing Johnson noticed was how big and uncomfortable she looked with her stomach protruding from her slim body like a missile.

"Hey, were you asleep?"

Marissa tried to wrap her robe around her belly, but it wasn't working. "I was watching *CSI*. Come on in. Let me go put on some clothes."

Johnson sat down in the living room and waited for Marissa to return.

When she walked back into the living room, she had on a pair of maternity jeans and a pink- and blue-striped maternity shirt that said "Baby on Board," and had an arrow that pointed downward. Johnson had thought he would one day watch Deidre walk around in funny-looking clothes like that, but she had dashed all his dreams with her revelation tonight. And in truth, he was beginning to think that the woman he loved and trusted was some kind of monster.

"So what's up?"

Johnson leaned his head against the back of the couch. "I just needed to get my head on straight."

Concern etched on her face, Marissa sat down next to Johnson. "What's going on? What happened?"

He put his hand over his forehead as if feeling for a fever. But the sad irony was that Johnson would have gladly weathered a fever rather than this aching feeling that was in his heart. He sat up, then hesitated for a moment as he tried to get his head around this nightmare that had become his life. "Do you remember me telling you that Deidre and I were desperately trying to have children, but so far nothing had happened?"

"Yeah. I also remember how you told me that it wasn't fair that unmarried women could just pop kids out like it was nothing but couldn't figure out how to take care of the kids once the delivery was done."

"I apologized for that comment," Johnson reminded her.

Nodding, Marissa said, "And I accepted your apology, so I shouldn't have even brought it up. My bad. Go on with what you were saying?"

"Deidre can't have children," Johnson blurted out.

"I thought you had already figured that she probably couldn't have children. Why is it an issue now?"

"I thought Deidre might have been the problem, but she confirmed it tonight."

"And . . . What's the problem? For better or worse—do you remember those vows?"

"I remember my vows," Johnson said irritably. "But Deidre knew she couldn't have children before we got married, and she never said a word."

"Ouch," was all Marissa could say.

"Ouch is right. I just don't know how I'm going to deal with this."

Marissa put her hand on Johnson's shoulder to comfort him. "I know this is hard, Johnson, but you need to find a way to get past it if you want your marriage to work."

"I don't know if I can make it work after this," Johnson confessed.

"Oh, come on, Johnson, you didn't marry Deidre because she would be able to have a hundred kids. Because if that were the case, you would have left already. The two of you have been married for seven years with no children, so there had to be another reason for marrying her."

"I loved her."

"And do you still love her?"

He closed his eyes, trying to get a hold on his emotions. "I'm not sure how I feel right now."

"Well, then, you better figure it out real quick, buddy. Deidre is a wonderful woman, and I know that she loves you to pieces. You don't want to end up alone, not if you possibly can work this out."

This was why he had come to Marissa. She wasn't a misery-loves-company type of person. She'd made her share of mistakes, but she had never blamed anyone else for them. She was a good friend, and he trusted her advice. "Could you trust someone who had lied to you for seven years?"

Marissa took a moment to answer, but when she did, she spoke the truth. "It would be hard. I don't know, Johnson. Maybe you need to listen to Deidre's side of this before you make any snap judgments."

"What if I don't like her side of things?"

"This one is too heavy for me. It sounds like you and Deidre might need a marriage counselor." She stood up. "And since I've never been married, I don't think I can help you with this one."

He stood up with her. "I didn't want to talk to you because of your marriage expertise. I've known you a long time, Marissa, and you've never sugar-coated things. You tell people what they need to hear, and that's that. So I just needed you to help me figure this out."

"I'm sorry, Johnson, I wish I could help you out with this." She walked to the door and opened it. "But if you really want my recommendation, then I'd say go home and talk this over with Deidre."

Shaking his head, Johnson admitted, "I don't know if I can do that." He walked out of Marissa's house and got back in his truck. He was more confused than ever now. Yes, Marissa was right, Johnson did love his wife. But could he trust her? Could he get past this deception she had visited on him for seven years? He didn't know, and until he could figure it out, he wasn't sure that he could go home. He pulled his car onto the road and drove until he found a hotel he could check into for the night.

Deidre desperately hoped that the slamming of the door hadn't awakened Kenisha. The children were upstairs in their bedrooms with the doors closed, but Deidre had let the bed out on the sectional in the family room for Kenisha. Deidre had thought it would be better if Kenisha didn't have to worry about climbing up and down the stairs. She just hadn't realized that Kenisha would have to deal with loud, yelling voices and slamming doors. What had she done?

Needing to talk with someone, but not wanting to burden Kenisha, Deidre tiptoed back into her bedroom, picked up the phone, and called her mother. She'd dialed her mother's number more in recent weeks than she had in the past few years. Her mother was truly a woman full of grace and mercy, because she hadn't said a word to Deidre about the way she had treated her family when all they had asked her to do was tell the truth.

Loretta's cheerful voice came over the line. "Hey, sweetie, how are you doing?"

As soon as her mother called her "sweetie," tears began flowing. Deidre blurted out, "He left, Mom. I did what you said, and he left."

21

Without Johnson lying beside her, Deidre had a fitful sleep. Most of the night was spent crying rather than trying to sleep, anyway. By morning, even though she had bloodshot eyes, she had to get up and help the kids get dressed and get them off to school. But when Deidre opened the door to the children's bedrooms, she noticed that only Kennedy was still in bed asleep. She tiptoed out of the room, not wanting to wake Kennedy, then she went in search of Jamal and Diamond.

They weren't in the upstairs bathroom, so she went downstairs. To her shock, Deidre found the kids seated at the kitchen table while Johnson scooped oatmeal into bowls. He then set the bowls on the table in front of the children. A smile crept across Deidre's face as she said, "I didn't know you were here."

He didn't look at her as he responded, "I came to take the kids to school and pick up a few items that I'm going to need."

"What items?" Deidre asked. The smile had left her face, and panic had replaced it.

"I need some underclothes and my uniform."

Was he leaving her? "Are you leaving me?"

"I need some time, Deidre."

"How much time, because I think we have a pretty big decision to make. And I don't think that can wait too long."

Johnson looked up, and his eyes bore into Deidre as he said, "Don't try to guilt me into anything."

She wanted to reason with him—tell him how much she loved and needed him—but she could tell that he wasn't ready to hear that right now. And she really didn't want to put the kids in the middle of this, so she simply asked, "Can I at least know where you're staying?"

"I checked into the Holiday Inn in Fairborn last night."

"Will you be home for Thanksgiving?"

"I don't know."

Deidre turned and walked out of the kitchen. She didn't want to break down in front of the kids. She went into the family room. Kenisha was awake and watching the Turner Network with the volume down.

She turned to Deidre as she walked into the room and said, "Are you okay?"

Deidre plopped down in the recliner. "You heard me and Johnson last night?"

"Yeah, couldn't really avoid it the way you two were yelling. I guess you told him, huh?"

"Yep, I did exactly what you and my mother have been after me to do. And now my husband is going to pack his clothes."

Kenisha didn't say anything. The two of them sat silently in the family room until Jamal and Diamond came in to give Kenisha a hug before leaving for school. "Hey," she said to Diamond and Jamal. "Give Mrs. Deidre a hug too."

Diamond and Jamal did as Kenisha requested and then ran out of the room. After they left, Kenisha turned back to Deidre and asked, "So what are you going to do?"

"I don't know," Deidre said in a helpless manner. "For a long time, I've dreaded that something like this would happen. I didn't want to be deceitful with him, but I was so afraid of losing him."

"If you want my two cents, I don't think he's leaving. Trust me, if that man didn't want anything to do with you, he would have gone to Wal-Mart and bought himself some more clothes. Plus, he's driving my kids around." Kenisha winked at Deidre. "He'll be back."

"I asked him if he would be home for Thanksgiving, but he didn't give me an answer."

Kenisha shifted in bed. "What made you tell him last night?"

"I watched how Johnson was with the kids last night, and then I thought about what you said about the two of us being able to help each other out, and I decided that you were right. But before I could ask Johnson about adopting the kids, I wanted to tell him what I had done."

"So, just like that, you told him?"

"I honestly don't know if I would have chickened out last night or not. But Johnson had already given up his dream of adopting a newborn, and he told me that he was willing to retire from the military if I would agree to adopt your kids. That's when I knew I couldn't hold the truth from him anymore. You see, I know how much Johnson wanted a newborn, and how much he loves being a soldier. I couldn't take that from him too."

"Wow, that's deep," Kenisha said as she sat up in bed. "Your husband was willing to throw his military career away to become a father to my children, and Kennedy's father gave her away for forty dollars."

"Hey, I just remembered that you didn't eat anything last night." Deidre stood up. "I'm going to make you some tomato soup. That ought to go down smooth enough."

"Aren't you going to work this morning?"

"No, I need to be here to meet your new nurse, and your wheelchair is being delivered today also."

"Why are you doing this for me? I have been so mean to you."

"You're all right, just a bit of a grouch sometimes," Deidre said as she walked into the kitchen.

Deidre opened a can of tomato soup, put it in a bowl, and microwaved it. She put Kenisha's soup on a tray with a bottle of water. When she returned to the family room, Kenisha had put the bed up and was sitting in the recliner. "You're tired of being in bed?"

"Yeah," Kenisha said. "As long as I've got the strength, I'd rather sit up. Never did like lying around all day long."

Deidre put the tray in front of Kenisha and then sat down and watched her eat. Deidre had thought Kenisha was thin when they first met, but she was positive that Kenisha had lost even more weight since then. "Johnson picked up your pain prescription yesterday. So if you're in any pain, just let me know, and I'll give you a pill."

"I had a friend who had been prescribed some pain medicine. She sat around her house looking like she was tripping off something. I don't want my kids to see me like that. So if I can avoid it, I'd rather just take it at night, after they go to bed."

"Okay, but they will be gone for several hours, so if you need one now, I can get it for you."

"I don't want to chance it. I need to go over Diamond's schoolwork with her when she gets in. She likes to pretend that she doesn't have any and will only do it if you force her."

"I caught a glimpse of that last night," Deidre said with a chuckle.

"She's a smart kid. She just doesn't believe it. Her dad was a thug, but he was no dummy. I always got pretty good grades in school also. So I know Diamond can do the work."

"She'll do it. She's just struggling with being a kid right now."

"Yeah, I just hope my dying doesn't stop them from making something of themselves."

"Kenisha, why do you choose to believe that you're going to die, rather than trust that God can heal you?"

Kenisha put her spoon down and laughed bitterly at that comment. "I can't believe you would ask me something like that. Even you believe that I'm going to die. You wouldn't have been talking to Johnson about adopting my kids if you didn't believe it."

"I admit that the signs are there. But I still believe that God can heal you. I'll be praying that prayer until there's no reason to pray it anymore. Do you understand what I'm saying?"

"Yeah, some of that 'hope for the best, but plan for the worst' stuff."

"I guess that's about the easiest way to explain how I'm feeling about the situation."

Kenisha pushed the bowl of tomato soup to the side of the tray and drank her water. After taking a few gulps of the water, Kenisha said, "Thanks, I'm done with this."

"You only ate half of your soup. Try to eat a little more, Kenisha."

Kenisha lifted her hand. "That's all I can get down right now, Deidre. I'll try to eat more later. Okay?"

Deidre got up to remove the tray, but Kenisha grabbed her arm and said, "Kennedy's crying. Can you go get her for me, please?"

Deidre hadn't heard anything, but she went upstairs anyway. And sure enough, Kennedy was sitting up in the bed crying her eyes out. "Don't be scared, princess. I'm right here." Deidre picked Kennedy up and noticed that the child was wet. "Did you have an accident?"

Kennedy shook her head.

"Okay, well, let me get you all cleaned up." Deidre grabbed some clean clothes and underwear out of the drawer, took Kennedy to the bathroom, and cleaned her up. For her effort, Deidre was rewarded with a hug. "Thank you, Kennedy. Now let's go see your mom."

A big smile appeared on Kennedy's face the moment she walked into the family room and saw Kenisha. "Ma-ma," the little girl said as she stretched out her arms for Kenisha.

Deidre took the tray out of Kenisha's lap and placed Kennedy there. "Sorry it took us so long. *Somebody* had an accident."

"Sorry, Ma-ma."

Kenisha looked at Deidre and said, "I forgot to tell you that I put a diaper on her at night. She's pretty good with going to the bathroom during the day—just needs a little more time to get the nighttime potty going right." Kenisha's eyes filled with sadness after she said the words "little more time." She then told Deidre, "We need to visit James, so I can get him to sign the release form so you won't have a problem adopting Jamal."

"Hold on, wait a minute, Kenisha. In case you haven't noticed, my husband has left me. I can't raise three children on my own."

"Please. I did it. Why couldn't you?"

"First of all, I work full-time. I wouldn't be able to give your kids everything they need without Johnson's help."

"You know, you've got more excuses than Kraft has cheese. I really wish you would just make up your mind, because I don't have a lot of time for these guessing games."

The doorbell rang. Deidre got up to answer it. Kenisha yelled at her, "We're not through with this conversation."

"Whatever," Deidre said as she left the room and went to open the front door.

"Hello, I'm Cynthia Harding. I'm here for Kenisha Smalls."

"Are you the home healthcare nurse who's supposed to start today?"

The woman smiled. "Yes, I am."

"Come in. She's getting a little feisty, so maybe you can help me with her."

"I'll try my best," Cynthia said as Deidre walked her to the family room.

Deidre made the introductions, and to her surprise, Kenisha was actually nice to the woman. Kenisha and Cynthia spent the day getting acquainted. Cynthia informed them that she could be there Monday through Thursday, but Friday was already dedicated to another patient. Deidre called Aisha and asked if she could sit with Kenisha on Fridays. Aisha agreed. All appeared to be going well as Deidre went to pick up Jamal and Diamond. When they returned home, the wheelchair was being delivered.

Jamal jumped out of the car and ran into the house. He watched as Cynthia helped Kenisha into the chair and then asked, "Why are you in a wheelchair? And who is she?" he asked, pointing at Cynthia.

"Don't I get a hello, a hug or something?" Kenisha asked while sitting in the wheelchair.

"Sure, Mama." He walked over and hugged her. He then stepped back and looked around the room. "Why are you sleeping in the family room? Why aren't you in a bedroom like the rest of us? And why are we still staying with Mrs. Deidre? You're out of the hospital. I want to go home."

As Deidre and Diamond walked into the family room, Deidre heard Kenisha say, "You've got an awful lot of questions for someone who don't run nothing. You let me handle this, and I'll tell you what's going on when I'm ready."

"But—"

"No buts, Jamal. Go do your homework, and I'll talk to you later. Okay?"

"Fine. Don't tell me what's going on. I don't care, anyway," Jamal said as he turned and stomped out of the room.

Deidre told Diamond to go do her homework also. When the two older children were out of the room, Deidre sat down next to Kenisha's wheelchair. She was trying to be patient with Kenisha, but this had gone on long enough. "He's not stupid, Kenisha. He knows something is wrong."

"I'm not saying nothing until I have some parents for them." And then through clenched teeth, Kenisha asked, "Now, do you want the job or not?"

Sometimes Kenisha's attitude was so bad that Deidre wondered why she even bothered. But Deidre didn't know how it felt to be given a death sentence, and she didn't know if she would be able to treat people with loving-kindness if her life was being abruptly cut short, either, so she endured. Sighing deeply, Deidre stood up. "Let me call Johnson, and then I'll let you know something for sure."

"Finally," Kenisha said as she rolled her eyes and shook her head at the situation.

Deidre didn't respond. She went upstairs to her bedroom and closed the door. She looked at the telephone but didn't pick it up. Instead, remembering that she hadn't prayed this morning, she got down on her knees in front of her bed and bowed her head. She didn't like neglecting to spend time with

God, and then having to come to Him in a time of need. So she said, "Father, I really need to talk to you about something, but first I want to ask your forgiveness. I haven't spent as much time in prayer as I ought to. Lately, I've been coming to You only when I need something, and that's not right. If I am going to have a true relationship with You, then we need to commune together on a regular basis."

In her heart, Deidre knew that she wasn't just saying words that were expected of her. She truly missed spending time with God and had allowed the circumstances of life to dictate her relationship with God, but that ridiculous behavior would stop now. Even if Johnson never came back, if she never became a mother, she would love God for a lifetime and be content with that. "Lord, I have been asking You to heal Kenisha, and I still believe that You can do it. Because I know that You can do the impossible. But Kenisha is asking that I adopt her children if she doesn't make it, and I need to give her an answer. I don't want to agree to do this if Johnson is not in agreement with me. He is still my husband, whether he wants to be or not. So, please, Lord, cause Johnson to have a change of heart where I am concerned. Allow him to see that Jamal, Diamond, and Kennedy need him just as much as I do."

When she had finished praying, Deidre remained on her knees for a while, hoping to hear God say all was forgiven and that He would go before her and speak to Johnson on her behalf. However, she didn't hear anything. But as the Bible said, faith without works is dead. So she got off her knees, choosing to believe that God would work everything out according to her prayers, and she called Johnson.

By the third ring, Deidre worried that she would be talking to Johnson's voice mail, but then he picked up. "What's up, Deidre?"

His voice sounded hurried, like he wanted to answer her question and get off the phone as fast as he could. "Kenisha wants an answer from us. She refuses to tell the kids about her situation until she knows what we are going to do."

He was silent for a moment, but then said, "I don't know, Deidre. You and I have a lot to iron out before we'll even know where we're going from here. Do you really think we should involve kids in this right now?"

"Johnson, you've been talking about adoption for months. And now that we have an opportunity to make that happen, you don't know what you want to do?"

"You know why I don't know, Deidre. So don't put this all on me."

"No matter how upset you are with me, Johnson, these kids didn't do anything to you. And if we wait too long, we could lose them."

Again he was silent.

"I need to let Kenisha know something."

"And I need to pray about this, Deidre. So I can't give you an answer this very minute."

"Thursday, Johnson. You have until then. When you come over for Thanksgiving, Kenisha and I will expect an answer from you." She hung up the phone and sat on her bed for a moment. She hadn't meant to sound demanding, but she couldn't let Johnson hem and haw around this issue. Kenisha deserved some peace in these terrible days to come. She would just keep praying that God would soften Johnson's heart.

22

Kenisha knew that Johnson had decided to be a father to her children the moment he walked through the door and set his suitcase down in the entryway. This had been a good day for her so far. She had been walking around and helping Deidre prepare the Thanksgiving dinner. She had been on her way to the bathroom when Johnson opened the front door. When she saw the suitcase, she wanted to run and give him a hug. But then sadness crept into her soul, because Kenisha knew that she would break her children's hearts today. "Hey, Johnson, how are you doing?"

He smiled. "I'm good, how about yourself?"

"Oh, you know how it is, I have good days and bad." She pointed at his suitcase. "Does that mean what I think it means?"

Johnson nodded.

"Have you told Deidre yet?"

"No, I haven't talked to her in a couple of days, but I'll tell her after I unpack."

"All right. Well, I've got to go to the bathroom before I have an accident," Kenisha told him as she walked into the bathroom. She was glad that Deidre would have someone to share her life with and that the children would finally have a real father figure in their lives, but as she sat on the toilet and blood that she knew had not come from her menstrual cycle began to trickle out, depression set in, and she silently cried for herself.

When she was done crying for all the days she would never see, the first dates, the prom dates, and the weddings that she would never know anything about, she cried for her children. Kenisha was not one to sit around with a cell phone attached to her ear, ignoring her children. She'd done things with them . . . taught them things. Her kids would miss her, that was one thing she knew for certain. And that was the most painful thing of all to swallow. Not that she could swallow anything anyway, with her throat hurting so bad it felt as if it were closing up on her.

She looked heavenward and asked, "Why, God, why? Couldn't you have found someone else to pick on?"

There was a knock on the bathroom door, and Kenisha jumped. "Mama, are you in there?"

It was Jamal. Kenisha smiled. He was her firstborn, the one she had spent the most time with. Would he remember her? "I'll be out in a minute," Kenisha said after she'd cleared her throat.

"What are you doing in there?"

"Just having a little private time, son. I'll be back in the kitchen in a minute. Okay?"

"All right, but hurry up. Mrs. Deidre went upstairs to talk to Johnson, and there's still a whole bunch of food that needs to be cooked before we can eat."

Kenisha wiped the tears from her face as she laughed at Jamal. He was always hungry. It didn't matter how much he ate, he could always make room for more. "Grab a banana and sit down somewhere, hungry boy." She flushed the toilet and then washed her hands. She threw a little water on her face to clear away any tear stains, dried her face, and then opened the bathroom door.

Jamal was still standing there. He whispered, "Did you do the number two?"

"No, boy, I just needed some time to myself."

"Good, because I need to go now," he said as he ran into the bathroom and closed the door behind him.

Kenisha went back into the kitchen and finished cutting up the peaches Deidre needed for the peach cobbler she was going to bake. She willed herself not to think about anything but the peaches in front of her and the wonderful meal her children would enjoy in a little while. But when Deidre walked back into the kitchen, Kenisha saw that she had been crying. But she didn't look sad. Kenisha knew that Deidre's joy came from the fact that she would soon become mother to her children.

All of a sudden, Kenisha was tired and needed to lie down. "I'm going to the family room for a while," she told Deidre and then left before they could say anything else to each other. Kenisha buried herself under the covers as she lay on the couch and watched some stupid old Christmas movie. She wanted to curl up in a ball to shield herself from the pain in her heart. But a shooting pain soared through her that was so fierce she had to bite down on her lip to keep from screaming.

Diamond and Jamal walked into the family room. She half smiled at them, trying desperately not to show how much pain she was in.

"You all right?" Diamond asked.

Funny how perceptive kids could be at times. They always seemed to know when something's going on. What was that saying—*If mama ain't happy, ain't nobody happy?* Maybe kids went through as much turmoil as their parents when there was a bunch of drama going on in the house. She wished she had thought of that when she was going through all that unnecessary stuff with Chico and his crack demon. "I'm okay. Why don't y'all sit down and watch television with me? You can watch whatever you want."

"Really?" Jamal said excitedly as he grabbed the remote.

Diamond tried to take the remote away from Jamal. "You don't get to pick all the time."

When the tug-of-war over the remote started, Kenisha realized that she had made a big mistake by not designating who would get to choose the first program they watched on television. But she was too weak to referee this remote smackdown.

Thankfully, Johnson came into the room and grabbed the remote. "If the two of you are going to fight over the remote, then nobody is going to get it."

"But Mama wanted to watch television with us. She said we get to choose," Diamond informed Johnson.

Kenisha gave Johnson a weak smile as he looked her way. "It's my fault," she admitted, even as she hoped that he would take care of the situation and not ask her to do it. She didn't want her children to know that she needed help to get off the couch right now. Not on Thanksgiving. She wanted them to enjoy this day, because, before they went to bed tonight, she was going to break their hearts.

"Okay, then," Johnson said. "You two sit down, and what we are going to do is alternate." He pulled a coin out of his pocket and told Jamal and Diamond to pick a side.

Jamal picked heads and Diamond was left with tails. The coin flipped in the air and fell to the ground so everyone could see the results. The coin landed on tails.

"Yes!" Diamond said as she jumped up and did a dance move around the floor.

"No need to gloat, Diamond," Kenisha said as she laughed.

"I'll take that." Diamond pointed at the remote in Johnson's hand.

"Okay, young lady, you get the first pick. But after your program goes off, then it's Jamal's turn. And I'm sure Kennedy will be awake by then, so after Jamal, you two have to give Kennedy a turn. Okay?"

"Okay," they said in unison.

Diamond then turned to Jamal and said, "I'm going to try to find something we both like."

Kenisha was so proud of her children. They hadn't been raised in the best of circumstances, but they were good kids. She was well aware of what people thought about project kids. But she had never raised her children to follow in her footsteps. She knew well that children raised in poverty grew up to live in poverty themselves. It had already happened to her. Martha had raised them in the projects with barely a dime to her name. And Kenisha and Aisha had both ended up in their own project homes with a houseful of kids and scattered daddies.

That's why it had been so important to Kenisha to find someone willing to adopt her children, rather than leave it up to the state to choose someone. She didn't want the state to piecemeal her children off to people who were only taking them in to collect a check. She wanted a better life for her children. And the moment she discovered that Deidre didn't have any children, Kenisha had hoped and prayed that this educated woman with the nice house would want to adopt her children. Kenisha realized that she had been pushy at times, but her children's lives were at stake. And Kenisha would look out for their best interests until she took her last breath.

By the time they had watched their second movie, Kennedy had awakened from her nap and dinner was ready. Johnson brought the wheelchair over and helped Kenisha into it. "We've got a spot for you at the head of the table," he told her while wheeling her into the dining room.

"Thank you," Kenisha said.

"Everything looks wonderful, Deidre. Were you and Kenisha up late last night preparing the food?" Johnson asked.

"We cooked the turkey and the ham last night," Deidre said, "but everything else was fixed this morning. Kenisha was feeling pretty good this morning, so we worked together."

"Yeah, Mama fixed the yams and the green beans," Jamal chimed in.

Johnson blessed the food, and then he and Deidre started filling plates. Jamal and Diamond ate as if they had just discovered food existed. Kenisha was so embarrassed, but she didn't say anything. She just couldn't bring herself to chastise her children—not today.

Kenisha, on the other hand, took slow, deliberate bites of her food. She was sure that Deidre thought she was eating so slowly because her throat was hurting. But the truth of the matter was, she would sit at this table forever if she could. But when dinner was finished and everyone had left the dining room, Deidre walked over to Kenisha and asked, "Are you ready?"

"No," Kenisha answered honestly. "Do we really have to tell them? Can't I just write them a note, and you or Johnson read it to them after everything is all over?"

"I don't think that's fair to the kids, Kenisha. They already know something is wrong. We need to talk to them. Okay?"

Kenisha wanted to continue expressing her objections, but Deidre was right. Her children deserved the truth, and she had just been too chicken to give it to them. She lowered her head, trying to adjust to the reality that had been forced upon her. When she raised her head, she was in control of the situation once again. "All right, let's go talk to them."

Deidre grabbed hold of Kenisha's wheelchair and pushed her into the family room. The kids were getting situated, while Johnson put in a DVD. He turned to the kids and said, "If you want to know what I'm thankful for, it is the birth of Jesus. I'm also thankful that I was able to share this day with all of you. Now, the next holiday that will be upon us in less than a month is Christmas, and I want you all to understand the true meaning of that day, before we get too busy making out lists for all the presents we want."

"But we are supposed to get presents for Christmas," Diamond, the gimme-gimme kid, chimed in.

"Yes, receiving presents is a fine way to celebrate Christmas, but this movie will show you the reason we give presents in the first place. It is a movie about the birth of Jesus and it's in cartoon form, so I think you all will enjoy. Okay?"

The kids nodded, and Johnson hit the play button.

Kenisha wanted to tell Johnson to turn that movie off. No sense filling her kids' heads with all that Jesus nonsense. But as long as the movie was on, she didn't have to talk. So she let the movie play and watched her children as they enjoyed themselves.

When the movie was over, which was way too soon as far as Kenisha was concerned, Johnson turned off the television and looked at Kenisha. Kenisha turned away from him. She looked at Deidre, hoping that she would call this whole "let's tell the children" thing off. But Deidre didn't look like she wanted to play the deception game anymore.

"All right, then," Kenisha said under her breath. She then turned to her children and said, "I need to talk to you guys about something."

"Is it about our Christmas presents?" Diamond asked with a gleam in her eyes.

How Kenisha wished she could talk to them about Christmas presents. Kenisha held back tears as she said, "No, baby, it's not."

The room was silent. Kenisha didn't want to break the silence, either. She was quite content with sitting here looking at her children without saying a mumbling word. But Johnson had to open his mouth and interrupt the peaceful atmosphere in the room.

"Your mother needs to talk to you all about something very important," Johnson said, giving Kenisha a gentle nudge.

Kennedy got off the couch, and went and sat down on Johnson's lap. To Kenisha that was a sign that her children belonged in this house and that they would be all right. She turned to Jamal and said, "Jamal, do you remember when you asked me why I needed this wheelchair, and why we were staying here with the Morrises?"

"Yeah. But you told me that you would tell me when you were ready."

Ready or not . . . "I think it's time for me to tell you what's going on." Kenisha took a deep breath and then said, "You know I had the surgery to get rid of my cancer, right?"

"And the doctor was going to make you all better," Diamond said matter-of-factly.

She had told them that, and naturally they had believed her. "That's what I thought. But a couple of months ago, Dr. Lawson told me that the cancer hadn't left and that it had spread throughout my body." She stopped talking again. Kenisha hadn't wanted to talk to her children about this because she knew it was going to be one of the hardest things she'd ever had to do in life. The pain of giving birth to the children was nothing compared to telling them that she wouldn't be there for their prom, graduation, first job interview, marriage. She wouldn't even get to see her first grandchild brought into the world, or know which one of her kids had the first grandchild, for that matter.

"Anyway, I've been getting sicker, and . . . and the doctors don't think I'm going to get any better."

"Are you dying?" Jamal asked with a horror-stricken look on his face.

The look on her son's face weakened Kenisha's resolve not to cry, and the tears began to fall. She would give anything to not have to say those words to Jamal. Living was so hard, why did dying have to be just as hard? She put her hand over her eyes and covered them while she tried to stop the tears from flowing.

Deidre put her hand on Kenisha's back and gently rubbed it. She leaned down and whispered in Kenisha's ear, "Do you need to stop?"

Kenisha shook her head. She wasn't going through this agony again; she was going to finish this tonight. Taking another deep breath and swallowing the lump in her throat, Kenisha looked at Jamal and said, "Yes, baby. I'm dying."

Jamal immediately stood up and screamed, "I don't believe you! That's not fair!" He then ran out of the room.

Deidre got up and followed Jamal.

Diamond's bottom lip began to quiver. She stood up and walked over to her mother and asked, "Why do you want to die?"

"Oh, baby, I don't want to die." Kenisha grabbed Diamond and hugged her close. "If it were up to me, I'd stay with you for a million years."

Diamond pulled away from her mother and asked, "Who is it up to?"

Shaking her head, Kenisha answered, "I don't know, sweetie."

"Jamal and I had the kids in the children's church pray for you when you were in the hospital. I think I'm going to ask the adults to pray when we go back to church."

Kenisha wanted to tell her daughter not to ask nobody for nothing. God wasn't listening to their prayers. He didn't care nothing about them, so don't waste your time, but she just brought her daughter close to her again and hugged her. She wanted to hug all her children as many times as she could between now and death.

Kennedy climbed down from Johnson's lap and walked over to her mother with a curious look on her face. She looked at Kenisha and asked, "What's wrong?"

"Everything, baby, everything," Kenisha said as tears blocked her vision.

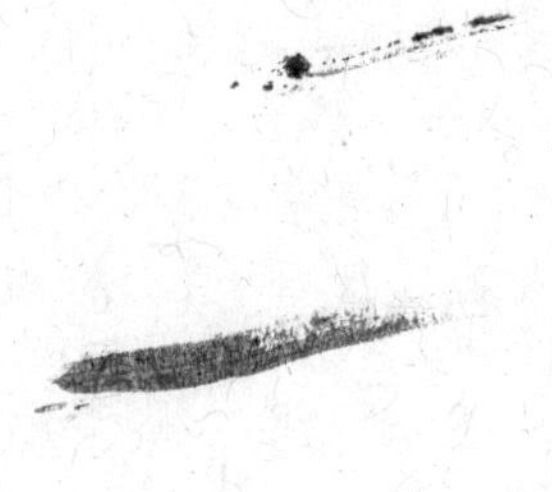

23

No!" Jamal yelled as Deidre walked toward him. "I don't want to go back in there."

After receiving the news from Kenisha, Jamal had run outside and was now huddled in a corner on the porch. "You don't have to, honey. Just wait right here for a second, I'll be right back." Deidre went directly to the entryway closet and grabbed Jamal's coat and hers and a blanket, and then ran back outside. "Here, put your coat on, and we'll get under the blanket so I can sit out here with you for a while. Okay?"

"Okay, but I'm not going back in there," Jamal told her as he put his coat on.

Deidre took the seat cushions off of the two chairs that were on the porch and handed one to Jamal as she sat next to him on the other one. She then put the cover around them. "I hate being cold. How about you?"

"It's not so bad. The worst for me is getting too hot," Jamal said.

"Well, is this cover making you hot?"

"No, it's fine."

After that, the conversation stalled. Deidre didn't want to push Jamal. Having your mother tell you that she was dying was a lot for an eight-year-old to take in. He needed to process the information, and she wasn't going to rush him.

They had been silent for about ten minutes when Jamal finally said, "You might want to go back inside. I don't want you to freeze out here."

She took that to mean that Jamal was starting to get cold. She shouldn't have given him the cushion for his bottom; maybe she would have been able to get him back inside faster if his backside froze off. "I might, but I'm not going in until you do."

"But that's silly."

"No sillier than you sitting out here freezing."

Jamal was silent another few minutes, and then he asked, "If she knew she was dying a couple months ago, why didn't she tell us?"

"Some things are hard to say, Jamal." Deidre knew that from experience, so she didn't have any rocks to throw at Kenisha. "Your mom has been trying to figure out a lot of things for herself and for you, Diamond, and Kennedy."

"Well, who is going to keep us if we're not going to have a mama no more?" Jamal asked, sounding angry.

"That's the other thing your mama wanted to talk to you about. I don't think I should tell you anything before your mother has a chance to finish talking to you all."

Putting his hand under his chin in a sulking fashion, Jamal said, "I don't want to hear it."

"You must want to know, Jamal, because you just asked me." Deidre stood up and held her hand out to Jamal. "Come on, let's go talk to Kenisha and get some of your questions answered."

After a minute Jamal grabbed Deidre's hand and lifted himself up. He walked into the house and back into the family room. Kenisha held her hand out to him, and he ran into her arms.

"It's not fair. It's not fair," Jamal kept repeating.

"I know, baby, but I can't do anything about it." Kenisha ran her hand down Jamal's back, trying to caress him.

He stepped back from her as his eyes lit with an idea. "What if I did extra chores at home? That way you could rest more and get better."

"I wish it was that simple, Jamal. But I don't want to lie to you anymore. I'm dying, and there's nothing we can do about it."

Jamal's hands clenched into fists as he angrily said, "Then what are me, Diamond, and Kennedy supposed to do? We're just kids; we can't take care of ourselves."

Kenisha looked toward Deidre and Johnson. Johnson stood up and put a hand on Jamal's shoulder. "Sit down for a minute, Jamal. Deidre and I would like to talk to you about something."

Jamal sat down, but his eyes now suspiciously scanned the room, connecting with the three grown-ups.

Deidre asked Kenisha, "Do you want us to tell him?"

Kenisha nodded.

Deidre asked Diamond to sit down next to Jamal. Kennedy jumped back on Kenisha's lap, and Deidre saw no reason to move her. Kennedy had no clue what was going on, anyway. Deidre turned to Jamal and Diamond and said, "I want you both to know that Johnson and I have grown to love you so m-much." Her voice broke with the weight of the emotion she was feeling, and she couldn't go on.

Johnson stepped in. "What Deidre is trying to tell you is that we want you all to live with us, as a family. Kenisha has asked us to adopt you, and that's what we plan to do."

Jamal shook his head. He turned to Kenisha and said, "I want to live with my daddy."

"Honey, your dad will be in prison for at least eight more years. You'll be sixteen by the time he gets out. If you don't live with the Morrises, you'll be placed in foster care, and I know you don't want that."

"He might come home sooner. You always said that he could get paroled at any time."

"That's not going to happen, Jamal. He'll be gone at least another eight years. I'm sorry, son, but that's the truth."

"What about Grandma Martha? She'll take us."

"You don't want to do that, Jamal," Kenisha said. "Your Grandma Martha has a drinking problem. She wouldn't raise you the way you need to be raised."

Deidre was a little surprised that Kenisha came right out and told Jamal that his grandmother had a drinking problem, but if she were trying to protect her children from harm, she would probably tell them some things they didn't want to hear too. She admired Kenisha for looking out for the best interests of her children at any cost.

Jamal pointed at Deidre and Johnson and said, "They don't even know us. Why would they take us in?"

Deidre crouched down in front of Jamal and said, "I know you. The first day you came to my office, I knew there was something special about you. I had no idea that we would one day become family, but Jamal, I have to tell you that each day I've spent with each of you I have fallen more and more in love. I tried to fight it for a long time, because I had no idea that Johnson and I would one day adopt the three of you. But that's what Kenisha wants, and I hope you'll want us too."

Diamond gave Deidre a hug and said, "Thank you for adopting us."

"Thank you for letting me," Deidre said with tears in her eyes. This was hard. It was so hard, but she would walk through the fire for these children. She only hoped that she would be able to help them through this.

"But I thought you were praying for my mother," Jamal said, that suspicious look in his eyes again.

"I was, Jamal. And I still am. You can pray for her too. And when we go to church—"

"No!" Kenisha's voice boomed throughout the room.

Deidre turned and looked at Kenisha.

"Stop taking my kids to church. I don't want you filling their heads with false hope."

Johnson said, "Wait a minute, Kenisha. You knew we were Christians when you asked us to adopt the children. I'm sorry, but we will be taking them to church. So you need to make sure that you want them to be with us, because we will share our faith with them."

"And that's a good thing," Deidre interjected. Now that she had agreed to take the kids, she couldn't bear to lose them. The only way she would willingly give them up would be if Kenisha received a miracle and survived this ordeal.

Incredulously, Kenisha asked, "How can you still trust God, with all the praying you've done for a child and for my healing, and nothing ever happens?"

Deidre sat down next to Kenisha and tried to explain her faith the best way she could. "I don't know why some of my prayers haven't been answered. But I still believe that God is able to do the impossible, and that is why I trust Him."

Unmoved, Kenisha said, "If you want to waste your time with church and all that whoopla, go ahead, but I'm going to make sure that my kids know the truth." Kenisha turned to her children and said bitterly, "God don't care nothing about us. We're from the projects, and that's where you'll end up when you're grown if you don't do something to change things. You hear me? Don't wait on no God in the sky to change things for you."

Jamal, Diamond, and Kennedy nodded.

"And don't pray for me at that church Deidre and Johnson takes y'all to, either. If God wanted to heal me, He could have done it already, right?"

Diamond jumped up, angry now too. "That's right. I'm not asking those stupid old kids to pray to God for nothing else."

"All right, then," Johnson interrupted. "Your mom is getting tired, so I think it's time for you kids to take your baths and get ready for bed."

"But I want to stay up with my mom," Diamond declared.

"And you can. But first you need to get in the tub and put your nightclothes on. If Kenisha is feeling up to company after that, then you guys can hang out in the family room all night long if you want. Okay?"

"Okay," Jamal said as he got up and made sure his sisters followed him upstairs.

Deidre was so grateful that Johnson had come home for this talk. She honestly didn't know how she would have stopped Kenisha from ranting on and on against God without starting an argument with the girl, but Johnson had handled it perfectly. There was no need to chastise Kenisha in front of her children. Kenisha had been given a death sentence. She knew people who lost faith for a lot less than that. Deidre would just have to pray, pray, and pray some more for Kenisha's heart to soften toward God.

Deidre stood and removed the pillows from the couch. "I'll put the bed out for you and change the sheets before you get in. Is there anything else you need before I go to bed?"

Kenisha grabbed Deidre's arm, and with a stricken expression on her face she said, "I need a pain pill."

"Are you sure? I think the kids are coming back down here."

"Tell them I went to sleep. I can't take the pain anymore. Please, I want the pain to go away."

Deidre got Kenisha a pain pill and then changed her sheets. Johnson helped her put Kenisha in bed. "Do you need anything else?" Deidre asked.

"Yeah, give me another one of those pills," Kenisha said, words slurring as evidence that the medication was already taking effect.

"These are pretty potent pills, Kenisha. You're only supposed to have one at a time."

"L-leave the bottle."

"You're going to be knocked out in a minute; just wait for the pill to do its job."

"Leave the bottle!" Kenisha screamed at her.

The look in Kenisha's eyes told Deidre that Kenisha wasn't looking for relief of physical pain as much as she wanted to check out from all the emotional pain she was feeling. Deidre shook her head. "I'll check on you in a few hours. If you need another pain pill, I'll give you one then."

Deidre and Johnson were headed upstairs when they spotted Jamal, with his Spiderman pajamas and a pillow under his arm, as he dragged his covers down the stairs behind him.

"Now's not a good time to go down there, son," Johnson said as he and Deidre met up with Jamal on the steps.

"Why, what's wrong?" Jamal asked in a panic.

Deidre quickly reassured him, "Nothing is wrong, Jamal. Your mom is tired, that's all. She went to sleep as soon as she got in bed."

"I want to sleep down there with her," Jamal said.

"Okay, Jamal, but please don't wake her up. Be very quiet when you go down there," Johnson instructed.

"Where are the girls?" Deidre asked.

"I just ran their bathwater; they're getting in the tub now."

"Okay, I'll go help them," Deidre said to Jamal's back as he ran the rest of the way down the stairs.

"Hurry up with the girls. We still need to talk, remember?"

When Johnson told Deidre this morning that he would accept responsibility for the children, he informed her that he still wasn't sure about where they stood, and that they would have to hash things out later. She just hadn't imagined that he had meant later that same night. "Okay, I'll be there as soon as I finish with the girls."

She then went into the bathroom. The girls were undressing. Deidre helped Kennedy into the tub and washed her up while Diamond washed herself.

Deidre pulled Kennedy out of the tub, dried her off, and then put a diaper on her so that she wouldn't soak the sheets through the night. Diamond got out of the tub, and Deidre handed her a towel to dry off with. The three of them then went into the girls' bedroom to put on their pajamas. Then Diamond asked, "Can we go downstairs and watch a movie with mama now?"

"No, baby, your mama was so tired that she fell asleep not long after you came upstairs to take a bath. But you don't have school tomorrow, so you can watch a movie with her then. Okay?" *Please say it's okay.*

"Okay," Diamond and Kennedy said in unison.

"Well, then, climb in your beds, and I'll read you a book before you go to sleep." Deidre looked on the bookshelf in the girls' room and grabbed a fairy-tale–princess book off the shelf while they got in bed and pulled the covers up. As Deidre pulled a chair in between the two beds and sat down, she thought that this book was exactly what they all needed tonight—a little make-believe.

24

Deidre was so exhausted by the time she reached her bedroom that night that she had completely forgotten that Johnson had told her that he wanted to talk. When she opened the door and saw Johnson sitting up in bed waiting for her, she wanted to turn around and go right back to make-believe land. But she closed the door behind her and said, "Thanks for all your help today. I honestly don't know what I would have done if you hadn't been here."

"That's what a partnership is all about, Deidre—being there for each other."

If he was starting their discussion like this, Deidre knew she didn't have enough strength left to defend herself tonight. "Johnson, do you think we can talk about this tomorrow?"

"No. I need to get this out now. We have so much more going on that I don't want this between us anymore."

"Okay," she said slowly as she sat down at the bottom of the bed. "I'm listening."

"Before we got married," he began, "I told you that I wanted children and lots of them if that was possible."

Deidre was silent. She was guilty, so what could she say?

"You knew all the while that you couldn't have children, but you never said a word. Marissa thinks that I should listen to your side of things before making snap judgments. But—"

Lifting her hand to stop Johnson in mid-sentence, Deidre said, "What does Marissa have to do with any of this?"

"She doesn't have anything to do with it."

"Then why did you tell her our business?"

"You told Kenisha. And before you told me, might I add."

"That's different," Deidre defended herself. "You should not be crying on the shoulder of a single woman. A woman who is about to give birth to a child whose father still remains nameless, might I add."

"That's another thing," Johnson said as he stood up. "Stop accusing me of things. Just because you are sneaky and underhanded doesn't mean the rest of the world is. Marissa doesn't want me. And for your information, she happens to think that you are a wonderful woman and that I should give you another chance."

Johnson's voice was escalating. She had pushed the wrong button, and she knew it. She had no right to accuse Johnson of anything after the way she had deceived him for so many years. She silently prayed, *Lord, please guide my tongue*. "You're right, Johnson, I was wrong for saying that. I don't want to fight with you, and I don't want you to come back home just to become a father to Kenisha's children. I want all of us to be a family. So please tell me what I can do to make this right."

Johnson sat back down, took in a couple of deep breaths to calm himself, and then said, "I just want to know why you didn't trust me enough to tell me the truth."

"I've been thinking about this a lot. And I don't know if the reason I didn't tell you had to do with my lack of trust in you or my own feelings of worthlessness." She hesitated for a moment. But Deidre was determined that Johnson know the truth of her feelings, so she forced herself to keep going. "From the moment my doctor informed me of my PCOS disorder, I have felt worthless. My mother tried to convince me that it didn't matter. She told me that I would find a man to marry who would love me despite everything. But I didn't believe her, and when my sister got married and started having children one after the other, I became so jealous that I didn't know what to do.

"Then I met you. And you were so wonderful that I didn't want to lose you. I kept trying to convince myself that it didn't matter, but when you started talking about kids, I knew it was too late to tell you the truth."

"Why?"

"As far as I was concerned, that would have been the final proof of my worthlessness. I honestly thought I would kill myself if you rejected me."

"So now you're telling me that I married a woman with suicidal tendencies."

"I don't have suicidal tendencies, Johnson. All of that happened between us before I gave my life to Christ. I have a better understanding of who I am now."

"And yet you still didn't tell me."

Putting her hands in her lap, Deidre tried to explain how they had gotten so far into their marriage without knowing everything about each other. "We were married two years before we committed our life to God, and although I no longer feared killing myself, I was ashamed of all the years I had deceived you. I kept trying to find ways to tell you, but then you would talk about children and I would chicken out. I have no excuse, but I love you. That has always been the truth, and I don't see it changing anytime soon."

"Okay, Deidre, I can accept what you say as the truth. But once we get through this difficult time with Kenisha, the two of us are going to the doctor together to find out if anything can be done concerning your condition. A lot has changed since you were sixteen, so we don't know if modern medicine has found a way around your condition by now or not."

"Is this your way of telling me that I'm old?"

"You're thirty-two, Deidre. I don't think that is old at all."

"Okay, just making sure."

Johnson smiled at her. It was the first smile he'd given her in over a week.

She reveled in it. "I'm sorry, baby. I promise I'll never keep anything from you again. Just please forgive me."

In answer to her plea, Johnson pulled his wife into his arms and held her through the night.

Kenisha felt better when she woke Friday morning. There were no more secrets, the kids knew what was going on, and they also knew that she had made sure that they wouldn't be left to the state. Jamal was asleep on the love seat. She propped her hands behind her head and just watched him. Kenisha still remembered how hard his delivery had been and how she'd begged God to ease her pain. But when her son had finally come out, she had felt as if he had been worth every minute of pain she'd had to endure.

But the pain hadn't been over when the delivery was done. Jamal had been a night owl; he would sleep for an hour and then be awake for two, expecting Kenisha to entertain him. Until Jamal was two years old, Kenisha hadn't known what a good night's sleep felt like. Then Diamond came along. She actually slept through the night but refused to take a nap during the day. Kennedy was the only child of hers who had slept through the night and who had taken naps during the day.

Kenisha had thought of Kennedy as her gift from God. But despite the difficulties her children had put her through with their erratic sleep patterns, she wouldn't have traded them for the world.

She turned her attention back to Jamal. He was snoring, but not so loud as to bother anyone. His future wife would appreciate that he was a light snorer. She would also like the fact that Jamal was handsome. Jamal looked more and more like his father with each passing day. Thoughts of James caused Kenisha to frown. She would have to see him soon in order to get those papers signed. But she didn't want James to see her like this. When he went into prison, she was young and vibrant, with hips that swayed and other attributes that men looked favorably on. But she had lost so much weight and looked so ghostly . . . if only James could remember her the way she had been.

But he was calling the shots, and James had demanded that she and the prospective parents come to see him before he signed off on anything. "I will see you soon, my love," she whispered.

A knock at the door brought Kenisha out of her lost-love dreaming. She knew it was Aisha, because she had been coming over the last few Fridays and sitting with her since her nurse didn't work on Fridays. Kenisha had actually been enjoying her Friday visits from her sister.

"Jamal," Kenisha called, trying to wake her son.

"Jamal, get up," she said a bit louder.

He stirred, stretched, and then looked toward his mother. "What's up?"

"Somebody is at the door. I think it's Aisha. Can you go let her in?"

"Sure, Mama, no problem." He stood up and walked toward the front door. When Jamal opened the door and saw who was standing on the porch, he ran back to the family room shouting. "Mama, Auntie Isha brought Chico with her."

"Where is she? I've got a right to see my daughter," Chico shouted as he stomped through the house.

"Calm down, Chico. This is not Kenisha's house, so you just can't act a fool in here," Aisha told him.

"Well, I want to see my child. I got a right to see her whenever I want," Chico said, like he was some expert on the law.

"She's in the family room. I'll take you in there, but I don't want you upsetting her. Do you hear me?" Aisha demanded.

"I didn't come over here to cause no trouble, Aisha. I just want to see my baby girl."

"Come on," Aisha said as she took him to the family room.

Kenisha was sitting up shooting daggers at Aisha with her eyes as she and Chico walked into the family room. "What do you want?" Kenisha demanded.

"You know what I want. You've been hiding Kennedy from me, and I want to see her."

Kenisha frowned, "I'm not hiding Kennedy from you."

"Then why haven't you been home?"

Deidre and Johnson walked into the family room, looking as if an intruder had just invaded their house looking for all the valuables. They weren't far off on that train of thought. It was for that reason that Kenisha never would have told Chico where the Morrises lived. Why Aisha had taken it upon herself to do such a thing, Kenisha didn't know, but she intended to find out.

"What's going on down here?" Johnson asked.

Chico swung around like he was big and bad. But he was too skinny to intimidate anybody. He pointed at Johnson and said, "So I guess you think you're my little girl's daddy now, but I got news for you. Kennedy don't need another daddy."

Tired of this whole scene, Kenisha said, "You already signed away your rights to Kennedy, Chico. You have no say over Kennedy. Not anymore."

Turning back on Kenisha he said, "That's because you tricked me with that lousy forty dollars. You knew I was having a weak moment, and you exploited that fact."

"You're always having a weak moment, Chico. You're on drugs. Look Chico, you did the right thing by giving up your rights to Kennedy. Don't turn back on that now. What you did was truly unselfish, and I was proud of you for that."

"But I love Kennedy," he protested.

"Again, I hate to remind you of this, but you are on drugs."

"That doesn't mean I can't be a father to my child."

"That's exactly what it means. Now please leave so I can rest," Kenisha said as she lay her head back down on her pillow.

"Look, Kenisha, I know you're sick. I'm not trying to cause you any problems, but I was looking for you and you weren't there. I got worried."

"I don't have any money, Chico. So save all the drama."

"Why you always got to think I'm after money?"

"'Cause I know you. You've got something up your sleeve, and I'm asking you to think of what's best for Kennedy for once in your life."

"What? You think these rich suckas can raise my child better than I can?"

"Yes, I do, Chico. Now please leave."

Chico turned to Johnson and said, "I could raise my child myself if some rich benefactor wanted to help me out too. But all that's neither here nor there because I want that paper back that I signed."

"No," Kenisha answered.

"You're not taking my baby girl away from me, Kenisha. I've got rights," Chico demanded.

"Do you have a place to stay?" Johnson asked Chico.

"I stay here and there, but if you want to loan me a couple hundred dollars to help me get on my feet, I can get a nice place for me and Kennedy."

"You think you can find a place for you and Kennedy with two hundred dollars?"

"It might not be as nice as yours, but a brother has to start someplace."

"All right, I'll tell you what," Johnson said as he put his arm around Chico's shoulder and guided him toward the front door. "I've got a hundred dollars on me. I'll give that to you if you want it. But I don't want to hear from you again until you have secured a place to stay for you and Kennedy. And if Deidre and I have already adopted her, then I guess you'll be out of luck. Okay?"

"Yeah, yeah, man. Whatever you say. Just hand me the money so I can start looking for an apartment."

Johnson pulled his wallet out of his back pocket and counted off five twenties. Before he handed it to Chico, he said, "Don't ever ask me for any more money, and if you come back here causing trouble, I will have you arrested. Do you understand me?"

"Ah, that's cold."

"No, but it will get very cold for you if you ignore my warning," Johnson told him with the same stern look that a captain gives to the privates in his unit. Then he opened the front door.

"All right, fine. Just give Kennedy a hug for me." Chico took the money and left.

When Johnson returned to the family room, Kenisha said, "Please tell me that you didn't give him any money."

"I did, but only because I didn't want him to continue upsetting you. I got rid of him, and I don't think we'll see him anymore."

"You gave him money; he'll be back."

"I think Chico and I understand each other."

Deidre put her arm around Johnson and asked, "Did you scare him, honey?"

"If he's smart, I did."

"Well, I'm sorry," Aisha said. "I didn't mean to bring all this drama over here. But Chico kept coming to my doorstep crying about how much he missed Kennedy, and about how he just wanted to see her, but he sure left after he got the money without seeing Kennedy."

"That's why you shouldn't have brought him here. Chico only cares about his crack habit."

"I'm sorry, Kenisha," Aisha said again as if that should settle everything.

But no matter how many times Aisha said she was sorry, Kenisha wouldn't be able to forgive her for this. There had to be some reason Aisha did this, and Kenisha would bet money that it had nothing to do with what Chico wanted. But she could badger Aisha on the subject from now until doomsday and she'd never get the truth, so she just told her, "There's only one person that you could bring to see me that I would appreciate seeing."

"I know you want to see Kevin, but I haven't heard from him, and I don't know where he is," Aisha said.

"Well, then, I'll tell you what, since you're all about helping the downtrodden—"

"Martha told me to bring Chico over here. I didn't want to do it," Aisha admitted.

Kenisha ignored her and kept on talking, "You go find my brother. Tell him that I want to see him before I die. But if you can't find him, then don't you come back, either. Okay?"

"Mama?" Jamal said, with an eyebrow lifted.

"Kenisha, how can you be so mean to your sister?" Deidre asked.

"As far as I'm concerned, I don't have a sister anymore. She's always thought that my kids were too spoiled. For all I know, she brought Chico over here to scare you and Johnson. She's hoping that my children won't have anyplace to go after I'm gone." Kenisha turned back to Aisha and said, "That'll teach my kids, won't it, Aisha? If they have to live in the projects with your kids, they won't think they're so much, then. Right?"

"I wasn't trying to scare Deidre and Johnson. Martha and I thought Chico really wanted to see Kennedy."

"Get out of my face, Aisha. Don't come back here anymore."

"Is that the way it is, Kenisha? First you disown Martha, and now you disown me too?"

"You brought Chico here, knowing that he steals to pay for his habit. What if he comes back here with some of his boys and robs Deidre and Johnson? What if one of my kids gets hurt because of what you did? No, I can't forgive what you did, and I don't ever want to see you again."

Aisha turned and fled out the door while everyone else remained stunned at how harsh Kenisha could be. She turned her back on them as she lay back down and went to sleep.

25

After the confrontation with Chico and Aisha, Deidre went back upstairs and prayed for Kenisha. It seemed that the more Deidre prayed for God to soften Kenisha's heart, the harder it got. But Deidre wasn't going to give up. If Kenisha was going to enter eternity, then Deidre wanted her to live it out in heaven. And there was no way that Kenisha was going anywhere near heaven with all the hatred, bitterness, and unforgiveness she carried around. "God, please mend Kenisha's heart. She's been through so much in her young life, and to tell you the truth, I understand why she's so angry all the time, but could You please help me show her kindness like she's never known?"

Johnson walked into their bedroom as Deidre was getting off the floor. "Were you praying?"

She wiped away the tears that were flowing down her face. "Yeah. I'm so worried about how bitter Kenisha is. I'm praying that God heals her heart before it's too late."

"I've been praying for her too, babe. So stop worrying; things will turn out for the good."

"I hope you're right, because I want Kenisha to live out eternity in heaven—whether she goes soon or much later."

"Since we're both off today, do you want to take the kids shopping?"

"We both can't take the kids shopping because Aisha isn't here, and somebody needs to stay here with Kenisha." Deidre then had a second thought and said, "Why don't you take the kids shopping, and I'll stay here with Kenisha? Pick up a tree. Decorating a Christmas tree should bring some joy into this house."

Johnson smiled. "Good idea, babe, I'll do it."

"And while you're off having fun with the kids, I'll go keep the dragon lady company." Deidre laughed at her own joke as she walked out of the bedroom and went downstairs to fix breakfast.

After everyone had eaten, Johnson and the kids left the house. Deidre sat in the recliner reading her Bible while Kenisha channel surfed. When Kenisha couldn't find anything on TV, she turned to Deidre and asked, "What's so interesting in that book?"

"I'm reading about Joseph this morning. He was a dreamer who became a very important man in the land of Egypt."

"I know the story," Kenisha said.

"Really?"

"Yeah, I'm not as ignorant as you think I am."

"I never said you were ignorant, Kenisha. You're putting words in my mouth. I was just a bit surprised that you were familiar with the story because you don't attend church."

"I used to sneak to this little church around the corner from my mom's apartment. The Sunday school teacher taught us about Joseph, the dreamer."

"What other lessons did you learn at that church?"

"Not too many. I started going to that church so I could pray for Jimmy to stop touching me. I had only been going a couple of weeks when my mother finally caught that perv and put him out."

"So you just stopped going?" Deidre asked, trying not to seem shocked about this new revelation.

"I guess I just lost interest. And maybe I was a little mad at God too. Right after I learned about Joseph and how he dreamed about stuff that later happened, I started dreaming that I was a butterfly. And that I was able to fly real high—so high that nothing could touch me. But every time I woke up, I'd still feel like this ugly little caterpillar, so I stopped going to that Sunday school class."

"But you are a human, Kenisha. There's no way you are going to turn into a butterfly."

"Yeah? Then why do I still feel like I'm getting stepped on like a caterpillar or any other common bug?" Shaking her head at the unfairness of it all, Kenisha continued, "Back then I thought God could do anything. But I guess he was schooling me so that I wouldn't be so disappointed later in life when He didn't do a thing for me."

Deidre silently prayed, *Lord, please give me the words to say to this girl. I don't know how to help her believe in You.* Then, just as if God was planting an idea in her head, Deidre said, "Have you ever told God that you're angry with Him?"

"Why would I want to waste time doing something stupid like that?"

"For one, it might make you feel better. There have been times when I was upset with God myself, but I prayed about it. I find that whenever I take the time to be completely honest with God about how I'm feeling, He always finds a way to help me get over whatever I might be going through."

"If I started telling God the things that have ticked me off about Him, I'd probably be dead before I finished, so like I said, why bother?"

Deidre didn't push. She picked up her Bible and finished reading the planned chapters, then she made lunch for herself and Kenisha. "Are you in any pain?"

"Yes, but I want to watch the kids put up the Christmas tree when they get back, so I'm trying to wait."

"Kenisha, can I ask you something?"

"I'm stuck on your couch, can't go anywhere unless I use that wheelchair, so I guess you can ask me all the questions you want."

"I don't mean to pry, but sometimes your behavior confuses me." Deidre hesitated for a moment, trying to find the right words. She didn't want to offend Kenisha, but she knew she couldn't let her continue on in this manner. "You are so good with your children, and it is obvious that you love them, but when it comes to your mother and your sister, it almost seems as if you hate them. Don't you think you owe your mother and sister an apology?"

"Nope," Kenisha said without giving the matter a second thought.

Deidre found it hard to believe that anyone could be that clueless about their behavior. So she tried again. "I have been in the room when you've had conversations with your mother, and I heard the way you talked to your sister this morning. Nobody should be treated the way you've treated them."

Sighing, Kenisha said, "I'm dying, Deidre. I just don't feel like holding my tongue anymore. Martha has never been a mother to me, and Aisha is going to be just like her. I feel sorry for my nieces and nephews."

"What about forgiveness, Kenisha?"

She huffed. "Out of all the things people have done to me, ain't nobody never asked me to forgive them for none of it. And if they did, I'm not sure I would let them off the hook that easily."

"People think that forgiveness is for the person who wronged you, but it's not. Because when we allow things to bottle up inside of us and we don't release it, or forgive the people who may have caused hurt to come in our lives, we just become bitter. And God can't use bitter people."

"Well, it doesn't look like He's going to use me anyway. I'm dying, remember?"

"What about your children, Kenisha? Do you want them to treat people with respect?"

"They already do."

"That's not a given. The Bible tells us that we must raise our children in the way we want them to go when they grow up."

"That's not my job anymore, is it?" Kenisha said with a frown as she looked away. She pulled the covers up over her shoulders.

"Kenisha—"

"I'm tired, Deidre. I don't want to talk right now. Wake me when the kids get back."

Deidre had so much more she wanted to say. She desperately wanted to tell Kenisha about eternity. Because if she didn't make it, and every sign pointed to that fact, Deidre wanted to help Kenisha make her journey to heaven. But Kenisha wasn't ready to hear about all that. So Deidre backed off. She left the family room and began straightening up around the house.

When Johnson returned with the kids, the atmosphere was once again filled with excitement. Deidre grabbed the ornaments out of the garage as Johnson put the tree up in the family room. Deidre popped popcorn, and Kenisha helped Diamond and Kennedy string the popcorn so that it could be hung on the tree. Jamal helped Deidre pick out the ornaments to be hung on the tree. All was going well in the Morris house, but Deidre worried that she was feeling too content with her newfound family. Something was bound to happen that would turn things upside down.

Kenisha and Deidre received approval for a special visit with James on Monday morning. Deidre had to call in at work again, but she did it without blinking an eye. Kenisha was grateful for that, and she now knew that Deidre would be the type of mother who would place her kids before her career.

They were seated in the visitor's area of Lebanon Correctional Institution waiting for James to take his seat and join them. Deidre was so nervous that her knees were knocking. Kenisha was just happy that she felt strong enough to walk into the prison and didn't have to be in that wheelchair. She spotted James's chiseled, chocolate form as he entered the room. The guard pointed in her direction, and she wanted to jump up and scream, "That's my man!" But she held her peace as she watched him walk toward her.

He smiled at her, and it felt like heaven opened up. The man was like a Greek god, all muscles and chocolaty goodness. He put you in mind of Morris Chestnut. Even the way he walked was smooth and rhythmic. James should have been making movies rather than doing time.

"Hey, baby," he said as he stood in front of her.

Kenisha stood up and put all her strength into hugging James. She kissed his cheek and then sat back down. "Look at you. You're shining like Mr. Universe or something."

"I'm not that big. I've just been lifting some weights and eating my carbs, that's all."

"Well, you're looking beautiful to me," she said and then touched her hair and turned away from him. "I'm sorry I don't look better, but I can't do nothing about all this weight I've been losing and how brittle my hair is."

"You still look good to me," James told her as his eyes danced over her hair and her face with all the hunger of a lovesick teen.

Kenisha turned to Deidre as if she'd just remembered that the room didn't only belong to her and James. "Deidre, this is James, Jamal's daddy."

Deidre stretched out her hand. "Nice to meet you. I'm Deidre Morris."

James shook her hand. "Nice to meet you too. I'm James Moore. You know, like my son is Jamal Moore."

Kenisha shoved James. "Don't start, we just got here."

"I'm not starting nothing, Ke-Ke. I just want everybody to understand that Jamal is my son."

"And we don't want to change that," Deidre said quickly. "My husband and I just want to do what Kenisha has asked us to do."

"What did you ask them to do?" James asked Kenisha.

"Baby, Deidre and Johnson are good people. They live in the suburbs in a nice house. Both of them have college degrees and got good jobs. Jamal can learn a lot from them. That's why I want the Morrises to adopt my children."

"Well, one of *your* children belongs to me. And Martha already told me that she would keep Jamal until I get out, so that he don't have to be adopted by nobody."

Martha was constantly messing with her. Deidre thought she was too mean to that woman, but every time Kenisha turned around, Martha was either doing something to her or one of her children. "James, you know my mother isn't fit to watch a dog, let alone Jamal. Our son is smart. He deserves a chance in life. Please help me give him that chance."

James pointed at Deidre while still talking to Kenisha. "You think that she's so much better than Martha just because she don't live in the projects. You need to check yourself, Kenisha, because we both grew up in the projects."

"Exactly, and look at us. You're in prison, and I never did nothing with my life but raise my children. I didn't even finish high school. But Jamal has a chance to do something with his life, but if you give him to Martha, he might end up in a cell with you. Now, is that what you want?"

James didn't say anything.

Kenisha stood up. "Well, I haven't got much time left, James, so I'm not going to fight with you. But Deidre is a praying woman, and she is going to make sure that God hears about how stubborn you are."

"You ain't right, Ke-Ke. Now you want to put God on me?"

"I don't want to. But you're not being reasonable. I love you, James, and Jamal does too. But you ought to love him enough to let him go."

"He's my son. He's all I have," James said with pain in his voice.

"You're in prison, James, and we can't wait on you anymore. I don't have much time. Please do the right thing."

James turned to Deidre and asked, "Why can't you just keep him for me until I get out of here? Why do you have to take my son away from me like this?"

"I didn't do this to you, James. All we want to do is give Jamal a home, and love and care for him just as you would have done if you weren't in here," Deidre said.

Kenisha plopped back in her seat and said, "I think I'm going to need the wheelchair to get back to the car. My body feels like it's locking up on me."

James jumped up and waved his arm for one of the guards. "What's wrong, Ke-Ke?"

"I'm just tired, James, that's all. Sit back down. I don't want you to get shot in here," she said with a smile.

"What's going on, Moore?" The guard asked as he walked over to them.

"She needs help," James answered while pointing at Kenisha.

"We need a wheelchair," Deidre said.

"We don't have one in here. We can carry her out if she can't walk. Hold on. Let me get a couple of guards to help you." The guard walked away.

Kenisha turned to James. She gently put her hand on his face. "I've got to go. Please mail the release form to the address I sent to you."

Tears glistened in James's eyes as he held onto Kenisha's hand. "I don't want to lose you, Ke-Ke."

"I'm sorry, baby."

The guard came back with a wheelchair. "I found one," he said, then asked. "Do you need help getting into it?"

"Yes," Kenisha admitted.

"I'll help her into the chair," James said, and he stood up and lifted Kenisha out of her chair.

Kenisha put her arms around James and imagined that he was carrying her over the threshold of the house they had said they would get when he got out. She wanted to stay in James's arms forever, but once he put her in the chair, the guard made him move away.

This was the last time she would ever see James. His last memory of her would be of the day he picked her up and put her in a wheelchair. Something just wasn't right about that.

26

Deidre knew that Kenisha would be upset after their meeting with James, so she scheduled appointments at a local day spa. She'd made sure to inform them of Kenisha's condition ahead of time. Deidre was glad that she had done so, because each technician treated them like royalty. Kenisha received a facial, a manicure, a pedicure, and a massage. Deidre only had enough money to pay for Kenisha's procedures, but the owner said that they were doing a two-for-one special that day.

Kenisha had to be wheeled from one room to the next, but even that didn't dampen her spirits. "This is great," Kenisha said with a genuine smile on her face.

"Isn't it? I get the works at least once a year."

"Wow. I never would have thought about doing something like this."

"A girl's got to treat herself every now and then," Deidre said as they walked into the massage room.

Kenisha lay on the table with Deidre on a table next to her. Instrumental music was playing softly throughout the room. The massage therapist pushed on Kenisha's back and began massaging the knots out of her back. "Mmm, this is nice," Kenisha said as she drifted off to sleep.

Deidre was thrilled at Kenisha's response to the day spa. She had hoped that an afternoon of pampering would help ease some of her pain, but later that night while she was in the kitchen stirring her chocolate, she heard sounds coming from the family room. Thinking that Kenisha might be moaning out of pain, she stepped closer to the room to assist her. But then she heard Kenisha talking, and she sounded like she was mad at the world, or better yet, from what Deidre could make out, Kenisha was mad at God.

It sounded as if Kenisha had taken her advice about telling God how she felt. However, Deidre felt like she had some explaining to do to God. Kind of like the way she'd felt years ago after she'd run into one of Michelle's ex-boyfriends in a grocery store. He'd asked for Michelle's new number because he said he still had some of Michelle's things and needed to know what she wanted him to do with them. Deidre had given him the number, and then he'd started a telephone harassment campaign. Deidre had apologized to Michelle for a month.

Kenisha said, "You knew that James was the only person who ever truly loved me, but You took him away from me anyway. You've never been there for me. Not when I was being raped and molested, not when my children needed food. Never."

The pain in Kenisha's voice was too much to bear. Deidre backed away from the entrance into the family room. She was sure Kenisha wouldn't want her to listen in on this very private conversation. Deidre grabbed her cup and headed back upstairs. But before she got out of the kitchen, she heard Kenisha say, "My own father didn't even want me. Night after night I prayed for my father to take me away from Martha. He paid child support to Martha, but he never came for me. Deidre is always praying to You, but I know that all this prayer stuff is a waste of time. Nothing but a waste."

Deidre remembered the name and location of the fast-food restaurant Kenisha had told her that her father owned. As Deidre walked up the stairs, she suddenly had a taste for a cheeseburger.

Deidre walked up to the counter and asked to speak with the owner. The twenty-something girl behind the counter said, "If you have a complaint, I can help you."

"No, I need to speak with Dwayne Smalls. This is an important matter, so please get him." Deidre had intended to order a burger and fries, but the burger smell was messing with her stomach. She didn't understand it, because she ate fast food often, and the smell of burgers had never bothered her before.

The girl walked away from the counter in a huff. When she returned, a short, overweight, bald man followed her.

He stood behind the counter and said, "What can I do for you?"

"I need to speak with you in private," Deidre told him. One of the women working behind the counter stopped working to glare at her. Deidre wondered if she was his child or an extracurricular affair who thought she was the work wife.

"I'm busy right now, I don't have time for no games," Dwayne told her as if women approached him on his job more times than he could count.

"It's about Kenisha, Mr. Smalls. I'm not here to cause you any problems. I'm just bringing you some unfortunate news."

"Let's go sit down at the tables." He walked from behind the counter and took Deidre to an empty table. When they were seated, Dwayne got right to the point. "Look, I just got remarried, and things are going good for me right now. So I don't need no drama. So you tell Kenisha and Martha that they're not getting another dime out of me."

Deidre took a deep breath. She hated giving people bad news, but this man needed a reality check for real. "I really don't know why you think being a father is all about sending a check, but that's none of my business. I came here to tell you that your daughter is dying. I thought you might like to see her before it's too late."

"Is this some kind of trick?"

He looked like he wanted to be sad for Kenisha but didn't really know what sadness felt like. And in that moment, Deidre truly understood why Kenisha had made so many bad choices. If her father had never said a kind word to her or couldn't even muster the emotion to feel bad for her, she might have gone from one man to the next trying to find the love she hadn't received as a child also. "Mr. Smalls, I really have better things to do with my time than to play games with you. Kenisha has cancer. I thought you might want to know, but I see now that I was wrong."

The woman who'd glared at Deidre from behind the counter came over to where they were sitting, put her hands on her hips, and asked Dwayne, "What's going on here?"

Dwayne turned to Deidre and said, "I'm sorry, but I forgot to ask your name."

"Deidre Morris."

He then turned to the woman and said, "Sit down with us, Brenda. This woman has brought me news about my daughter."

"Your daughter?" Brenda said, as if this was the first she'd heard of any daughter. "You have four sons with your first wife. You never told me about a daughter."

"She's grown, probably twenty-five by now."

"Twenty-three. She turns twenty-four on the fifth of January, if she lives that long."

This time a pained expression crossed Dwayne's face. "Do you really think she's going to die?"

"I've been praying all I know how for Kenisha. But to tell you the truth, she has been steadily declining. Unless God gives us a miracle, I don't think she has much longer."

Brenda turned to Deidre with a raised brow. "Did I miss something? Is something wrong with his daughter?"

"The doctors say that Kenisha doesn't have that much longer to live. She has cancer."

Brenda put her hand over her mouth as she said, "Oh, my God."

"The thing is, Mr. Smalls, I was hoping that you would come see Kenisha. She probably won't admit it, but she desperately needs your love."

He lowered his head in shame.

His wife put her hand over his. "What's wrong, baby?"

"I don't know what to say to her. I treated Kenisha so badly the last time I saw her." He looked up, eyes darting from Brenda to Deidre, looking for understanding. "I was going through a bad divorce a few years back. Kenisha came to see me. I hadn't seen her in years, but I was mad about all the money I'd paid out to her mother in child support, and I knew good and well that Martha hadn't done anything but drink the money up. So I didn't even talk to her. I told her I wasn't giving out any more, and she left with two little kids."

"Those are your grandchildren, Mr. Smalls. Kenisha now has three children, and my husband and I have agreed to adopt them, but they might want to know their grandfather."

"I don't know if I can face her after how I've treated her, but tell her that I'll pay for the funeral. Just call me when it's time."

How big of you, Deidre wanted to say. Instead she opened her purse and took a small notepad and pen out. She wrote down her address and handed it to him. "This is where Kenisha is staying. Tell her yourself." Deidre stood up and said, "Now if you'll excuse me, I have an appointment."

She left the burger joint feeling slightly dirty. She went home and showered before she, Kenisha, and Johnson went downtown to the Juvenile Court Building. Kenisha had called the woman she had been working with at the Action Adoption Agency and told her that she had prospective parents for her children. The woman suggested that they pick up a Pro Se packet at the Juvenile Court so they could file for legal custody. She then told them that they would need to have their lawyer file the adoption petition with the Probate Court. But the process should go smoother if Deidre and Johnson already had legal custody in the works.

Knowing all that, it was still hard for Deidre to hear Kenisha tell the clerk in the Juvenile Court Building that she needed the Pro Se packet because she was dying and her children needed legal guardians.

The clerk looked up at Kenisha and asked, "Are you serious?"

"Nope," Kenisha said. "I'm really just tired of being a mother, so I'm trying to throw my kids off on somebody so I can spend the rest of my days partying like a rock star."

Deidre jumped in front of Kenisha. "We have her medical records. She's telling the truth."

Shaking his head as if dealing with a naughty child, the clerk opened a file cabinet behind his desk and produced the forms needed to get the process started. He handed them the packet. "Fill this out and return eight copies to me."

They sat down at a table not far from the clerk's desk and began filling out the paperwork. The process was sobering for

Deidre because if James didn't release his parental rights, she and Johnson could end up as the parents of two children rather than three. Deidre kept trying to quiet her fears by reminding herself to trust God, but her heart was beating fast when she handed the papers to the clerk. "How long does this process take?"

"A couple of months."

Worry lines etched across Deidre's face. It was the second of December. Pretty soon people would be on vacation and out for the Christmas and New Year's break. What had she done? Had her procrastination cost her the children she dearly wanted? Would Kenisha even be alive long enough for this background check to go through? *Oh, dear Lord, please help us*, Deidre silently prayed.

27

On Friday morning, Deidre was preparing to miss another day of work so that somebody would be at the house with Kenisha when the doorbell rang. She went to the door and opened it. Her eyebrow rose as she stared into Aisha's smiling face. A young man, maybe mid-twenties, was standing next to her. "Hey Aisha, I didn't expect to see you today."

"I told you I would take care of her on Fridays, and that is what I intend to do. Kenisha is just going to have to deal with it," Aisha said firmly.

"You brought someone else to see your sister?"

"Yeah. But this one is cool. Remember, she told me not to come back without Kevin. So I brought him with me."

Now Deidre was smiling. "You're Kenisha's brother? Come on in. She has been wanting to see you. Thank God you showed up."

After Deidre walked them into the family room, she told Kenisha, "I'm going to go and get ready for work. Please be nice to Aisha."

As Deidre walked out of the room, Kenisha started to roll her eyes at her sister, but then Kevin walked into the room.

"Oh my God, I didn't think I would see you again. I didn't know if you were dead or alive."

Kevin walked over to the bed and knelt down next to his sister. "I've been doing what you asked me to do lil' sis. I went to a rehab. I'm trying to get clean so my nieces and my nephew can be proud of me."

Tears filled Kenisha's eyes. "I thought I would never see this day. Why didn't you tell anybody where you were going?"

"You know how our family can be sometimes. They say stuff to make you feel bad about yourself. I just didn't want to have all that in my head while I was trying to get clean, so I just walked off and didn't say anything to anybody. But I prayed before I left. I told God that if you were still alive when I got out of that rehab, I would stay clean for the rest of my life."

She wanted to tell Kevin that it was no use bargaining with God, because He was just going to do whatever He wanted anyway. But she didn't want to fill Kevin's head with the negativity he was trying to get away from, so she kept her feelings to herself.

Aisha loudly cleared her throat. When Kevin and Kenisha turned to her, she pointed at Kenisha and said, "You owe me an apology."

Kenisha thought about it for a moment and then admitted, "You're right. I shouldn't have been so mean to you. Come over here so I can give you a hug."

Aisha climbed on the bed with Kenisha, and the sisters hugged like long-lost friends.

"I'm sorry, Isha. I'll try to control my temper from now on. Okay?"

"All right," Aisha agreed, clearly happy just to be back in her sister's good graces.

"Hey, have either of you seen Angelina?"

"Not in a couple of weeks. She just finished taking her finals, and you know she don't come around when she's studying."

Kenisha knew that Angelina hadn't felt comfortable around her since Kenisha told her just what kind of pervert her daddy was. But just as Kenisha hadn't wanted to go to her grave without seeing Kevin, she had the same kind of feeling now about Angelina. "Call her for me. Tell her I'd like to see her," Kenisha asked Aisha.

"Sure, sis. What about Martha? Do you want to see her too?" Aisha asked.

Shaking her head vehemently, Kenisha said, "I'm not even sure if I want that woman to attend my funeral."

"Lil' sis, you've got to stop all this," Kevin said. "I know Martha wasn't the best mother, but my counselor at the rehab told us that the best way to free ourselves is to let go. And that's what you need to do. Kenisha, just let go of all the bitterness that you have toward Martha. I guarantee you'll feel a lot better—I do."

"You handle your bitterness the way you see fit, and I'll handle mine. Okay?"

"Have it your way, Ke-Ke. I'm just trying to help you take that heavy load off your shoulders."

"Listen to you, away at rehab for a couple of months and you come back a philosopher," Aisha said.

"I might not be a philosopher. But I'm a whole lot wiser than I was when I went in. My counselor helped me find a job. It's not much, but I'm going back to school."

"Shut up, Kevin. You are not," Kenisha said.

"Yes, I am, Ke-Ke. I'm going to be that architect I always dreamed about being. It's not too late. And I plan to live every day of the rest of my life to the fullest."

"Has my impending death put you in such a hurry to live life to the fullest?"

The brightness that had been in his eyes as he discussed his job and his plans for school left as he admitted, "Yeah, Ke-Ke. This shouldn't be happening to you. But it's made me realize that we shouldn't waste a minute with bitterness or with unfulfilled dreams, because we don't know when our end is going to come. And I'd rather mine came while I was doing something. That's the way I see life now. And it's all thanks to my little sister."

Kenisha put her hand on Kevin's head and leaned back against her pillow. Her eyes appeared to be looking far off as she said, "As the years go by and my children begin to forget me, would you tell them the story of how I inspired you to go out and make something of your life?"

"Every chance I get," Kevin told her as he leaned his head on her shoulder.

"Okay, you two are sounding too morbid for me," Aisha said. "What do you say I call Angelina over here, and we spend the day watching comedies?"

"Sounds good to me. But you need to call Deidre first, and make sure it's okay," Kenisha said.

After Aisha got the okay from Deidre, Angelina came over, and the four of them spent the day watching funny Christmas movies and other comedies. They laughed and joked with each other as they reminisced about the funny things they'd done when they were kids. Like the time Kevin rolled down their uncarpeted stairs on his big wheel, fell and busted his head and had to go to the hospital for stitches. Or the time Dynasty got caught stealing a bag of chips at the convenience store down the street from their house, and the store clerk whupped her all the way home, and then Martha whupped her some more.

"That girl was always doing stuff she didn't have no business doing," Aisha said with a laugh.

"She was kicks," Kenisha said.

"Hey, remember when we used to sing 'We Are Family'?" Angelina asked.

"Yeah, we really thought we were Sister Sledge back then. I remember how we would hold our play microphones and put on Martha's wigs and strut around the room singing." Aisha held her fist to her mouth as if holding a microphone and sang, "*We are family.*"

Angelina stood up, fist to her mouth like a microphone, and sang, "*I got all my family with me.*"

Kenisha sat up and joined in while Aisha and Angelina danced around the room. When they finished the song, Kenisha told Aisha, "You should do some of those moves for the next reality show you audition for."

Aisha stopped dancing and asked excitedly, "You really think so?"

"Nope," Kenisha said as Angelina and Kevin burst out in laughter. "But I think it will give the producers something to laugh about. You never know, sis, comedy might be your ticket in."

Aisha waved them off. "Forget y'all. I know I've got moves. Y'all are just jealous." Aisha started dancing around the room. "See that? One day that's going to be a signature Aisha move."

"That's right, Isha, don't give up your dreams," Kevin said, still laughing.

They continued on like that for hours, then Angelina put Tyler Perry's movie *Daddy's Little Girl* in the DVD player. They were enjoying the movie until Idris Elba got fed up and headed out to settle a score. That's when Sam Cooke's song "A Change Is Gonna Come" started playing. The four of them listened as the honesty of those lyrics poured out of Sam Cooke's mouth.

It's been too hard living, but I'm afraid to die. Those lyrics mesmerized Kenisha because she felt the same way. There were times that she would have gladly given up this crappy life that had been forced on her. But it was the not knowing what came next that had stopped her. Now that her life was being taken from her, Kenisha really wanted to know, as Sam Cooke said, *what's up there beyond the sky*.

When the song finished, Kenisha turned to Kevin and her sisters and asked, "What do y'all think is up there?" She pointed upward.

"Are you talking about upstairs or heaven?" Aisha asked.

"Heaven. Do you think there is such a place?"

"I sure hope so. After suffering like hell on earth, I'd love to think we get to go to a place like heaven when it's all over," Kevin said.

"I started attending this church on campus about a month ago," Angelina began. "And, well, the members have really been helping me get through some things."

Kenisha knew what things Angelina was trying to get through. And for the first time, she wondered if she had been wrong when she told Angelina how evil her father really was. He had never been that way to Angelina. So maybe she should have let the girl go on idealizing her father. "I'm sorry about the things I said to you, Angelina. I shouldn't have told you."

"I'm glad you told me what he did to you and Kevin. He had no right, and I don't need a man like that in my life."

"He's still your father, Angelina. You can't let what happened to me and Kenisha turn you into a bitter, unforgiving person," Kevin said, again sounding wiser than his twenty-seven years.

"I'm praying about it," Angelina admitted.

"You're going to church and praying. Oh goodness, what have I done to you?" Kenisha asked jokingly.

"You can joke if you want to, but because of this church, I now can tell you that I not only believe that there is a heaven, but that there is also a God and we must serve Him if we want to get to heaven."

"Okay, we're getting morbid again. This is supposed to be a fun day, remember?" Aisha said.

"Then we better change the subject before Angelina starts baptizing us," Kevin said, and they all broke out laughing.

The next day, Kenisha was still in good spirits as she told Deidre about her fun time with her family.

When she finished, Deidre said, "Wow. You really changed their lives."

"Not really. They could have done that stuff without me," Kenisha said. As far as she was concerned, she hadn't done anything right all her life, so how could she possibly have helped change anyone's life?

"Kenisha? I can't believe you don't see how you helped them. It might have been in an indirect way, but if you hadn't been alive, your brother might still be on drugs and Angelina might never have attended that campus church."

"So you're saying that I wasn't born for nothing? That I've made a difference?"

"Not only in the lives of your brother and sister, but in the lives of your children. You've made a difference in my life also."

Laughing, Kenisha said, "Yeah, right. What could I have helped you with?"

"Laugh if you want, but I'm telling you the truth. When I met you, I was so absorbed in my problems that I had only been praying for myself, and I was only concerned about what Johnson and I wanted. My prayers changed after meeting you. And believe it or not, you helped me get my faith back."

"How? None of your prayers have been answered."

"But the thing is, I have come to accept that whether God answers my prayers or not, I know that He is able to. And I have decided to serve Him the rest of my life even if He never does another thing for me, because I love Him that much. So, thank you, Kenisha."

28

The first thing Deidre did when she got to work that morning was call her mother and cancel their Christmas plans. "I was so looking forward to seeing you and Johnson," Loretta said.

"I know, Mom, I wanted to see you too. But I don't think we should leave Kenisha right now."

"That poor girl. My heart breaks for her every time I think about this situation," Loretta said.

"Mine too, Mom. We've all been trying to hold on the best way we know how."

"I've got an idea." Loretta sounded excited. "Why don't I come down there and spend Christmas with you? I would love to see Johnson and the kids. And I think I'd like to meet Kenisha before it's too late."

"But what about Michelle? Will she be upset that you aren't there with her family?"

"I spend Christmas with them all the time. I want to meet my new grandchildren. And anyway, I only live an hour away. I can speed up the highway and give my other grandchildren their presents too."

"Thanks, Mom, I'd really like for you to be here." They hung up, and then Deidre got to work. She didn't know how she was going to handle her position at the school and motherhood—because she'd been doing a lousy job so far. She'd missed more days of work this year than she had in the past ten years. Deidre just hoped she would get a handle on things quickly.

Stacks of files were on her desk. Teachers were waiting on her to approve numerous requests. So she put her nose to the grindstone and got busy. As she was halfway through her stack of files, Ms. Burn, the third-grade teacher came into her office with tears in her eyes and an angry set to her mouth.

"What's wrong?" Deidre asked, hoping that it was something simple, because she didn't have time for interruptions.

"I need to report a parent for child abuse."

Putting her pen down, Deidre asked, "Which child?"

"Ronny Nickels. This is the third time this year that his mother has beaten him black and blue, and then sent him on to school like it's nothing. I think Ronny's arm is broken this time, though. He kept wincing every time I touched his arm. So I asked him to stay in when everyone else went out for lunch."

"Did you have the nurse check his arm?"

"I sure did. She has called for an ambulance. Ronny has several welt marks on his back that are still bleeding."

Deidre closed her eyes and screamed inside. She had known that Shameka Nickels was abusive, but she had done nothing to stop the woman. Deidre remembered thinking that Ronny was so bad, he probably needed a good beating every now and then. But no kid deserved broken bones and bleeding welts. Deidre got up and went to the nurse's office with Ms. Burn. When she walked in, the paramedics were already there, looking over Ronny.

Ronny was sitting in a chair letting the paramedics look at his arm and his back. This was the first time that Deidre had looked at Ronny without seeing a kid on the fast track to prison. She saw a scared little kid who needed help.

"I don't want to go to the hospital, Mrs. Morris. My mom will get mad," Ronny said to her as soon as she walked into the room.

"Everything's going to turn out all right, Ronny. Your mom won't be able to hurt you again, okay?"

He nodded, but the fear was still in his eyes.

Deidre wanted to pull him into her arms and hug him. But she was afraid that she'd just cause him more pain. She didn't understand how a mother could victimize her own child like this. Jamal was only a year younger than Ronny. Kenisha was worried that her kids would be abused in other ways if they lived with Martha. But wasn't it all the same? Didn't it all leave scars?

Deidre was determined that nothing like this would ever happen to Jamal. Somehow, she would get around the stubbornness of Jamal's father. Those children would not go to Martha if Deidre had anything to say about it. They had a meeting scheduled with an attorney that evening. Deidre prayed he would have good news for them.

On the ride home, Deidre's heart was heavy. She thought that she would shout the victory once Shameka was arrested, but it had only made her sad for the breakup of another family—although, if any family needed to be broken up, it was definitely Shameka's. Hopefully, her five children could all be kept together, as Deidre was trying to do for Kenisha's children.

"What's wrong with you?" Jamal asked.

Jamal was in the front passenger seat, and Diamond was in the back. They had been riding home with Deidre the last few weeks. "Nothing's wrong. I was just thinking about something that happened at school today."

"Oh, I thought you were worried because you have to talk to that lawyer tonight," Jamal said.

She pulled up at a red light and stopped. She then looked at Jamal and asked, "Why would I be worried about that?"

He shrugged his shoulders. "Maybe you don't want us anymore."

The light turned green, but Deidre didn't notice. She was too busy looking at Jamal trying to gauge his mood. Deidre hadn't forgotten that when Jamal found out his mother was dying, he'd asked to stay with his grandmother. Maybe he was hoping that she would allow him to do that now. The car behind her honked its horn. Deidre drove off as she asked, "What do you want me to do?"

Shrugging his shoulders again, he said, "I don't know. You said that you wanted us. I just wondered if you had changed your mind."

"I haven't changed my mind, Jamal. Johnson and I are here to stay. You don't have to worry about that."

"I wasn't worried."

"Okay, then," Deidre said, letting him off the hook. When they got home, the kids sat with Kenisha while Deidre fixed dinner. Johnson would be home by 5:30 p.m., and their attorney was expected at 6:00 p.m. She wanted the kids fed and upstairs doing their homework so they wouldn't be eavesdropping on their conversation.

She was making burgers and fries for the kids, something quick and easy. But dinner wasn't as easy to make as Deidre had thought. The smell of the burgers turned her stomach just as it had when she'd visited Kenisha's father. She sat down at the kitchen table trying to get as far away from those burgers as possible. No way was she going to eat one of those. And that was strange for her, because she had never been one of those oh-no-red-meat-for-me kind of people. Maybe age was changing her taste buds.

"I see we're having our grand old American classic," Johnson said as he walked into the kitchen.

Deidre looked at her watch. "You're early."

"I was too excited. All I could think about was our meeting with the attorney tonight, so I knocked off a half hour early."

Deidre got up and said, "Good. Can you do me a favor and finish cooking those burgers? They're making my stomach turn."

"I can handle that."

"Thanks. The fries are in the oven."

Deidre went into the family room. Kenisha was watching *Judge Judy*, so Deidre sat quietly and let the girl enjoy the program. "You really like this show, don't you?"

"Judge Judy is my girl. She tells it like it is," Kenisha said with a smile on her face.

After the kids ate, Deidre sent them upstairs to do their homework. Not long after, the doorbell rang. Johnson opened the door and showed Daniel Walker into the family room.

"Thank you so much for meeting with us tonight," Deidre said.

"I'm just doing my job, so don't worry about it," Daniel told her. He walked over to Kenisha, and extended his hand. "You must be Kenisha. I'm Daniel."

Kenisha shook his hand. "Deidre told me that you are a good lawyer."

"I like to think I am."

"Well, we need you to be, because we have a problem," Kenisha told him.

Daniel sat down, opened his briefcase, and took out a notepad and pen. "I'm all ears."

Kenisha and Deidre took turns telling Daniel about the daddy problem they had with Chico and James.

When they finished with their story, Daniel asked, "Does Chico visit his child regularly?"

"He comes by once a month. But that's only because he likes to hit me up when he thinks I have some extra money."

"Has he paid child support in the last year?" Daniel wanted to know.

"He hasn't had a job since she was born. Chico is on drugs, so he's not trying to give me any money."

"That's all I need to tell the courts, then. He signed the release form, but even though he claims he wants to change his mind, he doesn't provide any support for the child. So the judge will revoke his rights, anyway."

"It's that easy?" Deidre asked, with wide, unbelieving eyes.

"If we were filing the adoption petition in Juvenile Court, it would be a lot harder. They tend to give the biological parent a lot more chances than the Probate Court judges do. Usually in Probate Court, all you have to prove is that the biological father or mother hasn't visited with the child in the last year, or that they haven't paid child support."

"So the same thing would go for James also, right?" Kenisha asked. "I mean, if he wasn't in jail, I know he would see Jamal all the time, and he would pay his child support. But he can't do either, because he's locked up and will be for at least another eight years."

"Same thing goes. We'll let the judge know that James refuses to sign the release form, but that he can't possibly take care of the child, nor has he been able to provide support." Daniel looked around the room at his clients and said, "Don't worry, we've got this petition locked up."

"What if I'm dead before the adoption goes through?" Kenisha asked as if she were saying that she might be on vacation on their court date.

Silence fell over the room as Deidre and Johnson turned toward Daniel. That was a subject that no one wanted to address but was nonetheless on everyone's mind.

Daniel cleared his throat before speaking. "Since the Morrises have already filed the application for legal custody, we shouldn't have a problem gaining the adoption. But I would like you to write a letter detailing why you feel that the Morrises would be the best people to parent your children. Can you do that for me?"

"Not a problem," Kenisha told him.

But no matter how much Kenisha tried to pretend that this meeting wasn't bothering her, Deidre knew that it was. If Deidre had been lying in that bed giving away her children, she would have a tough time with the process also. She wished that she could say or do something for Kenisha that would make her feel better. But Deidre couldn't think of a single thing that could take this kind of pain away.

Johnson walked Daniel out, and the two women were left alone for a while. Kenisha looked at Deidre, and with a voice full of sadness, she said, "Well, it's done. My kids will soon be your kids."

Deidre took Kenisha's hand in hers and gently squeezed it. "I'll never let them forget you. I will tell them how you helped Kevin and Angelina turn their lives around. I'll let them know about that meeting you caused my relationship with God to grow. And I will especially tell them how you wanted nothing but the best for them."

"Will you tell Kennedy that I taught her to read and spell at the age of two? She's my only child that could do something like that so early. And I'd like her to know that I had something to do with her smarts."

"I will."

"And tell Jamal and Diamond that their mother loved them so much that she wouldn't rest until she found them a home that was filled with love."

"I'll tell them every chance I get."

A tear ran down Kenisha's face as she said, "Thank you."

Deidre patted her hand as she stood up. "Get some rest, Kenisha, we'll talk some more in the morning. And I'll send the kids down so they can spend the evening with you. Okay?"

Deidre went upstairs. She opened Jamal's door. All three children were in his room. They were sitting on the floor, watching television. "Did you finish your homework?"

Both Diamond and Jamal nodded.

"Well, if you're done with your homework, your mom would like to hang out with you. So head on downstairs, okay?"

Jamal stood up and grabbed Kennedy's hand. The three began to walk out of the room, and then Diamond stopped in front of Deidre and asked, "If you're going to be our new mommy, what are we supposed to call you?"

Deidre hadn't given any thought to what the children would call her. She was sure that Kennedy would begin calling her Mom pretty soon, but Diamond and Jamal were used to calling Kenisha Mom, and she didn't know how they would handle saying those words to another woman, so she said, "You can call me whatever you like. Okay? Whatever feels comfortable."

"Okay, thanks, Deidre," Diamond said as they walked away.

Deidre smiled as she walked into her bedroom. Life had certainly changed for her and Johnson. A few months ago she had been praying for just one child, and now she was adopting three at one time. She didn't care what they called her, because

Deidre had made up her mind that she would love and protect her children as if she'd given birth to them; in her heart, it didn't matter that these weren't her birth children.

Deidre heard Johnson yell, "Stop running down those stairs. And don't carry your sister on your back down those stairs, either."

He opened the bedroom door, rolled his eyes, and closed the door behind him. "Is this what being a parent is all about? Am I going to be forever saying the same thing? Or are they going to learn to obey?"

"I don't know, baby." Deidre laughed at him. "My dad said that my sister and I didn't listen to a word he said, either. He was always repeating this and that rule. He said we drove him crazy."

Johnson fell on the bed, looking exhausted. "I guess I'm going to go crazy then, because I love those hard-headed kids."

"Are you sure this isn't too much change, too soon?" Deidre asked, worried that Johnson wasn't feeling as good about this arrangement as she was.

"No, baby, this is the way it is. And I'm fine with what we decided."

Deidre leaned over and kissed her husband. When they pulled apart, she said, "Have I told you how wonderful you are?"

He sat up and scooted Deidre closer to him. "Oh, so I'm wonderful now, am I?"

"Yes, I should have listened to you when you first brought up the idea of adoption, but I was being so bullheaded that I couldn't believe I could love children that I didn't birth."

"And now you're sure that you can?" Johnson asked.

"Are you kidding? I love Jamal, Diamond, and Kennedy so much already; I can only imagine that my love for them will grow with each passing day. I just hope we don't do a terrible job as parents. Kenisha has put a lot of faith in us, and I really don't want to let her down."

"We'll just have to stay in prayer on their behalf," Johnson said as he nibbled Deidre's earlobe.

"You want to pray for them right now?"

Johnson shook his head. "I had something else in mind for tonight," he told his wife as he softly kissed her neck.

"Okay, Johnson, but we have to pray first thing in the morning."

He agreed, but by morning their whole world would change.

29

Deidre put on her robe and went downstairs to fix breakfast for everyone. She was humming while she walked toward the kitchen. But the humming stopped when she heard Kenisha moaning. Her moans tore at Deidre's heart, because they sounded as if they came from the depth of pain. Deidre rushed into the family room and found Kenisha on the floor, trying to crawl but moving very slowly. Her body was drenched in sweat. "What's wrong, Kenisha?"

Kenisha stopped moving and looked around the room, trying to find Deidre. When their eyes locked, Kenisha said one word, "Pain."

Deidre ran to get the pain pills and a glass of water, and came back to the family room. She tried to lift Kenisha up so she could take the pills, and that's when Deidre felt how hot Kenisha was. "You're burning up." And that wasn't all. Deidre noticed that Kenisha had soiled her nightgown. She helped Kenisha take the pain pills and then said, "I'm going to call an ambulance."

After calling the ambulance, Deidre got a cold rag and wiped the sweat from Kenisha's face. She then told her, "I'm going to throw on some clothes so I can go to the hospital with you. She ran back upstairs, threw on a jogging suit, and then woke Johnson up. "I have to go to the hospital with Kenisha. Can you please make sure the kids stay up here?"

"What's going on?"

"She's got a fever again. She's in a lot of pain, and I think she's lost control of her bowels. The ambulance is on the way. Just don't let the kids come down until I can get everything cleaned up. I don't want them to see her like this."

Deidre ran back downstairs with clean clothes and washcloths. The paramedics arrived and helped her clean Kenisha up before putting her in the ambulance. Deidre was grateful that the man-and-woman duo allowed her the extra minutes it took to get those soiled clothes off of Kenisha. Deidre knew that Kenisha would not want to go to the hospital in that condition.

As the paramedics were preparing to roll Kenisha out of the house, Johnson and the kids came down the stairs. Deidre could kiss her husband for holding the kids back. From the time she let the paramedics into the house, she'd heard the kids questioning Johnson. Somehow he'd managed to hold them off until the last moment. Deidre put the soiled clothes in a trash bag and pulled the sheets off the bed as the children gathered around Kenisha.

"Where are you going, Mama?" Diamond asked.

"Hospital," was the only word Kenisha got out, as the paramedics wheeled her out of the house and into the ambulance.

"I want to go," Jamal said as he tried to run after the paramedics.

Johnson grabbed Jamal. "We're all going. That's why I had you wash up and put on your clothes. Now go get your coats so we can get to the hospital."

Deidre went into the bathroom to wash her hands. When she came out, she asked Johnson, "Do you think it's wise to take them?"

"Yes, I do. This might be it for Kenisha. And if it is, I don't want them to think we kept them from seeing their mother one last time."

Deidre nodded. "You're right. Let's go."

They spent the day at the hospital. The kids had eaten breakfast and then lunch in the hospital cafeteria before the emergency room doctor could tell them anything. But when he finally came out, the prognosis was so grim, Deidre wished she'd never met with the man. "There's nothing we can do for Ms. Smalls. Her oxygen level is decreasing, and her body is shutting down. We recommend that you contact hospice of Dayton and have her moved over there."

Deidre's hands started shaking. She had known that Kenisha was going to die. Kenisha had given her that awful news herself. However, everybody would die one day or another, anyway. But to be told that death was imminent and that they needed hospice was a different matter altogether.

Johnson and the kids were in the cafeteria eating lunch so she didn't have anyone to lean on for comfort. Tears filled Deidre's eyes, and she told the doctor, "I-I can't do it. You shouldn't be telling me to do it, either. Shouldn't you be in there trying to fix her?" Her voice elevated as she said, "Isn't this a hospital?"

The doctor guided Deidre over to a chair and helped her sit down. "Try to calm down. I'll have my nurse contact hospice because they will need us to provide a referral, anyway. We will let you know when the assessment nurse from hospice arrives. Is that okay?" he asked as if he were a hostage negotiator trying to keep the peace.

"Okay," Deidre said as she put her head in her hands and cried. She had spent a lot of time praying for God to heal Kenisha. Now that she supposedly had to face that the end was near, Deidre realized that she hadn't spent nearly enough time praying for Kenisha's salvation. Kenisha had been so resistant to the idea that Deidre had backed down the few times she had attempted to bring the subject up. Now Deidre worried that she had cost Kenisha an eternity in heaven.

"What happened?" Johnson asked as he rushed over to Deidre.

Deidre quickly tried to wipe the tears from her face as the kids walked over. "Hey," she said to the group.

"Is something wrong with my mom?" Jamal asked.

Deidre stood up and tried to calm her own shaking as she said, "She's not feeling well right now. But the doctor feels that she would receive better care if she were transferred to another hospital. The good thing about it is, all of us can be in the room with her anytime we want at this other hospital." Deidre tried her best to say those words in an upbeat manner. Like going to another hospital was like going to Disneyland.

Johnson mouthed the one word that answered everything, "Hospice?"

Deidre nodded. Then she asked Johnson, "Can you take the kids in to see Kenisha before they aren't allowed back there anymore? I need to call Aisha."

"Why wouldn't we be allowed back there?" Johnson asked.

"I've never been through this before, so I don't know if we would be able to have the kids back there when the nurse gets here or not, so can you please just take them now?" Deidre knew she sounded impatient with Johnson. She didn't mean to take this out on him, but he was available. She took her cell phone out of her purse and walked away from them.

Outside, Deidre took slow, deep breaths, trying to get a grip on the fact that she was losing a friend, and all the prayers in the world hadn't changed the situation. She looked to heaven and said, "I will trust You."

She opened her phone and dialed Aisha. When Aisha picked up, Deidre said, "I've got some bad news for you."

"No. No!" Aisha screamed. "I was just over there. Please don't tell me my sister is gone."

"No, she's not gone, Aisha. But we're at the hospital, and they are going to be moving her to hospice."

"Oh, my God," Aisha screamed again.

"Look, Aisha, I need to get back inside, but can you tell your mother and everyone else?"

"Yeah, okay," Aisha said.

Deidre hung up and then turned back toward the hospital. She'd give anything if she didn't have to go back in this place. She looked around, wanting to run—to act as if none of this was happening. Then as she silently prayed for strength, she went back into the hospital, went to the chapel, and prayed for Kenisha. "Please don't let her leave this earth without learning to forgive and accepting You as her Lord and Savior."

Kenisha was in and out of consciousness. She vaguely remembered seeing her children and Deidre and Johnson a few times during the day. She also remembered a bunch of people in white coats and light blue hospital uniforms coming in and out of her room. She couldn't say for sure, but she thought she had gone on a ride and then been placed in a different room than the one she had been in earlier. As she opened her eyes, it felt as if she were coming out of a fog. Her room was empty, which seemed strange to Kenisha because she could have sworn that a bunch of people had been surrounding her bed, talking to her. She hadn't been able to recognize the voices or even make out what they were saying, but she remembered the noise of people.

And now the room seemed so silent to her. Was this how death felt . . . empty and hollow? If this was how dying felt, she didn't like it at all.

Someone knocked on her door. Kenisha looked around, trying to find the door, then as it opened, a man peeked his head in. "You're finally awake," the man said.

As he opened the door wider, Kenisha saw that he had one of those white collars around his neck, and he was gripping a Bible in his hand like it was gold or something. "I just stopped by to see if you wanted prayer."

"A little late for that, aren't you, Reverend?" Kenisha said scornfully.

"It's never too late to pray. But I'm available if you just want to talk also."

Kenisha wanted to curse the man. She was dying. If God had wanted to help her, he could have done something to remove this cancer. But if she put the man out of her room, she would be stuck with the empty hollowness of her room, so she said, "Have a seat."

He sat down and said, "I'm Elder Lewis."

"All right, Elder Lewis. Why don't you tell me all about this good God of yours."

"I certainly can do that," he said with an enormous smile on his face. "What do you want to know?"

For a moment Kenisha couldn't think of anything she wanted to know about God. She thought she pretty much had Him pegged. But then she thought about the conversation she'd had with Kevin, Aisha, and Angelina the other day. She decided that this man was probably in a better position to answer than any of them. So she asked him, "Do you really think there's a heaven?"

"Yes" was all he said.

"That's not good enough, Elder Lewis. How do you know there is a heaven?"

"The Bible mentions heaven more than fifty times."

"Have you ever seen it?" Kenisha said skeptically.

"Have you ever seen Disney World?"

Rolling her eyes, Kenisha said, "No."

"But you believe it's there, don't you?"

"Well, of course. I know people who have gone."

"I know people who have gone to heaven," Elder Lewis countered.

"You can't say that for sure. Nobody has ever come back from heaven and told about it," Kenisha said as if she had studied the matter extensively and knew what she was talking about.

"All the people I know are smart. They don't want to come back from heaven once they get there. But there was a man who saw the ins and outs of heaven and wrote about it in the book of Revelation."

"Yeah, right," Kenisha said. Her skepticism was obvious.

Elder Lewis opened his Bible and flipped to Revelation. "If you don't mind, I'll read some of it to you."

Kenisha leaned back against her pillow. "Go ahead. It's not like I have anywhere to be or nothing."

He turned back to his Bible and began, "*I John, who also am your brother, and companion in tribulation, and in the kingdom and patience of Jesus Christ* . . ." He read from chapter 1 through chapter 7 of Revelation.

The seventh chapter of Revelation fascinated Kenisha. She asked Elder Lewis, "Do you really think that angels are up there bowing and worshiping God like the saints do at church?"

"I believe every word my Bible says, so I would have to say I do, indeed."

"That's got to be a sight to see." When the room was silent again, she turned to Elder Lewis and said, "You can read some more of your Bible if you want."

"I will, but first I'd like to know how you've been feeling about God since you got the news about your cancer?"

"Getting cancer didn't change my opinion of God. I've known He was unfair ever since I was nine years old."

"Do you mind my asking what happened when you were nine?"

Kenisha smirked. She was only too willing to let this good-tidings bringer know what a non-caring God he served. "My mother caught her boyfriend raping me and accused me of trying to steal him from her." Kenisha waited for the look of horror that was sure to appear on the man's face. Then she would let him in on a few other things. But the man's expression never changed.

All he did was say, "I know firsthand that life is hard sometimes. I was molested as a child myself. It took me a long time to get over what happened."

"Then you should agree with me. If God does exist, He is the most unfair person in the universe. Right?"

"No, sorry, Kenisha, I don't agree with you on that. You see, I came to find that God is loving and He is kind. The God I serve wants to take away all the pain and suffering that this cruel world inflicts on us."

Kenisha lay there for a moment, thinking about Elder Lewis's words. She could tell that he truly believed what he said. But the jury was still out for her. She turned to Elder Lewis and said, "I used to pray for God to take away my pain and suffering, but He's been a long time coming."

30

Frank Thomas called as Deidre was getting the kids ready to go visit their mother. "Are you coming to work today?" he asked snidely.

"No, the kids are out for winter break, so I gave my staff the day off."

"I didn't okay any day off for you or your staff."

"No, sir, you didn't. But I have family obligations that I have to take care of today, and there was no need for my staff to come in if I wasn't going to be there."

"And when do you plan to get the reports together that I need?"

Sighing deeply, Deidre said, "I'll come in on weekends if I have to, Dr. Thomas. You'll have your reports, but I can't come into the office today."

"You know what I think?" Frank Thomas asked.

"No, I don't." *But I'm sure you'll tell me.*

"I think you don't want to write that report on Shameka Nickels. It's going to be hard to explain how you called Children's Services on a woman who filed a complaint against you."

"Are you kidding me? I did my job. That woman broke her son's arm. She deserves whatever she gets."

"Well, let me tell you this, Mrs. Morris. You have missed quite a bit of work here lately. You are not setting a good example for your teachers or your office staff. I'm getting complaints every time I turn around about your behavior. So if you don't get yourself in to work today, I'm going to write you up."

Deidre had worked for numerous school systems and had held different positions, but she had always received glowing reviews and had never been written up for anything. Six months earlier, a threat like that would have caused Deidre to drop everything she had planned and hightail it back to work so she could continue to make a good impression. But life wasn't just about her and Johnson anymore. She had to think about Jamal, Diamond, and Kennedy. So she said, "Do what you have to do, Dr. Thomas. I'm going to spend the day with my family like I planned."

She hung up the phone and finished getting the kids ready to go to hospice. The doorbell rang and Deidre wanted to scream. She told the kids, "Grab your coats," as she opened the door. Dwayne Smalls, Kenisha's father, stood on her porch. Deidre was so relieved that this man had finally come to see his daughter. He was almost too late. "Kenisha's not here. She's at hospice. But we're on our way to visit with her. You can follow me if you'd like."

"I know she's not here. Martha came to my restaurant begging me for the money to bury her. But I'm not giving that woman another dime to go buy a beer with."

"But I thought you told me that you would pay for the funeral," Deidre said, looking dumbfounded by the callousness of this man.

He lifted the envelope that was in his hand. "Here's the money I promised. You should be able to give her a decent burial with that. I don't want anybody saying people had to go door-to-door begging for money to bury my daughter."

Deidre took the check, but she wasn't going to let this man off the hook that easily. "It would mean a lot to Kenisha if you would go see her."

"I told you before, I can't do that. Just call and let me know when and where the funeral will be. My number is in the envelope also." With that, he turned and walked away.

Deidre was burning up. She had never had a violent streak, but she wanted to attack this heartless man. She wanted to jump on his back and beat some sense into his head. She was still seething when she walked into Kenisha's room, so she sat down and began reading forgiveness scriptures while the kids talked to Kenisha.

When the kids sat down and started watching television, Kenisha turned to Deidre and said, "This man came to my room last night and read to me out of the book of Revelation."

Deidre was excited, but she tried not to let it show. She just hoped and prayed that God was answering her prayer and that Kenisha would come to know Him before she died. "Why'd he read out of Revelation?"

"We were talking about heaven and whether it really existed or not. So he wanted to prove to me that this dude named John had seen heaven and wrote about it in the Bible."

"So did he convince you of anything?" Deidre asked slowly.

"The Bible reading was all right. I didn't have anything else to do. But I still have my doubts." Kenisha pointed at Deidre's Bible. "What are you reading?"

Deidre feared that if she admitted to being angry and needing to forgive, Kenisha might think badly of her and then she wouldn't be willing to listen to anything else Deidre had to say.

But then again, Deidre didn't want to lie, so she said, "I've been looking up some scriptures on forgiving."

Laughing, Kenisha said, "What happened? Did Johnson make you mad or something?"

"Johnson always makes me mad," Deidre said jokingly.

"Well, let me hear some of what you're reading. Maybe it will help me forgive a few people." Kenisha propped herself up in bed and prepared herself for another Bible study.

"Well, I've read through several, but the one that really stuck out for me today was in Matthew when Jesus is talking about prayer. The scriptures that helped me see things the way God would see them, concerning forgiveness, were in Matthew, chapter 6, verses 9-15.

"After this manner therefore pray ye: Our Father which art in heaven, Hallowed be thy name. Thy Kingdom come. Thy will be done in earth, as it is in heaven. Give us this day our daily bread. And forgive us our debts, as we forgive our debtors.

"And lead us not into temptation but deliver us from evil: For thine is the kingdom, and the power, and the glory, for ever. Amen. For if ye forgive men their trespasses, your heavenly Father will also forgive you: But if ye forgive not men their trespasses, neither will your Father forgive your trespasses."

Kenisha's eyes were closed as Deidre finished reading. Deidre thought she had fallen asleep, so she closed her Bible and stood up to go to the restroom.

When Deidre sat back down, Kenisha said, "Do you think that's how it really works?"

"What?" Deidre asked, not sure if Kenisha was talking in her sleep or not, since her eyes were still closed.

"Do you really have to forgive others in order for God to forgive you?"

"I think you do. That's why I was reading those scriptures, to remind myself that I don't have a right to hold unforgiveness against anyone. Not when God has forgiven me for everything I've ever done wrong."

Deidre waited for Kenisha to respond, but when Kenisha started snoring, Deidre knew for sure that she was asleep this time. That's when the doubts came pouring in. Had she picked the right scripture to read? Had she answered her question right? Why hadn't she told Kenisha about salvation? Instead of dealing with her little forgiveness issue, she could just as easily have turned her Bible to John 3:16-17. But she had allowed Kenisha's father to get under her skin and make her lose focus. Deidre just hoped that God would give her a little more time. She lifted her head heavenward and silently prayed, "Please, Lord, don't let her die without confessing You as her savior."

"Why is she sleeping so much?" Diamond asked as she came back over to Kenisha's bed.

"She's tired, honey. But don't worry, we're going to stay here all day. So, when she's awake, you'll be able to talk to her. Okay?"

"Okay, but she sure is tired an awful lot."

Deidre lifted Diamond into her lap. She gave the little girl a hug. She planned to give her lots of hugs in the weeks, months, and years ahead. "Do you remember when your mom told you about her illness?"

Diamond nodded.

"Well, this is just part of the sickness. It makes her so tired that she has to sleep. But while she's sleeping, she's not in any pain. And that's good news, right?"

"Right," Diamond said and then jumped off Deidre's lap and danced back over to her brother and sister to draw some more Christmas pictures to tape to Kenisha's walls.

That's when Deidre thought about how she could bribe Kenisha to stay with them a little longer. She went over to the table and sat down with the kids and asked, "Hey, how would you guys like to bring the Christmas tree here?"

"What about the presents?" Jamal asked.

"Yes, of course, we'll bring the presents also. We can go to church on Christmas Eve, and then come here and spend the night. When we wake up on Christmas morning, you'll be able to open your presents with your mom. How about it?"

Diamond and Jamal jumped out of their seats and yelled, "Yes!"

A second later, Kennedy jumped up and mimicked her brother and sister, "Yes!"

Deidre walked back over to Kenisha's bed and whispered in her ear, "Did you hear that, Kenisha? We're going to spend Christmas with you. And I know you don't like to disappoint your kids, so you have to stay with us another week."

They put the tree up in her room, brought the presents, and then Deidre told her that she couldn't die until she had celebrated Christmas with her family. A tall order, since she was so weak all she could think about was closing her eyes and never opening them again. But her kids expected her to watch them open their presents on Christmas morning. So Kenisha was in a bargaining mood. She turned her face heavenward and did something she hadn't done in a long time—prayed. "I haven't talked to you in a long time. As I grew up, I started to think of You as this big, important being in the sky who didn't care what happened to the little people on earth. But Deidre keeps telling me that you do care. So I'm going to try You one last time. I'm not even going to ask You for my life, I know I'm dying . . . I can feel death closing in on me. But if you allow me to live to celebrate Christmas with my children, then I will give my life to You."

Kenisha knew that she wasn't really offering God a whole lot, seeing as she was dying and wouldn't be able to do much for Him on earth. But they had been keeping her drugged up, so she couldn't feel much of the pain. The drugs made her want to sleep, and during her sleep time, she'd been dreaming about heaven—streets of gold, angels bowing while people sang beautiful music. The place seemed so peaceful that Kenisha had actually decided to give heaven a second thought. But she couldn't go one more place without knowing for sure she was going to be cared for. So if God wanted her in heaven, He would have to prove it.

"Oh, and one more thing." Kenisha wasn't familiar with the proper protocol of praying. She just knew she had some things she wanted to talk to God about, so she was just going to say what was on her mind. "Could you answer one of Deidre's prayers, finally? I mean, come on, that woman really believes in You."

She turned over and went back to sleep. And as she began drifting, she realized that she was now going into an area that was very much the un-heaven. *Where am I going?* she wondered as she began to feel a strong gush of wind sweep in and knock her off her feet. She began swirling around and around this valley of dead people. *Oh my God*, she thought. *I am literally seeing dead people.*

She wanted to scream, but as she continued to swirl around and around, leeches began attaching themselves to her body. They covered every part of her as well as her mouth. Every time she reached up and pulled one off her mouth, another attached itself to her mouth so that she couldn't make a sound.

For some reason she was no longer just swirling around and around, but she was swirling and descending, swirling and descending. When her feet finally touched the ground, they landed on something sticky. Somehow Kenisha knew that she was standing on the blood of all those dead people she had seen while swirling her way into wherever she was. This was certainly not the heaven she had been dreaming about the past few days. This place felt hollow. Dreadful. Evil. Maybe she needed to rethink her whole strategy. Kenisha had thought that she would be doing God a favor if she forgave Him for His absentee Godship in her life. She had also thought that God would appreciate her being willing to live in heaven, but everything in her being told her that the place she was now standing in was the alternative. She would take that sweet, peaceful place she had been in over this horror show any day of the week.

"You belong here with me, Kenisha. You've been mine all your life. Don't change things now."

"Who said that?" Kenisha demanded. She hadn't belonged to anybody. Nobody had ever wanted her, not even God.

"Yes, that's right, Kenisha. You just keep remembering that God didn't do anything for you. Not when you were a kid, not when you had your own kids and the fathers left you one by one, and not when you got sick."

Whoever this person was who was whispering in her ear, he seemed to know a lot about her discontent. And he was right. She had been angry with God for a long time. Could she just let that anger go, even though God had never done a single thing for her?

"Don't let it go, Kenisha. You have a right to be angry with God. Just hold onto that anger a little longer and then you will be all mine. Stay here with me, and I will show you all. I'll show you things you've never even imagined."

"No!" Kenisha screamed. Something about this didn't seem right. She didn't want to belong to this man, whoever he was.

She started flailing her arms to get the leeches off so she could get out of this place. She didn't want to be here; she wanted the whirlwind to pick her back up and swirl her out of this sticky, hollow, dark place. But the wind wouldn't come, so she just kept fighting her way out.

31

What's going on? What's wrong with her?" Deidre asked as Kenisha thrashed uncontrollably around the bed. The monitors were flashing and beeping so fast, Deidre thought they were going to short out.

"She's having a seizure. This sometimes happens at the time of death," the attending nurse told her.

"Death! No. Christmas is two days away. She can't die right now. We're all spending Christmas together." Deidre's thinking was a bit irrational, considering that she didn't have the ability to grant life or death, but she leaned down and whispered in Kenisha's ear, anyway. "Calm down, Kenisha. Take deep breaths. We need you here for Christmas."

The noise from the monitors decreased. Her blood pressure level was coming down. The nurse said, "Keep talking to her. Maybe she's coming out of it."

"Johnson is on his way into the room with the kids. They brought presents for you. You have to be here to open them. Come on, Kenisha. I know you. You don't want to disappoint those kids, and I know it."

The thrashing stopped, and Kenisha slowly opened her eyes. When she saw Deidre standing over her, she said, "Thank God. Are the leeches gone?"

"What leeches?"

"They're all over me. They feel slimy," Kenisha said as she attempted to brush something out of her bed.

The nurse leaned over to Deidre and said, "Sometimes when patients are close to death, they have these out-of-body experiences. We can't explain it, but it looks like Kenisha has been somewhere she didn't want to be."

"I don't want to go back there," Kenisha said with tears in her eyes.

Deidre knew exactly where Kenisha had been. It was definitely time for the Roman's road-to-salvation talk.

"You don't have to," Deidre said as she sat down next to Kenisha and grabbed the girl's hands to stop her from trying to remove leeches. "You're safe now, Kenisha. You don't have any leeches on you."

"They weren't in heaven," Kenisha said as the horror of her experience finally began to subside.

"Who wasn't in heaven?" Deidre asked.

"The leeches. I didn't see them in heaven."

"When did you go to heaven?"

Kenisha shifted position as she turned toward Deidre. "I've been dreaming about heaven ever since that man and I talked about it. But the place I dreamed about today wasn't heaven at all. There was this voice in my ears, and he asked me to stay there with him. But it was too dark and too evil. Everybody was dead and their blood was all on the floor."

"Sorry it took us so long," Johnson said as he walked into the room with the kids. "They made me stop at the snack machines and buy them all sorts of unhealthy things."

Deidre had become so engrossed in Kenisha's retelling of her horrific experience she had forgotten that Johnson and the kids had been coming along behind her. She turned to her husband and said, "Babe, do you think you could eat that stuff with the kids in the waiting area? I was just getting ready to go over the Roman's road-to-salvation with Kenisha."

Johnson did an about-face. "Not a problem. Come on, kids. Let's go get some more junk."

Kenisha put her hands under her head as she asked, "What's this Roman's road thing about?"

"It's called the Roman's road-to-salvation because we can find a clear and detailed map for salvation and an eternal relationship with God in the Letter to the Romans. If you'll allow me, I'd like to read and explain these scriptures to you."

Kenisha nodded, giving Deidre permission to continue.

Thank you, God. Please keep her heart open to receiving You. "The first scriptures I want to read to you are found in Romans 1:20-21:

"For the invisible things of him from the creation of the world are clearly seen, being understood by the things that are made, even his eternal power and Godhead; so that they are without excuse: Because that, when they knew God, they glorified him not as God, neither were thankful; but became vain in their imaginations, and their foolish heart was darkened."

"So are you saying that because I didn't thank God for all the horrible things that happened to me, I now have to live in darkness?"

"No, Kenisha, that's not it. Let me keep going and then we can discuss. Okay?" Deidre said as she flipped over to Romans 3:23 and read: "*For all have sinned, and come short of the glory of God.*" She flipped some more pages and then read Romans 5:8: "*But God commended his love toward us, in that, while we were yet sinners, Christ died for us.*"

She then went to Romans 6:23: "*For the wages of sin is death; but the gift of God is eternal life through Jesus Christ our Lord.*"

Kenisha interrupted Deidre with a question: "So is that why I saw all those dead people? Was that a sign to me of what happens to people who die in their sins? Because the people in heaven seemed happy. There certainly wasn't any blood on the floor."

"I think God has blessed you with a unique ability to see into heaven and hell, and then make a choice as to which place you want to live out eternity. Most people don't get a sneak peek, Kenisha. So I'm hoping that you understand how special you are to God."

"I guess I don't understand how you can say that I'm special to God when I have suffered so much heartache."

"We all suffer from something, Kenisha. That's a part of life—since evil has come into the world, God has no choice but to let things play out, so that we can choose good over evil."

"But how do you choose good or evil? I don't understand." Kenisha said with a furrowed brow.

Smiling, Deidre said, "I'm glad you asked. That information is in the next two scriptures I want to read to you out of Romans, chapter 10: *If thou shalt confess with thy mouth the Lord Jesus, and shalt believe in thine heart that God hath raised him from the dead, thou shalt be saved. For with the heart man believeth unto righteousness; and with the mouth confession is made unto salvation . . . For whosoever shall call upon the name of the Lord shall be saved.*"

"So accepting good over evil is more like accepting God into your heart, and all you have to do to accomplish that is admit you have sinned, ask forgiveness, and believe that Jesus Christ is the Son of God and that God raised him from the dead. That's it."

Kenisha opened her mouth to ask another question, but that's when the party got crashed. Kevin, Aisha, and her four children burst into the room singing Christmas songs.

"Hey," Kenisha said as she looked at her family.

"Hey, yourself," Kevin said as he set his boom box down. "We thought you could use a little cheering up, so we brought the Christmas carolers over here to sing to you about Rudolph, Frosty, and the First Noel."

Kenisha smiled and the door burst open again, and Johnson and the kids came back in.

Jamal said, "We want to sing too."

"Well, come on, boy. Anyone can join this singing group," Kevin told him.

Deidre was smiling on the outside as the kids began to sing, but inwardly she worried that she might have missed another opportunity to close the deal. And she didn't know how many more chances she would have to talk to Kenisha about God.

"Y'all sound so good. Y'all should go door-to-door, every Christmas, singing for people," Kenisha said as she began to doze off again. She wanted to pull herself awake because she didn't know if she was going to drift into a nice place or a dark and evil place. But she was so tired that she couldn't make her eyelids stay open. As she drifted further and further into sleep, Kenisha began to see snapshots of Martha's life. She watched as one man after the next walked into her house and then walked out, taking a piece of her with him.

Kenisha's mind's eye focused on Martha sitting on a porch step, smoking a cigarette. She looked young, like she was in her twenties. A little girl ran up to her with a bruised knee. Kenisha quickly realized that that little girl was her. She remembered the incident. She had been five years old, and Billy Wilson had pushed her down on the playground. She'd run all the way home to tell her mama.

When Martha saw her, she put her cigarette down and pulled Kenisha into her arms. "What happened, baby?"

Kenisha pulled away so she could show Martha her knee. She pointed at it and said, "Billy knocked me down."

Martha picked Kenisha up and took her inside. She got a washcloth and wiped away the blood from Kenisha's knee. She held the cloth there until the bleeding stopped, and then she bent her head and kissed Kenisha's knee. "There. See, Mama made it all better."

Suddenly, Kenisha was at her ninth birthday party. Martha had made her a cake and had boiled hot dogs for her guests. But the big deal of the day came when Martha rolled a brand-new pink bike into the living room. It had a bow on it, so Kenisha knew it was hers. She jumped out of her seat and ran to the bike. She looked at Martha with a gleam in her eyes and said, "Is it really mine?"

"All yours, baby. I hope you like it." Martha gave her a hug and then whispered in her ear, "I love you."

That was the last time Kenisha remembered her mother hugging her or saying that she loved her. Soon after that party was when Martha had discovered that Jimmy Davis had been molesting her. Kenisha thought that Martha would come to her rescue, and then things would go back to the way they had been. But although Martha threw Jimmy out, things never went back to normal. It felt to Kenisha as though Martha blamed her for yet another man leaving her. But it hadn't been Kenisha's fault. All these years, Kenisha had wanted to know why Martha hadn't stood up for her. Why hadn't Jimmy been prosecuted for what he did? Why hadn't Martha loved her more than she had loved that monster?

When she woke again, Kevin and Aisha were still there. She waved them over to her bed.

"What's up, sis?" Aisha asked.

"I want to see my mother," Kenisha said.

Kevin and Aisha exchanged stunned glances.

"You sure about that, Ke-Ke?" Kevin asked. "She's been hoping that you would ask to see her."

"Yes. I'm sure. Bring her here on Christmas Eve."

32

Deidre's mother arrived on the morning of Christmas Eve. Loretta then spent the day helping Deidre prepare the Christmas meal that they were going to take to hospice with them the next day. The plan was that the children would go to church with them tonight, then Deidre and Johnson would drop them off at hospice so they could spend the night with Kenisha and the rest of their family, because Kevin, Angelina, Aisha, and her children were all planning to spend the night. Aisha told Deidre that she believed Martha was going to spend the night as well, but that all depended on whether Kenisha threw her out of the room.

Deidre was going to come back home and spend the rest of Christmas Eve with Johnson and her mother. Then in the morning they would pack up the food and head out to hospice to enjoy Christmas with the rest of their family. For that is how Deidre felt. She had truly bonded with Kenisha's family and hoped that they would want to be a continuing part of the children's lives.

"Okay, the sweet potato pies are in the oven, now what?" Loretta asked her daughter as they stood in the kitchen.

"I think that's everything. Let's go sit down for a little while, I'm tired," Deidre said. They stretched out on the sectional in the family room and listened to the Christmas music that was softly playing on the radio. Johnson had taken the kids out to see the Christmas decorations throughout the neighborhood. "Thanks for coming, Mom. I can't tell you how glad I am to have you here with us."

"I wouldn't have missed this for anything in the world. I got a chance to meet my grandchildren. I saw Johnson's smiling face, and tomorrow I get to meet Kenisha."

Deidre yawned. "I wish you could have met her before now, and then you could have seen just what a vibrant person she was. This illness has taken its toll on her. She's pretty weak now. I'm just praying that she'll live through tomorrow. I don't want the kids to remember Christmas as the day their mother died."

"That's a worthy thing to pray for. So I'll join my faith with yours on that," Loretta said.

"Thanks, Mom," Deidre said, then asked, "Is Michelle okay with you being here? Aren't the kids going to miss you?"

"Rod's mom is coming down for Christmas. So the kids will have a grandma there for them. She's just not as much fun as I am, though," Loretta said with a chuckle.

Deidre was thrilled that her mom had come to visit, especially while she and Johnson were going through so many changes. She needed the extra support, but she didn't want her nieces and nephews to be without their NaNa. So it made Deidre feel so much better to know that Michelle's mother-in-law would be there for the grandkids.

She dozed off and when she opened her eyes, Jamal and Diamond were jumping up and down in front of her saying, "Get up, get up!"

"W-what's wrong?" Deidre said as she jumped off the couch. *Lord, please don't tell me that Kenisha is gone. Not yet, Lord, please.* "Did something happen?"

"Calm down, De," Johnson said as he came into the room. "The kids are just wanting to get to church so they can see the Christmas play and then go to hospice for the sleepover with their cousins."

"Oh, okay. Let me go upstairs and get dressed. Give me twenty minutes."

"Twenty minutes?" Diamond said, as if Deidre had asked for six months.

"Yes, twenty minutes. Now, go in the kitchen and get a snack. I'll be back before you know it." Deidre headed up the stairs thanking God for yet another day of Kenisha living on earth.

Pastor Monroe was behind the pulpit welcoming the visitors when they arrived. Loretta had only attended their church once before. That was the first year that Deidre and Johnson had joined the ministry.

So Loretta stood up and proudly announced, "My name is Loretta Clark, and I am Deidre Morris's mother. I am so happy to be here celebrating Christmas with her, my son-in-law, and my new grandchildren." Loretta picked Kennedy up and hugged her as she retook her seat.

When the service ended and Deidre and Johnson prepared to leave, Deidre was feeling pretty good about her newfound freedom. So good in fact that when Mother Barrow came over to them, Deidre reached out and hugged the woman. "Merry Christmas, Mother Barrow. We haven't seen you around here in a while. Have you been okay?"

"I was in Maryland, visiting my son and his wife for Thanksgiving. I stayed on until last week."

"Well, it's nice to have you back," Johnson told her.

Deidre then introduced her mother to Mother Barrow.

Mother Barrow told Loretta, "It's nice to meet you. But I came over here to get a good look at these children." She looked at Jamal, Diamond, and Kennedy as if studying them.

She then turned to Deidre and said, "Yep, these are the children that God showed me you would have, but I must say, I thought they would come one at a time." Mother Barrow laughed at herself. "Isn't that just like God? He only lets us see what he wants us to see."

Johnson picked up Kennedy as he told Mother Barrow, "We're adopting them, but they're ours just the same."

Mother Barrow smiled as she asked, "Is the baby in the nursery?"

"What baby?" Deidre asked with a raised eyebrow.

"God showed me four kids. The smallest was a baby."

Deidre and Johnson glanced at each other questioningly. Okay, Deidre acknowledged that Mother Barrow had been right about the fact that they would become parents. But a fourth child? Would the courts let them adopt another child so soon after applying for the adoption of three at one time?

Mother Barrow put her hand on Deidre's stomach and closed her eyes. When she opened them, she said, "God didn't leave me wondering on this one. He's in there."

Johnson started ushering the kids out of the pew as he told Mother Barrow, "Good to have you back, but we need to get going. The kids have a sleepover to get to."

"Are you okay?" Johnson asked Deidre as they got in the car.

Deidre saw the look of concern in her husband's eyes. He was worried that she was going to flip out over Mother Barrow's prediction that she was pregnant. But Deidre had already passed through that storm, and she had learned to trust God. She wasn't running off to the drugstore to buy a pregnancy test or begin worrying that her period was going to show up any minute and dispute the prediction. If Mother Barrow was right, Deidre would be happy for the addition to their family; if she was wrong, it would not steal her joy. She told Johnson, "I am more than okay. I'm blessed to have all of you in my life." She then turned and looked toward the backseat and asked the kids, "So are you ready for your sleepover?"

"Yes!" they said in unison.

They drove the kids to hospice. Johnson took their sleeping bags out of the back of the truck and walked the kids in. Deidre latched onto her mother's arm as they slowly walked into the building. "I'm proud of you, Deidre. You have grown through this experience. You seem so content and self-assured."

Deidre patted Loretta's arm. "Thank you for saying that, Mom. None of this has been easy. And I really can't say how it happened, but I have truly learned to rest in Jesus."

As they walked into Kenisha's room, Deidre noted that Aisha, Kevin, and Angelina were all there, along with Aisha's children. But she didn't see Martha. While Loretta was meeting everyone, Deidre pulled Aisha to the side and said, "I thought you were going to bring Martha."

Aisha looked a bit embarrassed as she admitted, "I was, but when I got over there to pick her up, she was drunk. She claimed that she was drinking because she was so upset about Kenisha. But I told her I wouldn't bring her here in that condition."

"But Kenisha wants to see her," Deidre reminded Aisha. Matter of fact, Deidre believed that Kenisha needed to see her mother.

"Not like that, she doesn't. If I brought Martha here drunk, Kenisha would probably use all the strength she has left to tell both of us off." Aisha shook her head. "I just couldn't spoil Kenisha's last Christmas like that."

"Do you mind if I go pick Martha up?" Deidre asked as an idea struck her. Before she retired, Loretta had worked for Alcoholics Anonymous. She had had one of the highest success rates in the program. Deidre believed that was largely due to the fact that she told her clients about Jesus. Maybe God had sent Loretta down here this Christmas for Martha.

"Be my guest. Just don't bring her here drunk." Aisha walked away.

On the drive over to Martha's house, it started snowing. "Look at that," Johnson said. "The kids are going to have a white Christmas."

"And if God is merciful, they'll have this one last Christmas with their mother," Deidre said hopefully.

Johnson pulled up in front of Martha's house. "I'll go get her. Lock the doors and wait for me to come back out with her," he said as if he were planning a mission with his soldiers. He knocked on the front door, and to his surprise it opened. Martha had not closed her door all the way, so it had just eased open with Johnson's heavy-handed knock.

"W-who is it?" Martha slurred as she sat up on the couch.

"It's Johnson Morris, ma'am. I'm Deidre's husband."

"Oh, the people who are taking my grandkids away from me."

"We want to take you to see your grandkids and your daughter. Will you come with us?"

"Aisha said I was too much of a disgrace to go and see my own daughter," Martha said and then lay back down.

"No, now, don't go to sleep on me, Ms. Carson." Johnson entered the apartment and helped Martha sit back up. "Do you want to see Kenisha?"

At the mention of Kenisha's name, Martha began to cry. She wrapped her arms around herself and said, "I want to see my baby. But my baby don't want to see me."

"That's not true, Ms. Carson. Kenisha has asked for you. She very much wants to see you."

Martha looked up, hope creasing the corners of her eyes. "She does?"

"Yes, she does. Now I'm going to go get my wife so she can help you get a change of clothes together. We're going to take you to our house so you can get some coffee and some sleep. We'll take you to Kenisha in the morning, okay?"

Martha nodded and then said, "Thank you."

Deidre came in and helped Martha pick out an outfit and underclothes to change into. Then they drove home.

Deidre fixed a pot of coffee while Loretta and Martha sat at the kitchen counter talking. The two women talked as if they had known each other for years, but Loretta had always had that effect on people. She firmly believed that loving-kindness drew people in. It didn't matter who the person was, Loretta loved them and treated them with kindness and respect.

When the coffee was ready, Loretta cut into one of the sweet potato pies and gave Martha a slice. "This pie is good. The coffee ain't bad, either," Martha said.

"There's plenty more where that came from, so just let us know when you need a refill," Deidre told her, because in truth she thought it would take at least three cups to get Martha on the road to being somewhat sober.

"Thanks. You all are good people. I can see why Kenisha wanted you to take care of the kids. I just hope I get to see them from time to time."

"Johnson and I aren't trying to take the kids away from you. We want them to remain connected with all of you. I think Kenisha would want that also," Deidre told the woman.

Martha shook her head. "She don't want me around my grandkids. She thinks I drink too much. But I wasn't always like this." She lowered her head and started crying.

Deidre started to say something, but Loretta shook her head. She pushed the coffee cup in front of Martha and remained silent.

Martha drank the coffee and then said, "If it wasn't for that lowdown Jimmy Davis, I would have a better relationship with all of my kids. He owes me, but he never even said he was sorry." She took another sip of her coffee. "But like I told Kevin, God will get him."

"Ms. Carson, I hope this doesn't come off the wrong way, but why didn't you have him arrested?" Deidre asked.

"I thought about it," Martha said. "But Angelina hadn't done nothing to nobody, and she needed child support. Jimmy wouldn't have been able to provide for Angelina if he was locked up."

Deidre opened her mouth to condemn the woman for being so selfish, but again Loretta admonished her to keep quiet.

Martha said, "I thought I did the right thing. But I haven't stopped drinking since that monster did those awful things to my baby. Kenisha thinks that I was drunk when it was happening to her, but that isn't true. I started having problems getting to sleep, so Jimmy gave me these sleeping pills. But I never imagined that he was pumping me with sleeping pills so that he could rape my children."

They talked for several hours. Once Deidre started yawning, Loretta suggested that her daughter go upstairs with her husband while the two grannies retired to the family room. Deidre brought pillows and comforters to them and then asked, "Are you sure you don't want to sleep upstairs in the kids' bedrooms?"

"We're fine down here. We'll probably watch some Christmas movies until we fall asleep," Loretta said.

"Okay, see you in the morning," Deidre said as she went back to her bedroom.

She woke Johnson up. "I need to talk."

Rubbing the sleep from his eyes, he said, "What's up?"

"Before talking to Martha, I was condemning her as much as Kenisha does, but my heart goes out to Martha because I can see that she is in a lot of pain."

"From what you told me about their family situation, it sounds like Martha has a lot to be in pain about."

Deidre had only been looking at this from Kenisha's side. But Martha had to live with the knowledge that she was partly to blame for what happened to Kenisha and Kevin when they were children. Then she had to live through the murder of one of her children, and now she would have to stand by and watch Kenisha die. It's easy to judge, but much harder to walk in another person's shoes. "I'm nervous about taking Martha to see Kenisha tomorrow. I don't want Kenisha to disrespect her mother. That's just going to take her ten steps back from where she needs to be. And I've been praying fervently that Kenisha would learn to forgive and accept Jesus into her heart."

"Kenisha wants to see her mother, right?"

"Yes. I am positive of that."

"Well, then, let's pray about that and ask God to mend this mother/daughter relationship. And maybe in the process, it will even help ease some of Martha's pain."

They held hands and bowed their heads in prayer, confident that God was faithful to do exceedingly and abundantly more than they could ever hope for.

33

Kenisha was visiting with Dynasty again. It was just the two of them, and they were having a good time, laughing and joking like old times. One of Dynasty's favorite songs came on the radio, and she got up and started dancing around the room. That girl loved to dance, and Kenisha wanted to sit there and watch her forever. But then Clyde burst into the room, barking orders and pulling Dynasty away from her.

Kenisha stood up and grabbed Dynasty's arm. "Don't go with him, Dy. I'm afraid for you."

"I have to, sis. But stop blaming yourself. It's not your fault," Dynasty said as Clyde's grip tightened.

Kenisha wasn't ready to let go. So she tried to pull Dynasty back, but Clyde's grip was too strong. He pulled Dynasty away from her, and Kenisha stood watching as Dynasty waved good-bye to her. It was over, and she was not to blame for it, Kenisha finally realized as she watched Dynasty move farther and farther away from her. Clyde was to blame—him and him alone. From now on, Dynasty's death would be on his head. She wouldn't share the blame of it with him another day.

Kenisha heard her kids screaming at her to wake up. A simple thing for most people to do, but to reenter the world from her drug-induced state was getting harder and harder to do. However, today was Christmas, and Kenisha wouldn't miss sharing this day with her family for anything in the world. Slowly her eyes fluttered open, and she managed a weak smile.

"It's Christmas, Mommy! Here, open your present," Diamond said while shoving a box wrapped in shining green paper at Kenisha.

Aisha said, "Hold on, Diamond. Let me lift up your mother's bed so she can sit up and enjoy this day with the rest of us."

"Thank you," Kenisha said to Aisha as she raised her bed into a sitting position. To Kenisha, her voice sounded hollow.

Aisha smiled as a tear rolled down her face.

"Do I look that bad?" Kenisha asked, trying to lighten the mood.

"No, sis, I'm just glad to have you with us on Christmas." Aisha then added, "But I am getting ready to brush your hair. Good Lord, girl, it's all over your head."

Kenisha took the present from Diamond, but she could barely lift her arms to open it. Aisha came back to the bed with a comb and brush. "Can you open this for me?" Kenisha asked her sister.

Kevin got up. "I'll open your presents and show them to you while Aisha does your hair." He took the present out of Kenisha's hand, unwrapped it, and then held it up for all to see.

"A butterfly bracelet. How sweet," Kenisha said as she smiled at Diamond.

"Put it on, Mommy."

"Can you put it on my wrist, Kevin?" Kenisha asked.

"Sure thing, sis."

Kevin put the bracelet on Kenisha. She saw him look away from her as his eyes became glassy. He was trying to be strong for her, but Kenisha understood. It's hard to say good-bye. He would miss her, and although Kenisha wasn't sure what happened in eternity, she hoped that she would always remember her family.

Jamal came over to her bed. "I got you something too, Mama."

"Thank you, baby."

Kevin opened the package and pulled out an angel figurine. The angel wore a pure white gown, and she had golden wings. Kenisha touched the angel, and let her fingers trace the length of the robe.

"I know you don't like church, Mama. But I still want you to go to heaven. And I figured this angel could help you get there," Jamal said as Kevin lifted him up so he could hug his mother.

She kissed her son on the cheek and held onto him as long as she could. As he backed away, Kenisha tried to hold on, but there was no way she could. To never see her babies again was worse than death. She wanted to beg him not to forget her. Diamond and Kennedy were so young that Kenisha didn't think they would remember much about her. But Jamal was different. He had spent more time with her than any of them. He would remember . . . please, God, let him remember.

"Look at this," Kenisha said as she wiped the tears from her face. "Y'all got me crying. This is supposed to be a happy day. Don't give me any more presents. I want to watch everyone else open theirs. So go get 'em."

No sooner had Kenisha said the words than her children and Aisha's children started grabbing the presents from under the tree and acting like normal, greedy kids on Christmas morning. When they had opened all the presents, Deidre and Johnson walked into the room carrying a trash bag full of more presents.

"Ho, ho, ho," Johnson said in his jolliest voice.

Kenisha watched as Deidre and Johnson were mobbed by the kids. The door to Kenisha's room opened again, and Loretta walked in. Then right behind her Kenisha saw Martha. Her eyes lit up like they hadn't since she was a child. She had wanted to see Martha so bad that Kenisha had been about to ask Aisha to go get her. She stretched out her arms, saying, "Mama!"

Martha ran into Kenisha's arms and hugged her. When they parted, she said, "You haven't called me Mama in a long, long time. I like the way that sounded coming off your lips."

Kenisha didn't smell alcohol on her mother's breath, and for that she was thankful. But whether she had been drunk or not, Kenisha would have wanted to see her. This was her mother, the only one she would ever have. "I'm glad you came."

"Me too, baby." Martha started crying as she hugged Kenisha again. "I'm so sorry for everything that happened to you. I wish I had been a better mother to you."

Kenisha put her finger against Martha's lips. "Enough of that," she told Martha. "I learned something while I've been lying in this bed dozing in and out. Plain and simple, I need to forgive myself for Dynasty, and you need to forgive yourself for what happened to me."

Martha shook her head as if to say she couldn't do it.

"Life is too short, Mama. I forgive you. Now, if you want to do something for me, then stop drinking and be there for my kids."

"I will, baby. I promise you," Martha said.

The day was beautiful. The children played with their toys while the grown-ups played board games. They all ate the food Deidre and Loretta had fixed. Then Jamal came over to her and whispered, "We're going to make you some snow angels." He left the room with Diamond and two of his cousins.

Kevin and Johnson helped Kenisha into a chair by the window so she could watch the children make their angels. She watched them lie down in the snow and then flap their arms to make the wings. When the children got up and ran back inside, Kenisha stared at those beautiful snow images of angels. She didn't know if her eyes were playing tricks on her or not, but the images glistened. She was captivated, because it felt as if those snow angels were trying to tell her something. And that's when she remembered that she had one more thing to do.

They put her back in her bed, and as evening rolled in she told everyone that she needed to be alone and asked that they come back in the morning.

When her room was empty, Kenisha tightened her grip on the angel Jamal had given her and then turned her face toward heaven and smiled. "I got to spend Christmas with my family," she told the Lord as if He didn't already know it. "Thank You for helping me find a wonderful home for my children, but now I need a home. I've never really felt like I was special or that I really belonged anywhere." Kenisha could feel her body giving out, so she knew the end was near. Deidre had helped her believe that God loved her, and now she wanted God to know that she loved Him. "I know now that, just as it wasn't my fault what happened to Dynasty, what happened to me wasn't Your fault, either. And I'm so sorry for blaming You. Please forgive me for everything I've said or done to You or anyone else, and allow me to live in heaven with You forever."

The call came at five in the morning. Deidre called Aisha to make sure that the people at hospice had notified them—they had. She ran around the room frantically grabbing a shoe here, a sock there. She pulled on a pair of jeans and then threw on a sweater. Johnson grabbed her and pulled her into his arms. Holding her close, he said, "It's going to be all right, baby."

Deidre couldn't hold back the tears. She cried in his arms as she admitted, "This is hard, Johnson. This is so hard."

"I know, baby, but we've just got to believe that Kenisha will be out of pain and in a better place soon."

"Will she, Johnson? That's what worries me the most. I've been trying to help Kenisha accept the Lord as her Savior, but it hasn't sunk in yet. I'm afraid that it might be too late now."

"Where is your faith?" Johnson asked as he left the room to go wake the kids up.

"He's right," Deidre told herself. "God can do the impossible, and I just need to keep the faith." Deidre helped Johnson get the kids dressed and rushed them to the car.

Once they were in the car and headed to the hospital, Deidre decided to make one more phone call. When Dwayne Smalls picked up, sounding groggy and like the world was bothering him, she said, "This is your last chance. You need to get to the hospital to see your daughter now or regret it for the rest of your life." She hung up, hoping that he would do the right thing.

Deidre tried to remain calm, but then she heard Jamal's soft sobs. "We'll be there in a minute, Jamal. Your mama is waiting to see you."

"What if she dies before we get there? I forgot to tell her that I loved her yesterday," Jamal said with regret in his voice.

"She knows, baby," Deidre said, trying to comfort the boy. But she knew how he felt. She hadn't had much time to talk to Kenisha yesterday, either. Deidre's prayer now was that God had had a chance to talk to her.

When they arrived, Johnson and Deidre helped the kids out of the car. They ran down the hall toward Kenisha's room. When they opened the door, Deidre noted that Martha, Aisha,

Kevin, and Angelina were standing around Kenisha's bed praying.

Angelina was leading the prayer. "Lord, I am thankful that You have allowed me to get to know You while I live here on earth, but I'm asking You to receive my sister, so that she can meet You face-to-face. In Jesus' name I pray, amen."

"No!" Jamal shouted. "Stop praying over her like that." He pushed his aunts aside and stood next to his mother's bed. Kenisha's breathing had slowed, and she looked as if she was only half with them. But Jamal wasn't ready. He had to stop this . . . this dying that his mother was doing, so he blurted out, "Don't die, Mama. I swear I'll stop going to church if you just don't die."

Somehow Kenisha found the strength to turn to her son. She wearily put her hand to his mouth and painstakingly said, "Don't . . . say . . . things like that. I made my . . . peace with God. Make your peace . . . Meet me on the other side."

Hearing her friend's confession of faith, Deidre stepped closer to the bed. She put her hand on Kenisha's shoulder and said, "Thank You, God. Thank You."

As though looking far off, Kenisha said, "Not . . . caterpillar. Got my wings."

Tears bubbled in Deidre's eyes as she remembered the day Kenisha had told her that she felt like an ugly caterpillar but had dreamed of becoming a butterfly. The journey this caterpillar had taken in order to get her wings had been a hard one. But she would suffer no more. "Then fly away, my friend. We will meet again some day, I promise you."

As Deidre said those words, the door to Kenisha's room opened and Dwayne Smalls entered. He walked over to Kenisha's bed with hat in hand and tears streaming down his face.

"D . . . daddy," were the last words Kenisha said as her chest heaved, and then she died with a smile on her face.

EPILOGUE

Come up here and be my beloved."

Kenisha heard the words, but wasn't sure who had said it. Her body was on the bed, and her family stood around her crying. She wanted to tell them to stop crying over that body on the bed, because she wasn't there anymore. She was right here, only she didn't know where "here" was. And then as if someone was serenading her, she heard the words again.

"Come up here and be my beloved."

She turned toward the voice, and then as if she had wings, she began to move up higher and higher until there was no comprehension of height. When she stopped moving, Kenisha found herself standing before the most magnificent, pearl-laden gates, and as she stepped forward, the gates opened.

At first she didn't want to go in because she was self-conscious about being in her hospital gown, but then she remembered that Aisha had combed and brushed her hair, so she didn't feel like a total freak. As she entered the gates, Kenisha was swept away in an overwhelming feeling of love. She marveled that any single place on earth could make her feel this wonderful. And that's when she remembered, she wasn't on earth anymore—she was in heaven.

Two women walked over to her. One smiled at her as she helped Kenisha out of her hospital gown. The other woman helped her put on a white robe, which was brighter than any white she'd ever seen before. Directly behind the pearly gates was a massive space where a cushion of snowy-white clouds caressed the feet of its occupants. The tree of life stood bold and beautiful in the middle of the outer court. Its leaves were a heavenly green, and she knew its fruit was succulent and enjoyed by all. Sweet, blissful music could be heard throughout the great expanse of heaven. It was the harp, but it was better than any harp on earth; it was the guitar, but it was better than any guitar on earth.

There were thousands upon thousands of people moving through the joys of heaven, clothed in glistening white robes, and with bare feet. But what struck Kenisha was how happy and contented everyone seemed. There didn't appear to be any boogiemen in heaven. For the first time since she was a small child, Kenisha let her guard down and enjoyed the beauty of her surroundings without wondering what might be lurking just around the corner.

During her first days there she walked around heaven, taking in as much as she possibly could. There was just so much to see, and all of it was good. Just about everywhere she went, there were fields and fields of beautiful red flowers, which represented the blood Jesus shed for the sins of the world. Some days Kenisha walked through those fields of flowers. Other days she danced through them with the joy of a blood-bought servant of Christ.

One day as she was taking her walk through the field of flowers, an angel came to her and said, "Come with me. The One who was, and is forevermore, would like to see you."

If Kenisha had seen an angel on earth, she probably would have run the other way. But she wasn't afraid of these mammoth-sized beings now, because she saw them everywhere she went. She talked with the other occupants of heaven all the time, but she didn't get to speak with the angels much, because they were busy with their God-given assignments. So to be walking with an angel made Kenisha feel special.

In truth though, she found something that made her feel special every day. Like the time she visited the room of tears and discovered that she had been on God's mind. Even when she was going through her darkest moments, the Lord had cared enough to bottle her tears. The day when she had joined the praise choir had been pretty special also. Kenisha had never imagined that she would one day be singing praises to God, but she was and she enjoyed it.

The door to the Holy Place was opened, and the angel stepped aside. Her Lord stood up and held out a hand to her. "Come to Me, beloved."

There were those words again. Whenever she heard them, it was like being wrapped in a warm blanket, for she truly felt loved. She walked toward the throne of grace and bowed down before her King.

The Lord asked, "Have you been happy here, beloved?"

Still on her knees, she lifted her head and responded, "So very, very happy. Thank You for allowing me to come here with You."

"I want to show you something." As the Lord Jesus said those words, the clouds parted, and Kenisha was allowed to see her children. They were in the backyard, laughing and playing on a swing set. The one thing that struck her was the fact that there was no snow on the ground. With a raised brow, she looked toward her Lord.

"Yes, beloved, you have been gone for several months."

He answered her question without her even having to ask. Kenisha was amazed that she had been in heaven so long. It had felt like no time at all. Her eyes focused on the house. She saw Deidre in the kitchen, standing at the sink washing the dishes while she looked out the window in order to watch the kids play.

Johnson walked into the kitchen and came up behind Deidre and kissed her neck. She turned around, and Kenisha's eyes widened. Deidre was very, very pregnant.

Kenisha was happy that Deidre had finally conceived a child. But in truth, she felt sorry for all the people she had left on earth, because they wouldn't be able to dance through the fields of blood-red flowers as she did every day.

Discussion Questions

1. In the beginning of the book the reader discovers that Deidre is keeping a secret from her husband. That secret nearly destroys their marriage. Do you think it is ever okay for spouses to keep secrets? If so, why?
2. Life was hard for Kenisha Smalls, but it became worse after she was diagnosed with cervical cancer. Did reading Kenisha's story make you question God as she did? If so, what answers did you come away with?
3. Deidre Clark-Morris and Kenisha Smalls live in two different worlds, but their shared heartache and pain bring them together. The two women get to a point in their friendship where they stop judging and learn to accept each other, flaws and all. Have you ever judged the outward appearance of a person without taking the time to discover who they really are? How do you think God feels about our ability to judge the very people he is trying to deliver and set free?
4. Kenisha blamed herself for her sister's death and thought that cancer was her punishment from God. What do you think? Does God punish us with sickness and disease?
5. Deidre knew she couldn't have children but she was resistant to Johnson's suggestions about adopting. What do you think was holding Deidre back?
6. Deidre kept trying to get Christ's message of love and redemption across to Kenisha, but Kenisha wasn't receiving that message. Do you think Kenisha had a hard time receive such a message from Deidre because of the deceptive way Deidre treated her relationship with Johnson? Or do you believe Kenisha wouldn't have been able to receive this message of hope from anyone until the time was right?

7. In the end, Kenisha discovered the great reward that is promised to those who love God. She was in no more pain—only joy filled her days. Did this help you to see that even though God's ways are different from our ways, the end result is better than we could ever imagine? Or would you have preferred a different ending to this story?

Want to learn more about author
Vanessa Miller and check out other great fiction
from Abingdon Press?

Sign up for our fiction newsletter at
www.AbingdonPress.com
to read interviews with your favorite authors, find tips for starting a reading group, and stay posted on what new titles are on the horizon. It's a place to connect with other fiction readers or post a comment about this book.

Be sure to visit Vanessa online!

www.vanessamiller.com